This innovative book examines the careers of three performers whose professional lives spanned the period from the late eighteenth to the late nineteenth centuries, from the heyday of neo-classicism to the coming of realism. While the individual essays concentrate on the specific work of Siddons, Rachel, and Ristori, a wide-ranging introduction relates their collective achievement to social and cultural change. All three rejuvenated a national repertoire and experimented with new forms of dramatic literature, achieving fame far beyond the boundaries of their own country. As they redefined the nature of tragic experience so, as strong and independent women, they contributed greatly to changing concepts of gender and sexuality. Vivid reconstructions of their interpretations and unique accounts of theatrical conditions place the art of three very different but pivotal figures in context.

Three Tragic Actresses

Three Tragic Actresses
Siddons, Rachel, Ristori

Michael R. Booth
John Stokes
Susan Bassnett

CAMBRIDGE
UNIVERSITY PRESS

Published by the Press Syndicate of the University of Cambridge
The Pitt Building, Trumpington Street, Cambridge CB2 1RP
40 West 20th Street, New York, NY 10011–4211, USA
10 Stamford Road, Oakleigh, Melbourne 3166, Australia

First published 1996

Printed in Great Britain at the University Press, Cambridge

A catalogue record for this book is available from the British Library

Library of Congress cataloguing in publication data

Booth. Michael R.
Three tragic actresses : Siddons, Rachel, Ristori / Michael R.
Booth, John Stokes, Susan Bassnett.
p.   cm.
Includes bibliographical references and index.
ISBN 0 521 41115 7 (hardback)
1. Siddons, Sarah, 1755–1831 – Criticism and interpretation.
2. Rachel, 1820–1858 – Criticism and interpretation.   3. Ristori,
Adelaide, 1822–1906 – Criticism and interpretation.   I. Stokes,
John, 1943–   .   II. Bassnet, Susan.   III. Title.
PN2598.S5B74   1996
792'.028'0922–dc20   95–51228   CIP

ISBN 0 521 41115 7 hardback

Contents

vii

Illustrations

Acknowledgements

I am grateful to the staff of the Department of Prints and Drawings at the British Musem for their assistance in helping me to locate illustrations, and to the University of Victoria for two grants for research and travel which enabled me to pursue my work.

Michael Booth

I want to thank Barbara Cavanagh, who kindly allowed me access to the remarkable theatre collection assembled by her and her husband; Madame Noelle Guibert, Conservateur de la Bibliothèque-Musée de la Comédie-Française, for helping me obtain illustrations; the staff of the Theatre Museum in Covent Garden, the Bibliothèque de l'Arsenal in Paris, and the British Library Newspaper Library in Colindale for their patience with my enquiries; the University of Warwick for a period of sabbatical leave in which I was able to pursue my researches; and Faith Evans.

John Stokes

Thanks to Alessandro D'Amico and especially to Alessandro Tinterri and his colleagues at the Museo Biblioteca dell'Attore di Genova. Special thanks to Clive Barker, who offered helpful comments on the draft. Above all, I am deeply grateful to Giovanna Buonanno, who worked as Research Assistant on this project and without whom I would not have been able to complete the task.

Susan Bassnett

INTRODUCTION

The roots of tragic acting go deep into the remote pre-Hellenistic past, and nobody has any idea what dramatic performance was like then. Only very recently have attempts been made to reconstruct the acting of the Greek classical period. The nature and technique of tragic acting is obscure at least until the late seventeenth century; even then there is little hard evidence. Only when we reach the time when theatre people and interested critics begin writing books about the theatre, when actors begin to compose memoirs, when theorists write upon the subject of the tragic actor and the proper acting of tragedy, and when newspapers and magazines are sufficiently advanced and culturally sophisticated to review performances, only then are we presented with a great deal of information about tragic acting.

Generally speaking, this period is the eighteenth century. In the nineteenth, with the proliferation of theatre criticism, biographies and auto-biographies of actors, prints, drawings, paintings, and finally photographs, there is much more evidence on which to base an examination of tragic actors – except, of course, for the one insurmountable obstacle that mighty as was their power their art was writ in water and has gone for ever, to be recovered, very partially, only by words and frozen visual images.

The advent of the actress complicates the whole business of the examination of tragic acting. When Sarah Siddons began to act in the English provinces in her teens, women had only been able to practise upon the professional stage of England for a century, though in France and Italy the professional actress can be traced much further back. As these three essays make clear, while Siddons, Rachel, and Ristori operated on the stage within the general limits understood by their contemporaries of 'tragic' acting, which comprehended actors as well as actresses, their gender added the complexity of female emotional structures and the responses of female rather than male characters to the situations and extreme pressures of tragedy.[1] Each essay examines a particular image of the feminine embodied in the figure of an actress, conscious that there is nothing inevitable about the association of the human body with abstract value and that meanings are always historically contingent.

When Sarah Siddons began her acting career in the 1760s it was generally understood that tragic acting was larger than life, that it was elevated beyond any other kind of acting. As the epic was raised above other forms of poetry, so was tragedy exalted above other forms of dramatic writing. In *The Actor*, published in 1750, John Hill declared, 'The nature of this species of the drama requires that every thing about it carry the air of grandeur.'[2] Thus the tragic actor's bearing, gesture, movement, speech, and facial expression all had to be appropriate to this elevation. An 'air of grandeur' became one of Mrs Siddons' marked characteristics and the idea survived, being later attributed to both Rachel and Ristori despite their pronounced physical differences.

Eighteenth-century tragic acting also subscribed to the notion that the principal passions must be made distinct from one another and codified according to their visual and auditory attributes into a universal language of the stage. Indeed, the idea of universality and the importance of the general, which applied to all mankind, over the particular, which might be merely an individual idiosyncrasy of far less significance, was explicitly stated by Dr Johnson in poetic theory and by Joshua Reynolds in artistic theory; Sarah Siddons was their contemporary.

It is not surprising that in the nineteenth century, under the pressure of the Romantic movement and its concern with the value of individuality, and of the new psychology and its application to human behaviour, ideas of universality should begin to disintegrate and tragic acting should change. Such cultural and scientific developments always affect the theatre and the work of the player as much as that of the playwright. Romanticism had already led to an emphasis upon character in dramatic action and therefore the necessity of a unified conception of character in the playing of a tragic role, as in Mrs Siddons' Lady Macbeth. It also valued the individual rather than the general passion. This shift to a more internalised or psychological style of acting is marked by an increasing insistence that the performer should show the transitions from one moment to another, should act through reaction, should convey the thought processes that eventually issue in speech.[3]

Psychology, with its interest in abnormal states of mind and the scientific analysis of behaviour, allowed actors opportunities to develop striking portrayals based upon coherent interpretations of character and emotion. Such interpretations were just as relevant to the revival of classical roles as to the creation of new parts in modern plays. It became acceptable – as it usually was not in the eighteenth century – to give a completely new interpretation of a well-known part layered, by passing theatrical generations, with the accretions of tradition. On the English stage this is what Edmund Kean did in 1814 with Shylock, and Henry Irving in 1878 with Hamlet. Similar processes took place in the French and Italian theatre: Rachel's Phèdre both replaced and extended earlier interpretations by Champmeslé and Clairon; Mirra in Alfieri's tragedy became one of Ristori's principal roles, supplanting the hugely successful interpretation by Carolina Internari, whom Ristori credits with having helped her develop her own individualistic approach to the character.

Inevitably, the degree of innovation in any performing style tended to be measured by comparison with others. Sometimes these comparisons operated according to common standards and techniques, irrespective of gender: Siddons with Garrick, Rachel with Lemaître, Ristori with Salvini. More often the comparison was specifically with performers of the same sex, either contemporaries or antecedents: Siddons against Anne Barry; Rachel against Mademoiselle Georges; Ristori against Carlotta Marchionni. But from the eighteenth century onwards there was the elite context of the *tragédienne* too, Pan-European in its range, drawing upon a more limited number, among them most obviously Siddons, Rachel, and Ristori. These great names came to epitomise not only the the dominant styles of a particular epoch, the differences and the similarities between national traditions, but the universal aspirations of the female tragic performer.

'Siddonian' entered the English language in the 1780s and became a touchstone throughout the nineteenth century. When the actress in Mrs E. Lynn's three-volume novel of 1851, *Realities*, recites, she goes 'through

Siddonian attitudes' and her deep voice utters 'Siddonian melodrama'.[4] When Rachel performed in London in 1846 she was greeted with a sonnet that concluded: 'The Shakespeare of the Gaul was great Corneille / The Siddons' throne is graced by thee, Rachel!'[5] 'We have even forgotten what *the* Siddons has been in that which *the* Rachel is', the *Morning Post* had confessed in 1842.[6] The *Atlas* agreed: 'She holds now, relatively, the laurel crown which was last worn by Siddons.'[7] Comparison could cut both ways, of course; in 1856 Macready was complaining that Ristori ('. . . merely a melodramatic abandonment or lashing-up to a certain point of excitement') was not nearly as impressive as Rachel had been, let alone Siddons.[8]

The actresses were as conscious of precedent as their audiences. When she considered playing the role of Lady Macbeth in England, Rachel was warned that Siddons had exhausted every possibility, especially in the sleepwalking scene: 'Oh, but I have an idea of my own,' she replied, 'I should lick my hand.'[9] When Ristori played the part, she paused in the letter-reading scene, 'looked down at her bosom and gradually closing her open hand she seemed to tear in the very act the infant from her nipple and dash it to the earth'.[10] With hindsight we can see very clearly how, through relish for the violent gesture that expressed a brilliant insight, psychological realism might develop out of a previously melodramatic style.

Passion crosses boundaries and captures audiences. That point is made in Madame de Staël's novel *Corinne* (1807), when the heroine is taken by an English family to see Mrs Siddons in *Isabella, or The Fatal Marriage*:

> The noble figure and professional sensibility of the actress captivated the attention of Corinna so much, that during the first act her eyes were never turned from the stage . . . It requires so much the more genius to be a great actor in France, because very little liberty is allowed in that country for an individual or original genius; general rules being so much adhered to. But in England an actor may venture anything, if Nature inspires him. These lengthened groans, which appear ridiculous when they are related or described, startle us when we hear them. Mrs. Siddons loses nothing of her dignity when she throws herself prostrate on the ground. There is nothing that may not be admirable, when an innate emotion accompanies it, an emotion which comes from the centre of the soul, and governs those who feel much more even than those who are witnesses of it. There is among different nations a different manner of playing tragedy: but the expression of

grief extends from one end of the world to the other, and from the savage
to the King there is something similar in all men, when they are truly
miserable.[11]

Compare that fictional instance, the imaginary Corinna exposed to an
imagined Siddons, with the real-life Lady Arthur Lennox experiencing the
full force of the living Rachel in London in 1841. The moment the actress
left the stage at the end of *Horace*, we are told:

> . . . some very piercing shrieks were heard, which lasted some time. Much
> anxiety was manifested by a large portion of the audience, who might with
> the more reason suppose that Mademoiselle Rachel had uttered those
> distressing cries, as, whilst taking leave of the house, one of the performers
> in *Les Horaces* had hastened from the *coulisses* to render her support. On
> inquiring, however, we ascertained that the lady whose sensibility had been
> so far overpowered by the agony of the scene was Lady Arthur Lennox
> who occupied one of the stage boxes. Her ladyship's sufferings excited
> the universal sympathy of the audience.[12]

A sophisticated London audience could identify with its stricken member
because it, too, had felt the inspirational power of a great performance.

Given the shabby incompetence of the companies with which they frequently chose to surround themselves, it sometimes seems surprising that
the *tragédiennes'* capacity to create rapture should have operated so consistently. Was it, as George Eliot, who saw Ristori in Rome in 1869, rather
cynically complained, nothing but 'so miserable, stupid an egoism' that
made the star opt for 'a cheap company that turns the ensemble into a farce
or burlesque which makes an incongruous and often fatally neutralising
background to her own figure'?[13]

In fact Eliot's protest betrays her ignorance of an Italian tradition in
which Ristori's company policy was not unusual. The *mattatore*, or star
actor, was generally surrounded by inferior performers, so as to allow the
star to shine more brightly. The concept of ensemble was not developed at
all in the Italian tradition, and the companies were run as extended families, in which younger and lesser members of the social hierarchy deferred
to the more dominant figures. In France, by contrast, Rachel, who had
graduated from the Comédie-Française where hierarchy was thoroughly
institutionalised, attracted some hostile comment for drawing upon her
own relatives in a seemingly nepotistic way.

This question of cultural difference in company management and acting styles must add another dimension to the way in which we read the critical opinion of the time. Whatever Italian audiences saw when Ristori performed with her company was not the same as what English or American audiences saw, accustomed as they were to look differently at the interaction between performers on stage. None the less, even in the early years of the century, audiences would make their feelings plain if standards fell below an expected minimum. In 1841, the actor playing Orestes in Racine's *Andromaque* uttered his last speech 'amid roars of laughter and showers of hisses' from a London audience;[14] and this on the same evening that Rachel was applauded for her extraordinary intensity. That moments of the highest emotion could emerge out of what sometimes appears to us to have been near to chaos is partly because acting styles were still organised around significant moments or 'points', and partly because international audiences knew what they looking for in an individual performance. Even the Royal Family was seen to be laughing during *Horace* at the St James' in 1846 when 'an appeal was made to the "august visage" of one of the performers, who "did and looked the terrible" in the most novel style'. Yet 'the poverty of the accessories exhibited Rachel in a more exalted point of view – and in this small theatre we are enabled to follow every line of change in her countenance – a study of surpassing interest'.[15]

The qualification is significant. As we each demonstrate in our respective essays, 'face-acting' pre-exists realism, is subtle and psychologically nuanced long before the invention of the camera, and it survives the building of large theatres – though only those in the best seats could fully appreciate the power and subtlety of an expressive countenance. From the late eighteenth century until the late nineteenth, at a time when the female body was kept rigid by heavy costumes and elaborate under-garments, spectators looked to an actress for the kind of powerful facial expression that conveys strong emotions. Siddons' 'brilliant and piercing eyes',[16] Rachel's 'quick and restless action of the eye-lids'[17] and 'quivering nostrils',[18] Ristori's 'flexibility of countenance'[19] and 'wild eyes, dishevelled hair'[20] were the means by which they conveyed the inner turmoil of the exposed woman. Even the fashion for neo-classical drapery, for 'the statuesque', did nothing to inhibit the expression of stress: rather it provided a significant contrast. Hermione in *The Winter's Tale*, Phèdre, even Medea are all examples of roles in which a sculptural poise could coexist with a desperate awareness of an extreme situation.

It is surely significant that those three famous characters are all mothers. As Michael Booth stresses, maternity had played its part in some of Siddons' most celebrated roles; Rachel and Ristori were both candidates for the part of Medea, a legendary and troublesome mother, in Ernest Legouvé's imitation of Euripides.

In the course of the nineteenth century Medea became a important focus in the continual process of redefining the feminine, and Legouvé's romanticised version was to be regularly revived in English, as well as in French and Italian. On the London stage alone it was brought back at least six times between 1857 and 1872. There was even a burlesque, *Medea; or the best of Mothers with a brute of a husband* by Robert B. Brough, in which Medea was played by a man (Frederick Robson) and the ending turned into comedy by the survival of the children.[21]

At this distance Rachel's on-off plans to perform in Legouvé's version, which he offered first to her, are not easy to unravel. It is certainly true that she had requested a new play from the writer who, together with Scribe, had already provided her with a great success in *Adrienne Lecouvreur*, yet when *Médée* was presented to the Reading Committee of the Comédie-Française, she encouraged its rejection. A Russian tour intervened, in the course of which she seems to have agreed to appear as Medea after all. Then, in 1854, cast down by the death of her sister, Rebecca, she changed her mind yet again. This indecision seems to have had several causes since the written statements that have survived make quite different points.

In a letter to Legouvé, for instance, Rachel protests that the play does not suit her style:

> I see the part is full of rapid and violent movements; I have to rush to my children, I have to lift them up, to carry them off the stage, to contend for them with the people. This external vivacity is not my style. Whatever may be expressed by physiognomy, by attitude, by sober and measured gesture – that I can command; but where broad and energetic pantomime begins, there my executive talent stops.[22]

However other comments would suggest that it was the unsympathetic nature of the role that made Rachel nervous, which still seems odd because she was above all celebrated for her ability to convey ferocious feelings.

(G. H. Lewes' famous tribute, 'the panther of the stage', may well have been inspired by Jason's 'No woman but a tiger' in Euripides' play).

At the same time, the standard point of comparison between Rachel and Ristori, who did eventually take on the role, was that the Italian regularly supplied what was lacking in her French rival: womanly tenderness, not perhaps the most obvious requirement for Medea. Yet here is the actor George Vandenhoff reminiscing in 1860:

> This is the point, too, in which RISTORI, the Italian *tragédienne*, so far surpasses the French one; in loving sweetness, the outgushing of a trustful, unselfish woman's heart. Rachel might make you wonder at her energy, her force, her demonical intensity. Ristori makes you weep with her, and love her by her nobleness, the depth of her feeling, and its feminine expression. Even in Medea, the character which Rachel refused to play, Ristori is a woman; outraged, injured, revengeful, maddened with her wrongs, but still a woman: Rachel would have made her a tigress, or a fiend![23]

It is certainly true that, as Elaine Aston has pointed out, Legouvé's play tends to stress the heroine as betrayed wife rather than as child-murderer.[24] Indeed, perhaps it was the pathetic element that Rachel recognised in *Médée*, reminding her that her own tragic talent lay elsewhere. Rachel M. Brownstein has plausibly argued that from Rachel's point of view the problem with Legouvé's play might well have been that, although it had a classical subject, it fell far short of the harsh neo-classical tragedies in which she had first found her voice.

Conversely, it may have been the chance to play to some degree *against* her own most celebrated qualities that drew Ristori to Medea. When, in 1855, Legouvé, impatient with Rachel's vacillation, first offered the Italian actress the part, she read it with initial misgivings, but was soon persuaded. In her *Memoirs* she records how she felt the play to be superior to other versions that she had read, and significantly notes that it offered her 'magnificent situations'. By this she means that the play could afford a series of the melodramatic stage-pictures at which she excelled, but in her account of the preparation for the opening in Paris she describes her fascination with the role in terms bordering on the obsessive: 'I thought of nothing – dreamed of nothing – but Medea.'[25]

Although apparently a devoted mother and daughter in her private life, Ristori's choice of roles often emphasizes the alternative version of those conventional types: Mirra, the incestuous daughter; Medea, the murdering mother; Lady Macbeth and Phèdre, women who subordinate their mothering instincts to their pursuit of power or whose libidinous drives push everything else to one side. On stage these fearful dark figures of the imagination, these fantasy roles ruled by violence and supposedly unnatural passions, some of them already performed by either Siddons or Rachel and long associated with their names, were the opposite archetypes of the safely domesticated female, 'The Angel in the House'.

In her art the *tragédienne* could move far beyond the limits of the social worlds she inhabited as a woman; her theatre was therefore a profoundly paradoxical place, a public arena for the display of what was publicly disallowed, where the representation of suffering and of desire might be the first signs of resistance. Whenever acting is expressive of deeply hidden feelings it becomes both seductive and dangerous, to performer and audience alike. As a contribution to sexual politics, tragic acting involved both psychic assertion and an irresistible, often erotic, form of self-display. Although our insistence upon tragedy as a form of counter-ideology might seem to conflict with transcendent Aristotelian beliefs, all the evidence tells us that it was the most immediate and the most sensual, as well as the most individually heroic of genres. Lasting images of legendary women, of triumph as well as of submission, marked by strength as much as by swoon, by courage as much as by madness: these are the political legacy of the great tragic actress.

SARAH SIDDONS

MICHAEL R. BOOTH

The funeral of Sarah Siddons took place on the morning of 15 June 1831. She was seventy-five years old and had long been retired from the stage. Nevertheless, the funeral, ostensibly a private ceremony, became a national event. The procession, winding its slow dark way from her residence in Upper Baker Street to St Mary's, Paddington, consisted of thirteen blackly bedecked mourning coaches and a number of private carriages, at least eleven of the coaches being occupied by performers from Drury Lane and Covent Garden Theatres.[1] Five thousand people were said to have witnessed the funeral. Public tributes filled the press, as they had when she retired in 1812. That retirement was not final: she appeared on a few occasions after that, and it was upon one of these that William Hazlitt, in an act of homage to her greatness, remarked, 'She was Tragedy personified. She was the stateliest ornament of the public mind.'[2] William Charles Macready, no mean judge of acting, worshipped her, which was extraordinary for one of his distrustful mind and sceptical temperament. He declared, 'In no other theatrical artist were, I believe, the charms of voice, the graces of personal beauty, and the gifts of genius so grandly and harmoniously combined.'[3] Years after her death he worked tirelessly – and, finally, successfully – to erect a statue of her in Westminster Abbey. Macready was an eminent actor, Hazlitt an eminent critic, but their reaction to her art was only typical of a veritable cornucopia of praise and adulation poured out during her career, upon her retirement, and again upon her death. 'With her the sun of Melpomene will set',[4] wrote Thomas Gilliland gloomily, four years before she retired, and that about summed up how her contemporaries felt.

Never before, nor since, were such accolades bestowed upon an

1 'Mrs Siddons and her son in the tragedy of Isabella' (1), by William Hamilton. 1785.

English actress. By her own peers and by later generations of critics and historians she has been generally esteemed the greatest of all English actresses, a genius of tragedy, unrivalled in the expression of passion and tragic character upon the stage. How was this reputation achieved? What justifies her pre-eminence, not only among actresses, but among all the tragic actors of her time? What constituted the art and strength of her acting? What explains her remarkable effect upon audiences? To what extent was her femininity an explanation of her power? To these, and other related questions, we must address ourselves in this chapter.

Sarah Kemble was born into the theatre. Her mother and father were provincial actors, as was her maternal grandfather. Eight of her brothers and sisters went on the stage. At least two of them besides Sarah – John and Charles – established great reputations as actors. In the season of 1783–4 five Kembles were acting at Drury Lane and Covent Garden. One niece, Fanny Kemble, made a sensational début as Juliet in 1829, and for a short time was the bright star of a fading Covent Garden. Another niece, Adelaide Kemble, became a fine opera singer. All her life Sarah lived in the context of the Kemble dynasty.

When she was born, on 5 July 1755 at Brecon in Wales, the provincial theatre, then largely served by small strolling companies like her father's, constantly on the road, was on the verge of a significant expansion into a network of Theatres Royal, with brand new patents from the crown, and circuit companies. Each circuit was a collection, varying in number, of mostly small towns in the same geographical area, the manager moving his company from town to town according to the potential for good box-office generated by important local events like fairs, race meetings, and assizes. Some of these circuit companies were centred upon a Theatre Royal of competent management and high artistic standing: before she returned to Drury Lane in 1782 Sarah Siddons acted in important companies such as Tate Wilkinson's at York and John Palmer's at Bath and Bristol. At the end of the eighteenth century she could perceive, from her high prominence at Drury Lane, a golden age of provincial theatre (soon to end after 1815) which despatched promising actors along a much improved road system to permanent berths at Drury Lane or Covent Garden, fostered a rich and geographically extensive variety of circuit and lesser strolling companies, and entertained highly remunerative summer visits, when Drury Lane and

Covent Garden were closed, from touring London stars, including Mrs Siddons herself.

In 1775, when she first came out at Drury Lane, the London theatre scene consisted of the winter theatres Drury Lane and Covent Garden, the summer theatre in the Haymarket, and an assortment of popular entertainment on the fringes of the city, including that at Sadler's Wells and in the theatrical booths of the great London fairs like Southwark Fair and Bartholomew Fair. Drury Lane and Covent Garden were organised on true repertory principles, with the bill often changing nightly, and few new plays having a consecutive nightly run of any length; the population base – London in 1775 had a population of about 700,000 – being too small, and provincial visitors too few, to sustain the long runs that were first seen in the middle of the Victorian period. Each theatre, therefore, had to carry a large stock of plays and standard scenery, both equally interchangeable as the occasion demanded, and balance its repertory carefully according to the tastes and social composition of audiences and the strengths of the acting company. This meant that every performer played many different parts during the course of a season. Stars performed far less often than utility players, but even after she had attained stardom Mrs Siddons appeared eighty times in her first triumphant Drury Lane season of 1782–3 (in seven roles), fifty-three times in the next season (in twelve roles, seven of them new) and seventy-one times in 1784–5 (in eight new roles and nine repeated from the two previous seasons). In her maturity as the leading tragic actress of Drury Lane, she acted about three times a week; her workload was much heavier as a touring star in the provinces.

Working in the provinces at an earlier time, together with her actor husband William, whom Sarah Kemble married in 1773, the young actress did not take long to be noticed by London. David Garrick, on the eve of his farewell season in 1775–6, was advised by a friend and talent scout, the Revd Henry Bate, that she was well worth considering for a position in the Drury Lane company. Bate, who saw her play Rosalind at Cheltenham, was impressed. Her face, he wrote, 'is one of the most strikingly beautiful for stage effect that ever I beheld'. He did not care much for her voice – 'dissonant' – but believed that any vocal problems might easily be corrected. He was struck by her 'action', stage deportment, and intelligence in delivering lines: 'I know no woman who marks the different passages and transitions with so much variety and at the same time propriety of expression.'[5]

Negotiations then began, with Bate acting for Garrick. Soon he wrote again to the Drury Lane manager praising 'the universal good character they [Sarah and William] have presented here for many years, on account of their public as well as private conduct in life' – a character that was a significant part of Mrs Siddons' appeal throughout her acting career – and commending her for being 'the most extraordinary quick study I ever heard of'. Bate also sent Garrick a list of parts she was prepared to play, since the negotiation of roles was always important in a contractual agreement to bring a promising provincial performer to London.[6] Twenty-three roles were listed, with comic roles outnumbering tragic. The Shakespearean characters on the list were Juliet, Cordelia, Imogen, Portia, and Rosalind, and the list also included four characters that were among her great tragic parts when she returned to Drury Lane in the 1780s: Belvidera in Thomas Otway's *Venice Preserved*, Jane Shore in Nicholas Rowe's *The Tragedy of Jane Shore*, Calista in the same author's *The Fair Penitent*, and Euphrasia (itemised in Bate's letter as 'Graec. Daughter') in Arthur Murphy's *The Grecian Daughter*. At this stage in her career, Sarah Siddons believed herself at least as strong in comedy as tragedy.

After further negotiations, exchanges of correspondence – with William Siddons, not Sarah – and deliberation on Garrick's part, the unknown actress, late of the Cheltenham and Gloucester companies, came out as Portia at Drury Lane on 29 December 1775. Such a date, so far advanced in the season (which had opened in September), had to be chosen because Sarah had given birth to her second child at the beginning of November. Indeed, her physical condition at the end of December was not good, and her nerves were worse. The established actresses of Drury Lane were hostile, although Garrick himself showed her many favours. Her début was worse than inauspicious; it was close to disastrous. Recently remodelled and somewhat enlarged, Drury Lane was much bigger than any theatre she had played in, and clearly she could not, vocally, gauge the size of the house. Her voice was inadequate and she acted poorly; if she did not know this herself the reviewers told her so with some enthusiasm. Further appearances as Lady Anne in *Richard III* and several comedies did little to improve her standing or her critical reception. In any event, by the end of the season in June 1776, public attention was concentrated on Garrick's splendid series of farewell performances, and the obscure and undistinguished young actress from the country was quite forgotten.

Obviously, however, Mrs Siddons did not accept the public estimate of her, and expected another contract for the 1776–7 season from the new Drury Lane management, now controlled by the dramatist Richard Brinsley Sheridan. It was a great shock to her and to her husband when no offer was forthcoming, and when, perforce, she had to return to provincial acting. The years that followed were difficult. By 1782 Sarah Siddons had four children (a fifth dying in infancy) and lived on a salary – a good one in provincial theatre – of £3 a week, supplemented by benefit performances and the emoluments William Siddons sometimes received as an actor. She never forgot the humiliating treatment she felt she had received from the new Drury Lane management, and was also inclined to blame Garrick for problems she encountered during her season with him. After acting sojourns at Birmingham, Liverpool, Manchester (where she played Hamlet), and York, she became established as the leading actress of the Bath company, which shuttled back and forth between Bath and the Theatre Royal, Bristol. She spent four seasons at Bath, playing both comedy and tragedy, and her increasing reputation finally reached the ears of Drury Lane. In 1782, though dreading a return to London and esteeming her leading position in Bath, she accepted a contract from Sheridan for the 1782–3 season, in order to earn more money, and on 10 October 1782 found herself once more upon the stage of Drury Lane.

Undoubtedly these years of provincial toil, combined with the shock of her rejection by Drury Lane, gave Sarah Siddons a basic sense of insecurity, which never left her, as well as a keen appreciation of the value of money. In her own memoir of her early years on the stage, she avowed herself 'an ambitious candidate for fame',[7] and painted a grim picture of what followed the rebuff from Drury Lane. 'Who can conceive of this cruel disappointment, the dreadful reverse of all my ambitious hopes, in which too was involved the subsistence of two helpless infants. It was very near destroying me. My blighted prospects induced a state of mind, which preyed upon my health, and for a Year and a half, I was supposed to be hastning to a decline.' However, she exerted herself 'for the sake of my poor babies', and through 'indefatigueable' industry and perseverance – which was certainly true – finally attained her goal.[8] The necessity of providing for her poor babies and eventually ensuring the comfortable existence of a large and growing family, as well as helping her own brothers and sisters, made Mrs Siddons extremely careful to exact what she deemed an adequate remuneration for her labours.[9] Nevertheless, no matter how much she earned it was never enough, and she was always worrying about money. For example, she repeatedly told friends that once she had accumulated the sum of £10,000 she would leave the stage and live in a country cottage. By 1785, at the age of thirty, she had achieved this monetary objective, after only three seasons at Drury Lane and lucrative provincial tours. But she did not retire into the country. In fact the country cottage did not materialise until 1805, when she was still acting; she purchased Westbourne Farm in then rural Paddington.

Sarah Siddons' concern about money can be explained in part by the events of the 1770s, but it is also true that for many years of her career, until she and her brother John left Drury Lane for Covent Garden in 1802, she was in the hands of the financially unscrupulous but utterly charming Sheridan, who completely bamboozled the unfortunate William in matters of business and frequently defaulted in the payment of salaries. At times Sheridan's unreliability took her away from Drury Lane acting outside London, and her health also kept her on occasion from the stage. Thus she was compelled to do as well for herself as she possibly could when she made provincial tours, and some managers, like John Jackson of the Theatre Royal, Edinburgh, positively groaned at what he believed to be her extortionate terms. Jackson related how in 1784 the Siddonses insisted upon receiving half the receipts of an engagement plus a clear benefit – that is, a benefit for which the management made no deduction for house charges – instead of accepting Jackson's original offer of a clear benefit and £400, £200 of which was to be made up by a subscription among the nobility as an inducement for Mrs Siddons to come, since he could not afford to offer the extra £200 on his own account. As it turned out, Jackson claimed, Mrs Siddons was given the £200 directly on top of her half share of receipts, £467; a clear benefit, £180; and gifts worth, he estimated, £120. Altogether, then, she earned £967 from her Edinburgh engagement; Jackson's share was £347.[10] In 1786 Mrs Siddons went to the Theatre Royal, York. The manager, Tate Wilkinson, noted ruefully that she 'received from her profits no less a sum than *eleven hundred pounds*, or very near it, for 17 nights acting, without alluding to any presentations she might and certainly did receive most liberally from particular persons, at York, on her benefit night'.[11] Her enormous success at York filled her pockets rather than Wilkinson's, and for some time thereafter theatrical business was bad – a frequent consequence of the visit of a star to a provincial Theatre Royal.

Such a golden harvest from provincial tours would have been imposs-ible without Sarah Siddons' triumphant return to Drury Lane in 1782 and her elevation, in a very short time, to the throne of Tragedy. She was assisted in her speedy ascent by the fact that there were no other serious claimants. The Drury Lane company was strong in men, but poverty-stricken on the female side in comedy as well as tragedy, and Siddons had no real rivals at Covent Garden. In tragedy the two leading tragic actresses of Garrick's management, Susanna Cibber and Hannah Pritchard, Garrick's Lady Macbeth, had left the stage in the 1760s. Anne Barry, who became Mrs Crawford in 1778, had left London and was acting in Ireland. She returned to Covent Garden in 1783 to contest the throne with Mrs Siddons, but her best days were over and she retired in 1798. Mary Anne Yates, a majestic, powerful, if cold actress, was at the end of her career and left the stage in 1785. Elizabeth Younge, later Mrs Pope, Garrick's last Cordelia, remained on the stage until 1797. She was a commendable trage-dienne who played Lady Macbeth, Euphrasia, Jane Shore, and Calista, strong in declamation and in the roles of distressed wives and mothers, but no competition for Mrs Siddons.

The facts of the 1782–3 engagement at Drury Lane can be briefly told. Opening as Isabella in Garrick's *Isabella*, an adaptation of Thomas Southerne's Restoration tragedy *The Fatal Marriage*, she went on to play Euphrasia in *The Grecian Daughter*, Jane Shore in *The Tragedy of Jane Shore*, Calista in *The Fair Penitent*, Zara in William Congreve's *The Mourning Bride*, like Southerne's a tragedy of the 1690s, Belvidera in *Venice Preserved*, and Mrs Montague in Thomas Hull's new tragedy, *The Fatal Interview*, the only failure – Hull's rather than Siddons' – of her season. Of these performances Isabella was the most popular; she played it twenty-two times, followed by Jane Shore and Calista with fourteen, Belvidera thirteen, and Euphrasia eleven. All five characters she had previously performed in the provinces; they were in the standard repertory and familiar to London audiences.

Except for Mrs Montague, all the roles she played this season entered her London repertory.

To put it mildly, Sarah Siddons had a powerful impact upon her audiences, a fact amply demonstrated upon her return to Drury Lane but by no means confined to the season of 1782–3. To record and investigate that impact is necessary in order to answer, or begin to answer, some of the questions raised at the beginning of this chapter.

For one thing, it was difficult even to get into Drury Lane on the nights Mrs Siddons was acting during that season. Box seats were virtually unobtainable, and large crowds rushed into the unreserved pit and galleries when the doors were opened. Anna Seward, the Swan of Lichfield, a minor poetess and a prolific letter-writer, wrote that 'I saw her for the first time, at the hazard of my life, by struggling through the terrible, fierce, madding crowds into the pit.'[12] It was all worth it, and Anna Seward remained a devoted admirer of the actress and her art. James Boaden recalled that when Isabella laughed in the very act of plunging a dagger into her bosom – this climaxing the most harrowing scene Mrs Siddons ever played – the audience was electrified, 'and literally the greater part of the spectators were too ill themselves to use their hands in her applause'.[13] When the formerly adulterous but now repentant and expiring Jane Shore is reconciled with her husband at the end of the play and utters the line 'Forgive me! – but forgive me!' Boaden remembered, vividly, 'the sobs, the shrieks among the tenderer part of the audiences; or those tears, which manhood at first struggled to suppress, but at length grew proud of indulging . . . The nerves of many a gentle being gave way before the intensity of such appeals, and fainting fits long and frequently alarmed the decorum of the house, filled almost to suffocation.'[14] Horace Walpole was not overwhelmed by Mrs Siddons, as were so many of his acquaintance, thinking both her voice and gesture unvaried, but he admitted that 'were I five and twenty, I suppose I should weep myself blind, for she is a fine actress'.[15]

Walpole's reserved point of view was decidedly not that of the audiences that jammed Drury Lane, night after night, to adore, sob, scream, and faint. In that first extraordinary season many of them could not bear to watch the farce afterpiece that followed a Siddons tragedy, and left the theatre in large numbers when the tragedy ended. Their reaction was not uniquely English; foreign visitors were equally affected. Ernst Brandes, who visited England in 1784 and 1785, was deeply moved by Siddons' Jane Shore, and he was not alone: 'The sight is terrible. I saw two ladies among the spectators fall into hysterics, and one of them had to be carried out, laughing convulsively. Such representations of pain are too much for modern nerves.'[16] The moments following Euphrasia's slaying of the usurper, when Siddons knelt and prayed silently for heaven's forgiveness for the necessary deed, much affected Friedrich von Hassell in 1790; he reported that 'on all sides nothing was to be heard save sobbing and soft applause'.[17] Karl Gotlob Küttner found the realism of Siddons' Isabella terrifying, her voice and laugh in the death scene 'truly harrowing, arousing unpleasant, distressing feelings'. Several times she made 'such sounds as to cut me to the quick'.[18]

Küttner saw Mrs Siddons during the 1783–4 season, and it is apparent that if the mass delirium of the early reaction passed away, her power to affect her audience over the years was just as great. One did not even have to be present in the theatre to be affected. The anonymous author of 'Letters from a Lady of Distinction to her Friend in the Country', letters relating to Sarah Siddons' appearance in Dublin in 1785, was unable to recollect her Belvidera in any sort of tranquillity. When Jaffeir places Belvidera, against her will, in the care of the conspirators, her sorrows 'took entire possession of my soul'; her voice, her face, her struggles to get free from the conspirators, 'her scream at being torn away' – because of all this 'I could only express my feelings by tears; – and, even now, my agitation is so great, that I must lay by my pen.'[19] Similarly, the pain of remembering the conclusion of *Isabella* forced her to break off her letter.[20] Such testimonials to the actress' power over her spectators continued to the end of her career. Mrs Piozzi was unable to sleep after seeing *Isabella* in 1789,[21] and the woman who accompanied her to the same play in 1790 fainted.[22] In 1797 Crabb Robinson laughed hysterically at Siddons' playing of the murderously inclined Agnes Wilmot in George Lillo's *Fatal Curiosity* and was nearly turned out of the pit.[23] In her last season, Charles Leslie saw her Mrs Beverley in Edward Moore's *The Gamester* at Covent Garden; during Mrs Beverley's grief at the death of her husband 'a lady in the boxes went into hysterics and was carried out'.[24]

Interestingly, the tremendous success of Sarah Siddons and her overpowering impact upon audiences was achieved in that season of 1782–3 without recourse to a single Shakespearean part. Next season she appeared as Isabella in *Measure for Measure* and Constance in *King John*, but it was not until 1785 that she played her most famous part, Lady Macbeth, though not for the first time, since she had performed it in the provinces. The roles in which she rose to immediate and tempestuous fame were from the standard non-Shakespearean tragic repertory, and it is worth briefly considering these plays to see if we can show any reasons for their impact upon audiences, at least as she performed them.

The most sensational performance of that first season was in *Isabella, or The Fatal Marriage* (Drury Lane, 1757), a version by Garrick of Southerne's *The Fatal Marriage, or The Innocent Adultery* (1694). Garrick's adaptation was a vehicle for the pathetic powers of Mrs Cibber. The impoverished widow, Isabella, faithful to the memory of her dead husband, Biron, and caring lovingly for her young son, refuses the honourable advances of the prosperous Villeroy. Finally, driven by poverty and the oppression of her cruel father-in-law, Count Baldwin, who has never forgiven her for marrying his son, she yields to Villeroy's entreaties and marries him. The day after the marriage the living Biron returns, the news that he was alive having been suppressed by his father, and his letters to Isabella intercepted. Isabella despairs and grows distracted; Biron is assassinated by the agents of his villainous younger brother; Baldwin repents, too late, of his conduct; and the now insane Isabella kills herself. The emotions of the principal character are carefully structured, passing from a deep and passive melancholy to lamentation, despair, and madness. The notes of pity and sorrow are strongly marked throughout, as can be seen in the lines spoken as Isabella pleads for succour to the heartless Baldwin:

> I lost with Biron all the Joys of Life:
> But now its last supporting Means are gone,
> All the kind Helps that Heav'n in Pity rais'd,
> In charitable Pity to our Wants,
> At last have left us: Now bereft of all,
> But this last Trial of a cruel Father,
> To save us both from sinking. O my Child!
> Kneel with me, knock at Nature in his Heart:
> Let the Resemblance of a once-lov'd Son
> Speak in this little One, who never wrong'd you,
> And plead the Fatherless and Widow's Cause.   (1.i)

The part of Isabella's child was played by Mrs Siddons' son, Henry, aged eight, an appropriate casting in support of an actress who excelled in the portrayal of strong and tender maternal and filial relationships.

Arthur Murphy's *The Grecian Daughter* (Drury Lane, 1772) was the next tragedy Siddons performed after playing Isabella, and it is a sharp contrast. Euphrasia was Mrs Barry's role before her retirement to Dublin and her marriage to Crawford; it then passed to Mrs Yates at Covent Garden. The play is set in ancient Syracuse. The tyrant and usurper Dionysius has imprisoned the deposed king, Evander, Euphrasia's aged father, in a dreary dungeon deep in the side of a steep cliff, and denied him food and water. Euphrasia's husband has fled the city, taking their baby with him. As a relieving Greek naval force besieges Syracuse, Euphrasia at great peril to her life seeks out the cliffside cell and gives suck to the perishing Evander with the milk intended for her child.[25] This extreme of filial care and tenderness is succeeded by Amazonian heroism when Euphrasia actively participates in plotting the tyrant's overthrow, defies him to his face, scorning his threats, and finally slays him with her own hand as he is on the point of killing Evander. The play consists mostly of patriotic and heroic speeches and postures of determination, confrontation, and rage, fitting nicely into one critic's characterisation of contemporary tragedy as 'a mass of pompous declamation'.[26] One can taste *The Grecian Daughter*'s declamatory flavour in these typical lines from act I:

> Shall Euphrasia's voice
> Be hush'd to silence, when a father dies?
> Still not the monster hear his deeds accurst?
> Shall he not tremble, when a daughter comes,
> Wild with her griefs, and terrible with wrongs,
> Fierce in despair, all nature in her cause,
> Alarm'd and rouz'd with horror? Yes, Melanthon,
> The man of blood shall hear me; yes, my voice
> Shall mount aloft upon the whirlwind's wing,
> Pierce your blue vault, and at the throne of Heav'n
> Call down red vengeance on the murderer's head.
> Melanthon come; my wrongs will lend me force;
> The weakness of my sex is gone, this arm
> Feels tenfold strength; this arm shall do a deed
> For heav'n and earth, for men and gods to wonder at!
> This arm shall vindicate a father's cause.

2 'Mrs Siddons.' As Euphrasia in *The Grecian Daughter* (v.ii), by R. E. Pine. 1784.

At least the rhetoric is energetic, and the character of Euphrasia skilfully conceived for a tragic actress who could combine with great effect – as Mrs Siddons could – unbounded filial love with heroic virtue and superhuman courage.

Jane Shore, the third of the characters she undertook in 1782–3, is the heroine of Rowe's eponymous tragedy, first performed in 1714 and long a stock play, one of the so-called 'she tragedies' for which Rowe was renowned. *The Tragedy of Jane Shore* is much closer to *Isabella* than *The Grecian Daughter*; the central character is essentially passive and resigned to suffering, and the dominant tragic feature is pathos. Jane Shore, formerly the mistress of the dead Edward IV, indignantly refuses Gloster's request to urge Hastings to agree with the former's determination to remove Edward's children from the succession. She suffers the fatal consequences of this refusal: her bosom friend Alicia, entrusted with money and jewels, turns against her; Gloster denies her food and shelter anywhere in the city; she is turned away brutally even from Alicia's door and pitiably wanders the streets of London, growing steadily weaker. (Mrs Siddons' physical suffering at this point was fearfully realistic, too realistic for many in the audience.) Despite the best efforts of her estranged but now forgiving husband, Shore, to whom she is lovingly reconciled moments before she dies, she expires peacefully in his arms.

Jane Shore opens the play, not luxuriating in royal comforts and favours, but already on the edge of the abyss that will shortly engulf her, contrite and repentant, grief in her countenance. From that early point the mood and tone of the play darken, and as her woes multiply the note of pathos becomes stronger. Even her defiance of Gloster is touched with pity and maternal feeling:

> The poor forsaken Royal little Ones!
> Shall they be left a Prey to Savage Power?
> Can they lift up their harmless Hands in vain,
> Or cry to Heaven for Help, and not be heard? (IV.i)

Of all the Siddons roles, this one most powerfully evoked compassion in the audience, especially when Jane Shore knocks at the door of the merciless Alicia and pleads for help, identifying herself as

> A very Beggar and a Wretch indeed;
> One driv'n by strong Calamity to seek
> For Succour here. One perishing for Want,
> Whose Hunger has not tasted Food these three Days;
> And humbly asks, for Charity's dear sake,
> A Draught of Water, and a little Bread. (v.i)

The pathetic emotions are not so strongly emphasised in the other Rowe tragedy that Sarah Siddons played in that Drury Lane season, following the

3 'Mrs Siddons in the Tragedy of the Grecian Daughter' (1), by William Hamilton. 1789.

failure of *The Fatal Interview* by Thomas Hull. *The Fair Penitent* (1703) is remembered today only for bequeathing the name Lothario to English usage and the lexicon of lovers and love-making. In the eighteenth century, however, like *Jane Shore*, it was frequently performed, its central character the tormented Calista, a part previously played by Mrs Cibber, Mrs Barry, and Mrs Yates. Calista is married against her will to Altamont – against her will because she has already given herself to the selfish and heedless Lothario. Calista is a much more complex character than Isabella, Euphrasia, or Jane Shore: proud, full of rage against her situation, perceiving herself as a victim of the world, yet hating herself for what she has done and consumed with guilt, loathing Lothario for his seduction of her and yet loving him, furiously resenting both her father, Sciolto, for arranging the marriage and Altamont for marrying her. Altamont refuses to believe the growing evidence that Calista has slept with Lothario until he catches the two together; Lothario is slain in the ensuing swordfight. In a grim Gothic chamber hung with black, with Lothario's body on a bier, her father sternly demands that Calista – '*in Black, her Hair hanging loose and disordered*' – kill herself, even though he expresses his love for her. Sciolto rushes out and is murdered by Lothario's friends; Calista, hearing the news, adds parricide to her sins and stabs herself. Throughout, her expression of emotion is extravagant, as in the following act IV speech to Sciolto:

> Yes, I will fly to some such dismal Place,
> And be more curst than you can wish I were;
> This fatal Form that drew on my Undoing,
> Fasting, and Tears, and Hardship shall destroy,
> Nor Light, nor Food, nor Comfort will I know,
> Nor aught that may continue hated Life.
> Then when you see me meagre, wan, and chang'd,
> Stretch'd at my Length, and dying in my Cave,
> On that cold Earth I mean shall be my Grave,
> Perhaps you may relent . . .

Writing to a friend in 1783, Anna Seward said that if she were allowed to see Mrs Siddons in only one character it would be Calista, 'because it exhibits such a conflicting and sublime variety of passions',[27] a character on the rack, as Campbell puts it, between virtue and vice.[28] Of the characters she played in the season of 1782–3, Calista is the only one tinged with guilt, a character that required different acting techniques from the others; playing her, Siddons was louder, more vehement, and 'walks with greater precipitation, her gestures are more frequent and more violent, her eyes are restless and suspicious, pride and shame are struggling for superiority, and guilt is in the abstraction of her brow'.[29] Boaden believed that in the acting of Calista Mrs Siddons anticipated her Lady Macbeth.[30]

The best-known of the non-Shakespearean tragedies Sarah Siddons performed at Drury Lane is *Venice Preserved*, and it is the only one occasionally revived today. Otway's tragedy had held the stage for a hundred years when she played Belvidera, a character all the leading tragic actresses had undertaken. The plot of *Venice Preserved* is simply stated. Poverty-stricken and bitterly suffering a haughty rejection from his wife Belvidera's father, a Venetian senator, Jaffeir becomes involved in a conspiracy against the state at the instigation of his best friend Pierre. Belvidera, in the care of the conspirators as a hostage against Jaffeir's loyalty to the plot, suffers an attempted rape. Furious at her news, Jaffeir is persuaded by Belvidera, horrified at the bloodthirsty plan to murder all the senators including her father, to reveal the conspiracy. Pierre and the conspirators are taken and executed; Jaffeir, in agonies of remorse at his betrayal, kills himself; Belvidera runs mad and dies.

Pathos is Otway's strongest suit, and Belvidera, like Isabella, is a passive and pathetic character: except for her single act of convincing Jaffeir to talk, things are done to her and she reacts with lengthy grievings and lamentations. For example, she complains to Jaffeir,

> Yes, yes, there was a time
> When *Belvidera's* tears, her crys and sorrows,
> Were not despis'd; when if she chanc'd to sigh,
> Or look'd but sad; – there was indeed a time
> When *Jaffeir* would have ta'ne [*sic*] her in his Arms,
> Eas'd her declining Head upon his Breast,
> And never left her 'till he found the Cause.
> But let her now weep Seas,
> Cry, 'till she rend the Earth; sigh 'till she burst
> Her heart asunder; still he bears it all,
> Deaf as the Wind, and as the Rocks unshaken.   (iii.ii)

The character of Belvidera was enshrined along with those of Isabella and Jane Shore in Mrs Siddons' pantheon of woe; it was the performance of these three, throughout her career, that drew the most generous libations of tears from her audience.

Other significant parts followed Belvidera. The jealous and vengeful Zara of Congreve's *The Mourning Bride*, torn, like Calista, between rage and love, but without pathos, concluded her list of new roles in the 1782–3 season. In 1783–4 she added Lady Randolph in John Home's *Douglas* (Edinburgh, 1756) – previously a great part for Mrs Barry – and Mrs Beverley in Moore's *The Gamester* (Drury Lane, 1753). Lady Randolph combines heroic stature with powerful maternal feeling. The basic story of the play is her discovery that her child, whom she thought dead, is still alive in the person of Young Norval, the son of the slain Douglas, to whose memory she is still faithful despite her second marriage to Lord Randolph. Very soon after this joyful discovery, however, Norval is mortally wounded by the villain and dies in front of his horrified mother; unable to bear his death she throws herself over a precipice to her own. Mrs Beverley is the wife of a compulsive gambler caught inextricably in the clutches of the villain and sinking ever deeper into debt. In remorse and despair he takes poison in a prison cell moments before his wife arrives with the happy news that his uncle has died and left him a goodly fortune. Boaden complained that *The Gamester* was but a bourgeois tragedy, that scenes of domestic distress were too common and ignoble for the tragic muse.[31] Nevertheless he praised Mrs Siddons' emotional power in the role. In Edinburgh, years after her first Drury Lane performances of the part, she played Mrs Beverley to the Beverley of Charles Mayne Young. In the prison scene she uttered a speech to another character with an exclamation of 'such piercing grief that Mr Young said his throat swelled, and his utterance was choked'. He was unable to speak or continue in the part until Mrs Siddons came up to him and asked him quietly to recollect himself.[32]

Thus it was in Isabella, Euphrasia, Jane Shore, Calista, Belvidera, Lady Randolph, and Mrs Beverley that Sarah Siddons made her great impact on London audiences, all of them given at Drury Lane before Lady Macbeth, before she had any kind of London reputation as a Shakespearean actress. Jacques Henri Meister, who visited the London theatres in 1789 and 1792, remarked of Shakespeare in England that 'as much as his tragedies are admired, they are not those by which audiences are now the most affected. None of his tragedies have caused so many tears to be shed as I have seen drop at the representation of Jane Shore, Venice Preserved, The Grecian Daughter, or The Gamester.'[33] In all her time at Drury Lane and Covent Garden, until she retired, Mrs Siddons played sixteen Shakespearean characters: Isabella (in *Measure for Measure*), Constance, Lady Macbeth, Desdemona, Rosalind, Lady Anne, Portia, Hermione, Ophelia, Imogen, Queen Katharine, Juliet, Volumnia, Gertrude, Cordelia in Nahum Tate's version of *King Lear*, and Queen Elizabeth in Colley Cibber's adaptation of *Richard III*. These parts were greatly outnumbered by some sixty roles in other plays during the same period (1782–1812) and at the same theatres. Of course no eighteenth-century actor or actress could subsist on Shakespeare alone, and many Shakespearean roles, especially in comedy, were entirely unsuited to her. Yet one must remember that much of her reputation came from outside Shakespeare, even though she was poorly served by contemporary tragic writers, who fed her with a steady diet of box-office failures. Of the Shakespearean parts, only her Lady Macbeth, Constance, and Queen Katharine were considered outstanding in her time.

English audiences, said Meister, need to have their attention constantly aroused, their passions strongly excited; they 'delight only in tragedies which become interesting by the great strength and variety of situations'.[34] Christian August Gottlieb Goede, who visited England in 1802 and 1803, declared that English actors were especially effective in the tragic expression of agitated and immoderate passion, and convey wrath, grief, despair, hatred, and revenge 'with unrivalled effect'. They are not so effective, he thought, in expressing 'soft and inward emotions'.[35] Certainly these strong and varied passions are abundantly found in the characters in which Sarah Siddons first distinguished herself at Drury Lane, as well as the 'soft', if not 'inward', emotions. However, their presence as attractively prominent, generalised aspects of text and character, as well as the opportunities they offer a tragic actress of superior abilities, do not entirely explain Mrs Siddons' enormous success and profound impact upon audiences when she played these roles.

The passions Sarah Siddons acted are the passions of suffering women, and those in the audience most affected by her performances were women, who obviously came to the theatre in very large numbers whenever she acted. Men wept quietly, but women sobbed aloud, screamed, went into hysterics,[36] and fainted. It is unlikely that such behaviour could have been caused solely by an actress' technique. In almost all the plots and characters described above, Mrs Siddons played the part of a more or less helpless woman suffering at the hands of men, and powerfully portraying that suffering. This is also true of two of her most popular Shakespearean characterisations, Constance and Queen Katharine.

Isabella is savagely rejected by her father-in-law and left to sink into poverty; Count Baldwin has also kept information from her that her husband is still alive. When Biron returns to her at last, the shock of knowing that he lives but that she is married to the importunate Villeroy drives her to the edge of madness, over which she topples when Biron is swiftly murdered by her vicious brother-in-law's agents. Jane Shore is admittedly an adulteress when the play begins, but remorse and penitence for past errors immediately place the audience on her side, as does her now dangerous position as the out-of-favour mistress of the dead King. Hastings vigorously attempts to seduce her and fails; Gloster pressures her to persuade Hastings to concur in his scheme to have Edward's children proclaimed bastards. When she refuses he decrees that she will starve in the streets of London, without succour from any household or passer-by. A woman, Alicia, turns her away when she begs for food, a dreadful act of cruelty by a professed friend.[37] But Alicia herself has been driven distracted by Hastings' rejection of her and his new affection for Jane Shore. Like Jane Shore, Calista is guilty of past sexual misconduct, but the text makes it clear that Lothario was the active seducer in the case; her remorse for what she has done, and the agony it brings her, more than compensate in the audience's eyes for the guilt incurred. So does her situation. Her overbearing father forces her into a marriage with a man she does not love, and the only man she has some feeling for, Lothario, acts basely towards her and then is slain by the bosom friend of her new husband. Indeed, directly after a scene of stormy abuse from her father, who commands her peremptorily to be happy in her marriage, Calista expresses herself on the subject of male oppression:

> How hard is the Condition of our Sex,
> Thro' ev'ry State of Life the Slaves of Man?
> In all the dear delightful Days of Youth,
> A rigid Father dictates to our Wills,
> And deals out Pleasure with a scanty Hand;

To his, the Tyrant Husband's Reign succeeds;
Proud with Opinion of superior Reason,
He holds Domestick Bus'ness and Devotion
All we are capable to know, and shuts us,
Like Cloyster'd Ideots, from the World's Acquaintance,
And all the Joys of Freedom; wherefore are we
Born with high Souls, but to assert our selves,
Shake off the vile Obedience they exact,
And claim an equal Empire o'er the World?   (III.i)

Mrs Beverley is just as helpless as Calista, placed in an impossible position by the gambling losses of her husband, and the sexual object of the villain's intrigues. Belvidera, whose only positive act is to persuade Jaffeir to confess to the conspiracy in order to save her father and Venice from a bloody massacre, becomes a mere pawn of this male conspiracy: abandoned by Jaffeir, forced into the hands of the conspiracy, and nearly raped. Her initial plight is prompted by her father's refusal to acknowledge her marriage to Jaffeir and to aid them as they sink into poverty. Lady Randolph's son is killed by the villain who schemes to obtain her own person; despite her heroic qualities she cannot survive in a world of male deceit and treachery. Euphrasia is quite a different sort of character from the others, yet her heroic virtues and superhuman courage are a necessary reaction to the usurpation of the tyrant Dionysius and his cruel starvation of her old father.[38] Even Queen Katharine in *Henry VIII* and Constance in *King John* suffer terribly at the hands of men: Katharine manipulated into divorce by the selfishness of Henry and the arbitrary authority of the Church, as represented by Cardinals Wolsey and Campeius; Constance's hopes for her son Arthur blighted by the power politics of a cynical, temporary alliance between England and France, and then by the battle that makes him John's prisoner.

All this female suffering Sarah Siddons represented on the stage of Drury Lane; almost all of it is caused by the calculated actions or deliberate neglect of men. On this stage she enacted huge and powerful images of female misery and anguish, which had a devastating impact upon at least the female part of her audience. The late eighteenth century was a sentimental age, particularly in the novel, the drama, and social attitudes. Crying audiences have been documented in English theatres well before the time of Siddons, but the sheer mass and scale of the reaction to her acting was new; not even Garrick provoked such a response. In the playing of Isabella, Jane Shore, Belvidera, and the others, Mrs Siddons touched the deepest chord of emotional truth in her audiences, who were defenceless before her. The substantial female component of those audiences lived in a world of men who defined and circumscribed them, and denied them what we would consider the most basic of civil rights. Unless they were rich and could make special legal arrangements, married women had no control over their own income or property, which passed to their husbands upon marriage. They could not conduct affairs of business on their own account without their husbands, such as signing contracts, suing, or making valid wills. Fathers had exclusive custody of children and absolute authority over them; there was no divorce, and of course no woman, not even a property holder, could vote. Unless women were independently wealthy they passed – as Calista points out – from the complete dominion of a father to the complete dominion of a husband. What Richard Steele wrote about women in 1712 still passed as current in received, conservative opinion when Mrs Siddons returned to the stage of Drury Lane:

> The utmost of a Woman's Character is contained in domestick life; she is Blameable or Praiseworthy according as her Carriage affects the House of her Father or her Husband. All she has to do in this World, is contained within the Duties of a Daughter, a Sister, a Wife, and a Mother . . . they will in no Part of their Lives want Opportunities of being shining Ornaments to their Fathers, Husbands, Brothers, or Children.[39]

The outpouring of emotion when Sarah Siddons played Isabella or Jane Shore or Belvidera must surely be placed in the context of a woman's position in the legal and social framework of late eighteenth-century middle-class English society, and in the imaginative and sympathetic life of women in this society. Mrs Siddons herself was a part of this context and this life; her personal situation is also relevant.[40]

By 1782 she had four children living, and she was to have two more. She lived a blameless private life and seemed the perfect wife and mother to the outside world. Several of her most sympathetic characters are mothers, and all witnesses testify to the power and humanity of her depiction of the maternal emotions. These emotions manifested themselves strongly as soon as she returned to Drury Lane. As Isabella she played with much pathos the role of a grieving, inconsolable widow and a loving mother to her son Henry. Euphrasia is also a mother. Constance, the archetypal mother, expresses the maternal emotions with great force:

> O Lord, my boy, my Arthur, my fair son,
> My life, my joy, my food, my all the world,
> My widow's comfort and my sorrow's cure![41]   (III.iv)

Maternal grief is strongly expressed in Lady Randolph's final speech:

>   My son! my son!
> My beautiful! my brave! how proud was I
> Of thee, and of thy valour! . . .
> Now all my hopes are dead! A little while
> Was I a wife! a mother not so long!   (v.i)

The 'Lady of Distinction' who saw Siddons as Lady Randolph in Dublin believed that maternal grief was more affecting than paternal grief:

> There is something in maternal affection, that, I think, melts the soul to a degree of tenderness superior to what any other sensation can inspire; being composed of the softness of love, divested of its selfishness, blended with a warmth of affection equalled only by the paternal: I therefore doubt if this play would have been so affecting, had the father been substituted for the mother of Douglas.[42]

After Siddons as Lady Randolph listened to her (as yet unidentified) son's well-known speech beginning 'My name is Norval', G. J. Bell, who saw her in Edinburgh, noted, 'The idea of her own child seems to have been growing, and at this point overwhelms her and fills her eyes with tears. Beautiful acting of this sweet feeling throughout these speeches.'[43] Acting Jane Shore, who is not a mother, Siddons nevertheless enjoyed one of her finest moments when she fearlessly and contemptuously defied Gloster on behalf of Edward's children, calling on Providence to 'save the friendless Infants from Oppression'.

In these portrayals of agonised mothers projecting powerful feelings for their children, Siddons was very much part of a theatre that had begun to sentimentalise children and realise the potential for tragic and pathetic emotion in their stage plight. At this time there may also have been a change in social and familial attitudes to the child and the child–parent relationship, attaching more importance to the former and more emotional weight to the latter. The trend towards pathos and tragedy in this theatrical area reached full expression in the suffering children of nineteenth-century melodrama and their distraught mothers, but the sentimentally inclined tragedy of the second half of the eighteenth century began to work this new vein with great profit; it was ideally suited to an actress of strong pathetic powers.

Such stage indulgence in maternal feeling was in some quarters deemed excessive; in 1800 one critic complained that 'the peculiar abilities of this justly celebrated actress, for the representation of matrons, though excellent in all parts, has occasioned love in almost every new tragedy to give place to *conjugal* and *maternal* affection; indeed, so much has the latter got possession of the theatre, that the introduction of a *nursery* is become almost a hackneyed stage-trick'.[44] Even as Volumnia in the 1788–9 season Siddons had infused the victory procession that Kemble inserted into the second act of *Coriolanus* with a gigantic maternal pride: 'Sensitive to the throbbings of her haughty mother's heart, with flashing eye and proudest smile, and head erect, and hands pressed firmly on her bosom, as if to repress by manual force its triumphant swellings, she towered above all around, and rolled, and almost reeled across the stage.'[45]

The image of the good wife and good mother in adversity which Mrs Siddons offered to her audience was not only emotionally affecting but was also elevated into a moral standard that in itself was powerfully sympathetic. It was argued that the catharsis through pity and terror available through her characterisations strengthened virtue and the moral principle in audiences. A poem published anonymously in 1783, entitled *The Theatrical Portrait* and concerned with Siddons' portrayals of several leading characters, is not about her acting at all, but about the moral lessons to be learned from her performance and its laudable tendency 'to keep awake in the Mind the various Virtues and Vices of each Character, that the One may be pursued with more Alacrity and the Other shunned with the greater Detestation'. The presentation of moral virtue on stage is noble and essential:

Siddons pursue the glorious work divine,
To copy Nature let the Task be thine!
Each growing Grace and Sentiment impart
That warms the Passions and amends the Heart.
Long live to charm and captivate the Soul,
Correct the Manners and refine the whole.   (lines 382–7)

Although Calista and Jane Shore do not qualify for the category of good wife and good mother in adversity, moral conclusions were also drawn from them, since they are characters from which moral instruction can profitably be derived. Much of *The Theatrical Portrait* is concerned with them. In a long, thoughtful article in 1783, Thomas Holcroft used the suffering of Calista, conveyed through the medium of Mrs Siddons, as a lesson for the better class of people who went to the theatre:

> So perfect is her conception of the infamy of her crime and the horror of its consequences, and such is her detestation of herself and of the ruin she has induced, that we think it impossible for an innocent female to behold her agony, without feeling an additional dread of the like sin; or if she had begun to cherish vicious inclinations, not to be terrified from putting them in act. It is no hyperbole to say we congratulate the nation on the happy effects that are likely, at least for a time, to follow from its being so much the fashion among those of high rank to attend the performances of Mrs Siddons.[46]

Shakespearean characters could also be enlisted in the ranks of morality. Siddons' Queen Katharine was much praised for her moral dignity; conversely, the actress was so associated with virtue and moral beauty on the stage that the poet John Taylor worried about her choice of Lady Macbeth for her farewell performance in 1812:

> Ah, why not leave on the delighted eye
> A part where Virtue might with Genius vie,
> Energetic, gentle, dignified and kind!
> Such not the ruthless partner of the Thane . . .[47]

In an earlier poem, Taylor was concerned that Siddons was to play the evil Millwood in George Lillo's *The London Merchant*. She should not, Taylor said, 'paint the dread extreme of ill / That marks a MILLWOOD's mind' because as an actress she had not been, and must not be, associated with stage vice:

> We know thy worth too well,
> To think that Vice will touch that breast
> Where all the Virtues dwell.[48]

Sarah Siddons' popularity as an icon of female suffering and a dispenser of instructive stage morality was subsumed in the immense appeal she had for both sexes and for all theatre-going classes, especially those audience members of rank and fashion, and of social, artistic, and political distinction. Everybody who mattered in any sort of fashionable, artistic, or political circle went to see her act, and everybody wrote about her in letters to their friends and confided opinions of her to their journals and autobiographies. This is why there is so much primary evidence about her acting; in fact the sheer bulk of commentary from people not professionally associated with the theatre probably equals the amount of material on her available in the writing of actors, playwrights, critics, and theatrical biographers. As Anthony Pasquin put it,

> Her greatness is such that all classes adore it,
> Like Africa's whirlwinds, it sweeps all before it:
> She touches the boundaries of all we desire.[49]

Luminaries such as Pitt the Younger, Fox, Burke, Gibbons, Erskine, Windham, and Malone were frequent in their attendance. Sir Joshua Reynolds could often be seen at the front of the pit; the Prince of Wales, the Duke of Northumberland, the Duchess of Devonshire, and many other nobility were admirers, as were innumerable writers and painters. The Royal Family also extended its patronage. George III and Queen Charlotte had little liking for tragedy, and rarely went to Drury Lane; they preferred comedy and Covent Garden. However, in January 1783 they made an exceptional series of visits to Drury Lane and witnessed Mrs Siddons' Euphrasia, Belvidera, Calista, Jane Shore, and Isabella. The actress noted that 'the King was often moved to tears which he as often vainly endeavoured to conceal behind his eye-glass, and her Majesty the Queen, at one time told me in her gracious broken English that her only refuge from me was actually turning her back upon the stage at the same time protesting "It is indeed too disagreeable."' Shortly afterwards Mrs Siddons was appointed official Reader to the Royal Family, which meant that she visited Windsor and Buckingham House 'frequently' and read to the King and Queen; we do not know what, but it was probably Milton and Shakespeare. George III was a keen theatre-goer and a good critic of acting. He told her that 'he had endeavoured vainly to detect me in a false emphasis' and 'commended the propriety of my action, particularly my total repose in certain situations', contrasting this stillness with the perpetual fidgeting of Garrick.[50]

The presence of Reynolds in the pit of Drury Lane indicates another level of Sarah Siddons' appeal: to artists. Indeed, like Ellen Terry a century later, she achieved cult status as an art object, and there are far more paintings and engravings of Siddons than Terry. Indeed, the *Biographical Dictionary of Actors, Actresses, Musicians* . . . records 189 portrait paintings, drawings, and engravings of Mrs Siddons, and another 152 of her in stage roles, with a further number of caricatures, busts, statues, models in wax, paintings on porcelain, engravings on glass, and a chess set with Siddons as the Queen.[51] She was painted by Reynolds, Lawrence, Gainsborough, Romney, and a veritable host of other artists: Hamilton, Stothard, Rowlandson, Harlow, Downman, Westall, among others. Several of these artists painted her many times. The most famous of the paintings is Reynolds' *The Tragic Muse,* which borrowed from Michelangelo to universalise and dignify his own art and his enthroned subject.[52] There is no tradition of heroic and dominant women in eighteenth-century British painting; such paintings as Kneller's *Lucretia* and Romney's *Cassandra Raving* show women in attitudes of physical strength and courage, but when one considers what happened to the subjects, the paintings are hardly suitable for inclusion in any treatment of heroic women in art. Richard Westall's imposing *Lady Macbeth,* painted, like *Cassandra Raving,* for the Boydell Gallery, is said to be of Mrs Siddons in the role. *The Tragic Muse* is as near as any eighteenth-century painting gets to the empowerment of women. When Professor Bell saw Mrs Siddons giving one of her magisterial readings of Shakespeare in Edinburgh, he commented that Reynolds' painting 'gives a perfect conception of the general effect of her look and figure in these readings'.[53]

The artistic cult of Mrs Siddons is not hard to explain. By the time she played Lady Macbeth in 1785 she was thirty, and in her physical prime. She was then remarkably beautiful, on the tall side, imposing in appearance, dignified and even regal in bearing and movement, with an expressive and well-proportioned face, the characteristic Roman nose of the Kembles,[54] and a pair of piercing black eyes. She was also acclaimed and lionised, the unchallenged Queen of Tragedy. Celebrity attracts celebrities, who thronged to the theatre to see her, and, if artists, to paint her. Many of these paintings reflect the new taste for the heroic in contemporary culture.

James Boaden thought that Mrs Siddons' attitudes on stage were 'fit models for the painter and sculptor alike';[55] she was 'Blest with a form for happy sculpture's hand', as John Taylor put it.[56] The comparison of an actress to a statue was common enough in the pictorial theatre of the nineteenth century – Rachel was so compared – but Mrs Siddons is an early example of such comparative method, although it was a standard practice in eighteenth-century acting manuals to urge performers to study classical statuary in order to perfect bodily grace and physical force on stage. Siddons herself took up sculpture around 1790 and evidently achieved the level of a gifted amateur. Thomas Gilliland believed that this accounted for her perfection of stage form, although she was praised for her attitudes well before 1790. It is not therefore surprising that she played Hermione, which Hazlitt remembered for her monumental dignity and her exact resemblance to an antique statue.[57] Campbell agreed: she looked the statue 'even to literal illusion; and, whilst the drapery hid her lower limbs, it shewed a beauty of head, neck, shoulders, and arms, that Praxiteles might have studied'.[58] Hermione's amply folded drapery was carefully chosen to be strong in texture, and Siddons in her pose was compared to a muse in profile.

A by-product of her interest in statuary was an experiment with a simple hair style and classically draped costume instead of the traditional powdered head-dress and hooped skirt of the tragic actress. Reynolds advised her to abandon the old styles in favour of something classical and timeless, advice consonant with his views on the function of costume in painting. The change-over can be seen in Lady Macbeth's sleep-walking scene, which Siddons first played in white satin, the traditional dress of a heroine run mad, and then in shroud-like white drapery. Boaden declared that this development was significant for the technique of the tragic actress, and that the old, restricting style of dress hampered this technique:

> It might be called the swimming or voluptuous; and the actress seemed to
> totter under the weight of her *superior* charms. The spectator's eye was
> attracted to the visible palpitations of the heroine; and as the spread of the
> hoop below kept the arms in a nearly constant movement of floating grace,
> – the hand, more frequently than it is now, was prest upon the bosom: it
> was the MODE, and *perhaps* perfectly decorous. Mrs Siddons never *thought*
> it so.[59]

Hermione in 1802 was the last new Shakespearean role Sarah Siddons played; indeed, the last new role of any description. Reaction to it was

4 'Mrs Siddons' Dress as Zara.' *The Mourning Bride* (III.v), by Mary Hamilton. 1805.

5 'Mrs Siddons' Dress as Lady Macbeth.' *Macbeth* (III.iv), by Mary Hamilton. 1805.

respectful, if not enthusiastic, and largely confined to her beauty and reality as a statue. Reaction to her first major Shakespeare part at Drury Lane, Lady Macbeth, which she performed for her benefit in 1785, was, on the other hand, breathless and awestruck. It was a great characterisation and a splendid performance, a touchstone for tragic acting for many years; every Lady Macbeth for the next century had to play against its memory, handed down through theatrical generations by actors and critics alike, a huge shadow looming over every new interpretation. Because Lady Macbeth showed Siddons at the apex of her powers and indicated the absolute limits of tragic force upon the English stage, and also because it was the most important Shakespearean role she undertook, it is worth briefly sketching in the outlines of what she did.

She originally conceived the part, according to her undated 'Remarks on the Character of Lady Macbeth', which she handed over to her biographer Campbell about 1815, as 'fair, feminine, nay, perhaps, even fragile . . . captivating in feminine loveliness'. Only a combination of this attractive femininity with energy and strength of mind could have enthralled her husband – 'a hero so dauntless, a character so amiable, so honourable as Macbeth' – into doing such a dreadful crime. He becomes 'the infatuated victim of such a thraldom'. Macbeth's letter immediately sparks her 'vaulting ambition and intrepid daring' and she persuades him to her 'horrible design'. In the second act, however, Macbeth's 'naturally benevolent and good feelings resume their wonted power' and he renounces the scheme. But his 'evil genius' taunts and reviles him, and 'drives before her impetuous and destructive career' all the loyalty, gratitude, and humanity that Macbeth possesses. She is a savage creature by ambition, not by nature. The 'daring fiend' now pushes the plot to its conclusion, easily suppressing any humanity in herself that would hinder it. The third act shows her lost to heaven and abandoned to hell, with all peace of mind gone. Her wretchedness requires the actress to assume 'the dejection of countenance and manners which I thought accordant to such a state of mind'. Such affliction has subdued her pride and reduced her strength of will, and she strives to support her husband in his own suffering. At the banquet, she entertains her guests 'with frightful smiles, with over-acted attention, and with fitful graciousness; painfully, yet incessantly, labouring to divert their attention from her husband'. It is her own 'restless and terrifying glances towards

6 'Mrs Siddons as Lady Macbeth.' *Macbeth* (I.v). Artist unknown. Undated.

Macbeth', as much as his own behaviour, which amaze the guests. The breakup of the banquet is extremely difficult for the actress since she must simultaneously depict terror, remorse, hypocrisy, and other varied emotions in rapid, agitated succession. The last appearance of Banquo's ghost is also visible to Lady Macbeth because it is she who has suggested to Macbeth the murder of Banquo and Fleance with 'But in them Nature's copy's not eterne.' The sleep-walking scene must be terrible in effect, for, wasted in form and haggard in countenance, burning with the fever of remorse, the restless spirit wanders dismally in her apartment re-enacting her crimes; this scene is the most appalling in the play. Lady Macbeth's basically 'feminine nature' and 'delicate structure' have been crushed, not only by the enormous pressure of her crimes, but also by the burden of her husband's miseries, placed upon her at a time when she herself has 'perseveringly endured in silence the utmost anguish of a wounded spirit'. Macbeth's robust and less sensitive constitution enables him better to endure his pain, but this endurance also allows him to commit further crimes. As a couple, 'their grandeur of character sustains them both above recrimination . . . in adversity', for Macbeth, though impelled into destruction by his wife, feels no loss of love for her, yet she appears to have no tenderness for him until, 'with a heart bleeding at every pore, she beholds in him the miserable victim of their mutual ambition'.[60]

Thus it is clear that Mrs Siddons' Lady Macbeth comprehended both the feminine, delicate woman and the ruthless fiend; ambition for the crown turned the one into the other with great celerity during the letter scene and the following soliloquy. Some critics and at least one actress, Ellen Terry, have been puzzled by what they saw as a discrepancy between Siddons' conception of a fragile, feminine Lady Macbeth and the 'fiend-like queen' that emerged on stage. If her 'Remarks on the Character of Lady Macbeth' are read carefully, however, there is no discrepancy. One problem is the dating of her comments. They probably look back on thirty years of playing the part rather than forward to a role that still had to be developed and tested fully in the theatre, a summary rather than a plan. Possibly her performance altered after her brother John began playing opposite her as Macbeth. Her Macbeth until 1788 was Gentleman Smith, who was not regarded as effective in the role and was weakly subservient to Lady Macbeth. Siddons may have dominated him much more forcefully than she did Kemble.[61]

After a perusal of the 'Remarks on the Character of Lady Macbeth' and an examination of what Sarah Siddons did on stage, one is aware that the preparation of the role was exhaustive and the execution most thorough in detail. Everything in this execution was subordinate to the overall conception of a woman losing her femininity and humanity to the dictates of an overweening, murderous ambition and then finding the fruit of crime to be only fear, depression, agony of mind, and disintegration of the soul. Such a subordination of the parts to the whole was an essential aspect of Mrs Siddons' (and Kemble's) methods, what Macready referred to as 'one great excellence that distinguished all her personations. This was the unity of design, the just relation of all parts to the whole, that made us forget the actress in the character she assumed.'[62] In this respect Siddons can be contrasted with Mrs Barry, who, like Edmund Kean a generation later, acted from situation to situation and climax to climax, coasting in between, playing each promising moment with energy and force as it occurred, but not taking a general view of the character. The new Romantic emphasis upon the paramountcy of character in dramatic action, especially in Shakespeare, manifested itself in the work of actors as well as critics and was significantly related to a controlling passion in the demonstration of unity of character in performance: in Lady Macbeth's case, for Mrs Siddons, the passion of ambition; in the case of Mrs Beverley, devotion to her husband; in Lady Randolph, love of her child.

The principal source for a reconstruction of Sarah Siddons' performance of Lady Macbeth is a set of notes written on the text of the play as edited by Mrs Inchbald, notes made by G. J. Bell, Professor of Law at the University of Edinburgh, and evidently made very soon after the performance. Bell recorded his comments about 1807, which meant that he saw a Siddons with over thirty years experience of the role (which she had played in the provinces before 1775). These comments were published by Fleeming Jenkin in 1887.[63] Other descriptions of her performance, or moments of this performance, abound. With all this evidence available, it might be useful to indicate a few examples of Siddons' intelligence of interpretation and intensity of performance, and to convey some sense of the impression it made upon audiences.

Professor Bell was particularly struck in *Macbeth* by Mrs Siddons' 'turbulent and inhuman strength of spirit' through which she makes Macbeth 'her mere instrument'. There is little evidence in his notes of the fragile femininity of the actress' conception, but then it disappears, according to her, during her very first scene, and there is almost no time in which to establish it – surely a weakness in her idea. In the second half of the play Bell found morality in her acting: 'The flagging of her spirit, the melancholy and dismal blank beginning to steal upon her, is one of the finest lessons of the drama. The moral is complete in the despair of Macbeth.'[64] When Lady Macbeth tells him,

> Glamis thou art, and Cawdor, and shalt be
> What thou art promised,

Bell noted Siddons' 'exalted prophetic tone, as if the whole future were present to her soul'.[65] The stress on 'and shalt be' was heavy, and Boaden says that 'the amazing burst of energy upon the words "shalt be" perfectly electrified the house. The determination seemed as uncontrollable as fate itself.'[66] Bell goes into some detail on the soliloquy immediately preceding the entrance of Macbeth in i.v and on the ensuing dialogue. The phrase 'Come, you spirits' is spoken in a low voice, with 'a whisper of horrid determination'. For the few lines beginning 'Come to my woman's breasts' the voice is 'quite supernatural, as in a horrid dream. Chilled with horror by the slow hollow whisper.' On 'never shall sun that morrow see' – Siddons repeated the 'never' – she again spoke on a low, slow sustained note, and 'her self-collected solemn energy, her fixed posture, her determined eye and full deep voice of fixed resolve never should be forgot, cannot be conceived or described'.[67] One could continue quoting Bell for his sharpness of observation, descriptive ability, and richness of detail, but two more examples from *Macbeth* must suffice to illustrate Mrs Siddons' pantomimic powers. When Macbeth gives the speech 'We will proceed no further in this business', Lady Macbeth's silent reaction over the five lines is strikingly varied: 'The sudden change from animated hope and surprise to disappointment, depression, contempt, and rekindling resentment is beyond any powers but hers.'[68] In ii.ii, when Macbeth describes the behaviour of the sleeping grooms in Duncan's bedchamber, his wife's reaction is 'as if her inhuman strength of spirit [is] overcome by the contagion of his remorse and terror. Her arms about her neck and bosom, shuddering.'[69]

For many spectators the sleep-walking scene was the crown of

Siddons' achievement in the role. She glided on – too swiftly, Bell thought – and broke with tradition, over the strong objections of her mentor, Thomas Sheridan, by setting down the candle in order to rub her hands. Hazlitt was much impressed by her entrance: 'In coming on . . . her eyes were open, but the sense was shut. She was like a person bewildered, and unconscious of what she did. She moved her lips involuntarily; all her gestures were involuntary and mechanical . . . She glided on and off the stage almost like an apparition.'[70] Leigh Hunt termed sublime 'the deathlike stare of her countenance while her body was in motion' and admired 'the anxious whispering with which she made her exit', but considered that she washed her hands in too domestic and commonplace a manner.[71] Bell remarked that her cry 'O, O, O!' at the end of the 'perfumes of Arabia' speech was not a sigh, but 'a convulsive shudder, very horrible', with an audible 'tone of imbecility'.[72]

Sarah Siddons' involvement with the play did not end with her retirement from the stage. She gave public and private readings of Shakespeare on many occasions, including *Macbeth*, interpreting all the parts herself.[73] These were dignified, almost religious occasions: the priestess speaking the words of the oracle in the sacred temple. Boaden makes just such a comparison in describing a reading: 'She was dressed in white, and her dark hair à la Grecque crossed her temples in full masses. Behind the screen a light was placed, and, as the head moved, a bright circular irradiation seemed to wave around its outline, which gave to a classic mind the impression that the priestess of Apollo stood before you uttering the inspiration of the deity in immortal verse.'[74] It was neither the first nor the last time that Siddons in practising her art had been compared to a priestess exercising her divine function. In any case, her sensitivity to the text was as great as ever. Attending a reading in 1819, Mrs Piozzi remembered her treatment of Macbeth's lines

> Hence, horrible shadow!
> Unreal mock'ry, hence!

The actress, 'when she has said "hence!" recoils into herself, and adds, in a low and terrified tone, "horrible shadow!" then recovering, cries out triumphantly – ".unreal mockery – hence!".[75]

The performance of Lady Macbeth in 1785 came midway through

Sarah Siddons' third season at Drury Lane, or fourth, if the season of 1775–6 is counted. By this time she was the leading performer in the country. Her salary had risen from ten guineas a week for the 1782–3 season (Garrick gave her £5 a week) to £20 for the next season to £24 10s. in 1784–5. For this sum she appeared not less than three times a week. She was also profiting handsomely from lucrative benefits and provincial tours, to the total extent of £4,000 or £5,000 a year – a princely sum for an actress in the eighteenth century. By the season of 1809–10 she was receiving fifty guineas a night from Henry Harris at Covent Garden and guaranteeing thirty-five appearances in the season, for a total of £1,837 10s. Both Siddons and John Kemble, at last unwilling to tolerate any more broken promises and financial double-dealing from the erratic Sheridan, had moved to Covent Garden in 1802, where she remained until she retired.

Ill health had been as much a problem as Sheridan, and there had been times when one or the other, or a combination of both, kept her away from the London stage for long periods. She did not act at all at Drury Lane in 1789–90, spending her time in the provinces, and her health prevented her from making more than seven appearances during the following season, after Sheridan had finally persuaded her to return at the end of 1790. Another difficulty was the paucity of a modern tragic repertory in which she (or any other actress) could distinguish herself in good new parts, refreshing her own art and giving spectators something new and appealing at the same time. This did not happen. In a sense, apart from maturing in the same roles and the same proven attractions year after year, she had met all her challenges and conquered them by the end of the 1788–9 season, when she played Queen Katharine for the first time. In Shakespeare, only Gertrude and Hermione lay ahead of her, and a long series of failures by tragic authors, such as Fanny Burney's *Edwy and Elgiva* (1795), Robert Jephson's *The Conspiracy* (1796), William Godwin's *Antonio* (1800), and William Sotheby's *Julian and Agnes* (1801). The only big successes of her later seasons probably owed more to the plays themselves than to her undoubtedly fine acting in them. One was Augustus von Kotzebue's *Menschenhass und Reue*, adapted by Benjamin Thompson as *The Stranger*. A sentimental drama about a sinful but repentant woman and the misanthropic husband from whom she fled with another man years before, the play ran for twenty-six nights in the first few months of 1798, exciting controversy because it dealt sympathetically with a modern adulteress unpunished by society. Mrs Siddons played the erring wife, Mrs Haller, and once again drew floods of tears and cries of anguish from her audiences. It was one of a small minority of modern-dress parts in her repertory; Mrs Beverley was another. The other success was Sheridan's version of Kotzebue's conquistador drama *Pizarro*, which played for twenty-five nights in 1799, a spectacular production with Kemble (who had taken the role of the Stranger) as the Inca hero Rolla and Siddons as an idealised camp-follower and Pizarro's mistress, Elvira – a seemingly quite unsympathetic part which she elevated into something respectable, passionate, and even heroic.

As she got older, Sarah Siddons put on a great deal of weight (evidenced by the two Mary Hamilton water-colours), and this combined with various physical ailments hampered her movement. John Genest noted that she did not play Isabella and Belvidera as well as she used to because she could not throw herself upon the stage as required, or 'make such bodily exertions as she had formerly been accustomed to'. In her last season, when as Isabella in *Measure for Measure* she knelt to the Duke, 'she could not get up without assistance'.[76] Despite infirmity her appeal to audiences was almost as strong as ever. She never lost her supreme position; indeed, she never really had any serious rivals in tragedy. Only Eliza O'Neill, who appeared at Covent Garden in 1814, was considered in any way comparable: excellent in soft, pathetic, sentimental, and sorrowful roles – 'the very beau ideal of feminine weakness', Fanny Kemble said[77] – and a graceful and beautiful actress with a deep, strong voice, she had little of Siddons' power, majesty, or ability to excite fear and horror.

When Mrs Siddons as Lady Macbeth left the stage at the end of the sleep-walking scene in her farewell performance on 22 June 1812, the audience insisted that the curtain be dropped on the play and the farce not be acted. It was not, however, to be her final Lady Macbeth. Between 1813 and 1819 she made nineteen more appearances, eight at Covent Garden, one at Drury Lane, and ten in Edinburgh. She acted three times for the benefit of the Theatrical Fund, three times for the benefit of her brother Charles and his wife, and twice (Lady Macbeth) at the particular request of Princess Charlotte. All the Edinburgh performances, in 1815, were for the benefit of her recently deceased son Henry's family.[78] She played Lady Macbeth for the last time in 1817 and her last stage performance of all, at Covent Garden in 1819, was as Lady Randolph. Critics noticed that her once famously precise enunciation had gone and that her voice was occasionally indistinct. After she retired in 1812, she wisely resisted a considerable effort to persuade her to return to the stage. 'Her advancing old age is really a cause of pain to me,' wrote Crabb Robinson in his diary in 1811, 'she is the only actor I ever saw with a conviction that there never was nor ever will be her equal.'[79]

Professor Bell's comments upon Mrs Siddons' acting of Lady Macbeth show how much she had *thought* about every line she uttered and every gesture she made. Those contemporaries who knew her remark how thoroughly she prepared her roles. She had a reputation as a quick 'study'; the word in its common meaning characterises her approach to her art. She told Macready that he would be successful if he worked hard: 'study, study, study, and do not marry till you are thirty'.[80] Her own early marriage and the obstacles a growing brood of children placed in the way of the solitude and concentration necessary for the learning of lines and the study of a part must have been almost insurmountable difficulties as she struggled towards the top. Here was a woman with an indomitable will, a consuming ambition, and a fierce determination to succeed; only such a combination of character and motive could have taken her through the problems of her personal life to her ultimate goal.

Sarah Siddons did not speak her lines aloud as she learned them, and eighteenth-century rehearsals consisted principally of the performers muttering quickly through their lines, or just saying their cues, confirming stage business and arranging exits and entrances. They were also few in number, rarely more than seven, eight, or nine even for a new play. It was private study, then, that accounted almost entirely for Siddons' preparation of a part. According to her own word, she never repeated a performance without studying the part afresh.[81] Campbell said that her whole life 'was one of constant study and profound reflection on the characters she played, and on their relation to surrounding parts'.[82] The last comment is interesting, and illustrates her concern for unity and the relation of the parts to the whole. Most actors of the time, and in the next century, were concerned with their own parts, not those of others; it was a period when actors were completely responsible for their own characters. There were no directors to show them ways of developing characters in rehearsal or executing them adequately in performance. A unity of ensemble might develop in a good company, but this only happened when a group of talented actors played together for several years, and was in no way a matter of artistic conception or direction.

Mrs Siddons' propensity for study led some critics to accuse her of showing too much art in her acting and too little nature, especially towards the end of her career. Leigh Hunt believed this, as did George Steevens, and there were others. Frances William Wynn found her acting too artificial: 'her attitudes were fine and graceful, but they always seemed to me the result of study'.[83] It may be, as some thought, that as she got older she became more deliberate and seemed more studied. However, audience preferences were changing, and the climate of taste was growing more sympathetic to the likelihood of a fiery and seemingly impulsive Edmund Kean, who made his sensational London début as Shylock in 1814, than to a middle-aged actress who had been on the stage for a generation, a representative of an older classicism rather than a new, exciting romanticism.

Another aspect of Mrs Siddons' preparation for a role was a deliberate effort on her part to identify herself, in advance of performance, with her character's emotions. In her own remarks about playing Constance, she says that a real difficulty for the actress is always to keep in mind those events in the play which have such a dreadful effect upon her character's fortunes, although she is off-stage when they occur. Even when she is behind the scenes, therefore, the actress of Constance must focus upon these events. Siddons' own practice was to keep her dressing-room door open so that she could hear the cynical deals being arranged between King John and the King of France, and to place herself with Arthur to hear the march played when a reconciled John and Philip enter Angiers to ratify the marriage between Blanche and the Dauphin: 'The sickening sounds of that march would usually cause the bitter tears of rage, disappointment, betrayed confidence, baffled ambition, and, above all, the agonizing feelings of maternal affection to gush into my eyes. In short, the spirit of the whole drama took possession of my mind and frame, by my attention being incessantly riveted to the passing scenes.'[84]

Many observers noted that when Mrs Siddons played a part she seemed possessed by it; she wept real tears on the stage and the storms of emotion lashing the character she played seemed, in part at least, to be her own personal storms. In 1797 a newspaper review of her performance of the heroine Arpasia in Rowe's *Tamerlane* commented on Arpasia's reaction to the death of her lover Moneses, strangled before her eyes by deaf mutes at the order of Bajazet. She utters the following wonderfully grandiloquent lines and then swoons and dies:

> Distraction! Blast the Tyrant, blast him!
> Avenging Lightnings! snatch him hence, ye Fiends!
> Love! Death! *Moneses*! (v.i)

According to the reviewer, 'Mrs Siddons's manner of receiving the death of Moneses, and the struggle that ended in her own, was one of the best efforts of the art we ever beheld. This effort, however, was too much for her powers; for after her fall, her groans were so audible that the curtain was properly dropped, and it was some moments before she could be removed from the stage.' The audience would not allow the succeeding farce to begin until they were reassured from the stage that she had recovered.[85] Corroborating the incident, Campbell says that 'she wrought herself up in the character to a degree of agitation that was perilous almost to her life'.[86] Here, in a character that suffers extremes of emotional pain, Siddons had crossed that fine line between identification with a role and the actor's conscious control of that identification. This episode illustrates the point about possession. There is nothing 'studied' here.

The physical expression of emotion on the eighteenth-century stage reached thrilling moments of climax in scenes like the death of Moneses and the collapse of Arpasia. Prevalent theories of acting stated that the passions must be shown in bodily attitude, gesture, and facial expression as well as in the speaking of lines. Audiences would recognise each passion because its outward signs were universally known and peculiar to that particular passion; the performer's face, attitude, and gesture would be harmonised in the expression of any one passion. This visual and external language of the passions was an essential part of eighteenth-century theatre, in practice as well as theory. The emphasis on facial expression and the eyes was understandable in a theatre auditorium that had not yet grown too large for the whole audience to see the actor's face distinctly, especially as that actor was careful to come down to the footlights at crucial emo-

7 Seven attitudes by Mrs Siddons, the first attitude being a man. From left to right in
the upper row: Calista, Euphrasia, Constance. From left to right in the lower row:
Calista, Imogen, Lady Randolph, Belvidera. Gilbert Austin, *Chironomia*, 1806.

tional moments, to catch both the illumination they provided and the light
from the auditorium, whose candles were always left burning. Only when
Drury Lane and Covent Garden were rebuilt or greatly enlarged in the late
eighteenth and early nineteenth centuries were many spectators unable to
catch an actor's expression unless they were seated in the front of the pit or
the boxes nearest to the stage.

The passions were clearly registered in the face of Sarah Siddons, who,
like Garrick, was capable of rapid changes of expression. Thomas Holcroft
noted in 1783 that since her features are 'so well harmonized' in repose and
'so expressive when impassioned' people think her more beautiful than she
is. 'So great too is the flexibility of her countenance, that it takes the

instantaneous transitions of passion, with such variety and effect, as never to tire the eye.'[87] Siddons so often impersonated afflicted heroines that it was noticed that her face in repose assumed a permanently mournful cast; perhaps this was responsible for the 'unusual grandeur of mien' that Edward Mangin remembered. He said that 'by her countenance alone, she could signify anger, revenge, sarcasm, sorrow, pride, and joy, so perfectly that it was impossible to misunderstand her, though she had not spoken a word'.[88] Anger, revenge, grief (or sorrow), and joy are four of the major passions whose necessary stage characteristics are described and illustrated in eighteenth-century acting manuals, and it was the actor's job to show them in the face alone, if required by the action of a scene. The by-play of facial expression was far more important to the eighteenth-century actor than it is to the modern stage actor, and in Mrs Siddons it was especially impressive.

The eyes were of course a vital part of the facial expression of the passions, and critics often remarked upon their effect in the performance of tragic actors. Mrs Siddons was endowed, all agreed, with a striking pair of black eyes that transfixed the spectator (and other actors) with meaning and passion. (Today, reviewers do not comment on the eyes, even in performances that occur in small theatres.) Mrs Siddons' eyes were appropriate to contemporary ideas of the passions:

> Thy piercing eyes, through Passion's maze that roll,
> Mark all the painful feelings of the Soul.[89]

To express 'painful feelings' was indeed one function of the eyes on the eighteenth-century stage. 'Piercing' was a word frequently used to describe Siddons' eyes. Mangin said that they were 'brilliant and piercing, and could be seen to sparkle and glare at an incredible distance on the stage'.[90] Their effect was enhanced by the movement of the eyebrows and the muscles of the forehead. The actor George Bartley, playing with her in 1809 or 1810 in Thomas Franklin's tragedy *The Earl of Warwick* (she first acted Margaret of Anjou in 1784), remembered that Margaret made a sudden and electrifying entrance, which rendered him breathless, and stood motionless in an archway. It is worth quoting his description as another illustration of Mrs Siddons' power of making her effects without speaking a word:

Her head was erect, and the fire of her brilliant eyes darted directly upon mine. Her wrists were bound with chains, which hung suspended from her arms, that were dropped loosely on each side; nor had she, on her entrance, used any action beyond her rapid walk and sudden stop, within the extensive archway, which she really seemed to fill. This, with the flashing eye, and fine smile of appalling triumph which overspread her magnificent features, constituted all the effort which usually produced an effect upon actors and audience never surpassed, if ever equalled.[91]

Siddons regularly distinguished herself in this kind of prolonged pantomime, a characteristic of tragic acting in the eighteenth and nineteenth centuries. Her use of the eyes in such pantomime was notable. Early in her triumphant Drury Lane career, Thomas Davies, who had acted with Garrick, declared that her eye is 'so full of information that the passion is told from her look before she speaks'.[92] Twenty-five years later a critic wrote that at a glance from her eyes 'a spectator may possess her thoughts before she has opened her lips', these eyes revealing 'all the emotions of the heart with astonishing intelligence'.[93] Again, to speak with the eyes, to convey the requisite passion at a glance, was an ideal of acting theory, aimed at by all tragic actors but rarely achieved with such success and such startling impact as by Sarah Siddons.

The voice was just as important in the expression of the tragic passions as the face and eyes, and should be in harmony with them in giving strength and meaning to any passion. When Meister said of Siddons that 'there is a certain force of expression in her eyes and mouth which can only be compared with the tone of her voice, which is at once melodious, clear, articulate, and thrilling',[94] he was exemplifying this desired harmony. As we have seen, Henry Bate thought her voice was her weak point when he scouted her at Cheltenham, and this weakness was one of the reasons for bad reviews in her first Drury Lane season. Even when she returned victoriously in 1782, doubts about her voice were still heard. Horace Walpole thought it clear and strong but not sufficiently modulated.[95] The general opinion, however, was different. The actress herself had at last correctly gauged the size of the house while rehearsing for her début as Isabella and had satisfied herself, despite her fears, that any previous vocal problems had been overcome. Critics immediately praised her articulation – 'clear, distinct, and penetrating', said Holcroft[96] – her vocal power, her melody, and a plaintive quality that must have been advantageous in the playing of primarily pathetic roles like Isabella, Belvidera, and Jane Shore. Her habitual tragedy tones in the intercourse of daily life amused many, as did her tendency to speak in blank verse off-stage. The painter Benjamin Haydon once saw her at a christening addressing baby and onlookers 'with a voice like the Delphian priestess'.[97] Her 'ahs!' and 'ohs!' – essential ejaculations of grief in contemporary tragedy – were renowned: plaintive, and, as Davies put it, 'sweetly moving'.[98] Foreign visitors to the London theatres in the 1790s noticed that these 'ahs!' and 'ohs!' were a feature of English tragic acting, with the sounds of cries and exclamations measurably prolonged. Possibly Mrs Siddons' example had proved catching, for Holcroft said in 1783 that her manner of 'pronouncing the exclamation oh! in all passages where the passions are violently agitated' was peculiar to herself and one of her chief beauties.[99] As for the loudness of her voice, another visitor, Goede, exempted her and a mere handful of other actors, including Kemble and George Frederick Cooke, from the impropriety, as he termed it, of speaking too loud in order to be quite intelligible to the audience.[100]

The enlargement of Covent Garden in 1792 and the opening of a huge new Drury Lane in 1794 might be thought responsible for the loudness of the tragic actor's voice, although Goede claims that actors were as loud in a small theatre as a large. Mrs Siddons does not appear to have raised the volume of her voice to accommodate a larger auditorium, but Boaden suggests that a smaller stage hampered her movements, which were freer and more impressive on the new larger stages: 'When the area is considerable the step is wider, the figure more erect, and the whole progress more grand and powerful; the action is more from the shoulder, and we now first began to hear of the perfect form of Mrs Siddons's arm.'[101] Whether on a smaller or larger stage, Siddons was rarely included in the animadversions against English tragic actors by domestic and foreign critics, who objected not only to loudness but also to over-declamatory speech or rant, mechanical movements, a stress upon and lengthening of cries and exclamations, sudden tricksy starts, and, in the women, a forced vibrato and an artificial heaving of the breasts. Falling down upon the stage to die was surprising and shocking to foreign observers, whose tragedians died with grace and dignity upon a chair or sofa, but they came to realise that these apparent excesses of tragic style in English acting had, as Meister remarked, 'an infinite degree of expression, and produce a wonderful theatrical effect'.[102]

From the European point of view the rough edges and over-exuberance of English tragic acting were compensated for by a thrilling intensity and powerful theatricality. In Sarah Siddons this intensity and theatricality were especially concentrated in key moments of performance, big situational and emotional climaxes that were touchstones of her acting. The distraction and death of Isabella in the last act of Garrick's adaptation is one such climax, famous not only for the power of the acting but also, as we have seen, for the devastation it wrought upon audiences. The most sensational single point of this scene, as far as audiences were concerned, was Isabella's act of stabbing herself and simultaneously laughing ('Now, now I laugh at you, defy you all / You Tyrant-Murderers'). Even here she preserved a dignity of grief which all her despair, tears, terror, and madness could not take away. The mad laugh was so dreadfully real that it petrified audiences. Küttner said that Siddons 'produced the last frenzied cry of the dying with such horrible realism and several times made such sounds as to cut me to the quick, so that I veritably shuddered'. The whole last act was appalling, Isabella appearing 'with the genuine pallor of death'.[103] Other aspects of the scene were almost as shocking: the wild stare by the body of the dead Biron, Isabella's screams when her attendants try to separate her from the corpse, her attempt to drag the corpse away with her, and her increasing insanity, the cumulative effect of which Holcroft describes in answering those who would doubt the actress' superiority:

> Let them observe during her progression to madness, with what distinct shades sanity and reason are depicted, let them behold her frenzy increase till she attempts to stab her husband, let them watch the inexpressible anguish of her looks, while she clings to his body when dead, let them view her in her last agonies give her laugh of horror, for having at last escaped from such inhuman persecutors and insupportable miseries, and then, while their passions are warm, let them declare who is her equal.[104]

Or, as Anthony Pasquin puts it more poetically, writing of the same scene:

> Our pulses flow faint, as the ear drinks her sigh,
> While Murder and Savageness glare in her eye.[105]

55

8 Mrs Siddons as Queen Katharine in *Henry VIII* (II.iv). Artist unknown. Undated.

Another high point of Mrs Siddons' acting career was her performance of Queen Katharine in *Henry VIII*, a role in which murder and savageness – or madness – play no part. Here the two scenes constantly praised by spectators are what used to be called the Trial Scene (II.iv) and the scene in which the queen is dying (IV.ii). The power of the Trial Scene lies in the courage of a proud and persecuted woman, unshakeable in her sense of right, turning on her tormentors, the Cardinals Wolsey and Campeius, in defence of her own integrity and her marriage to the King. In this scene Mrs Siddons was at her most dignified and majestic, mighty, one could say: sorrowful, affectionate, and noble in her speech to Henry; vexed, indignant, and contemptuous in her address to Wolsey. The climactic moment in her playing of this scene came as she begins to speak to Wolsey. In what was obviously her own piece of business, Campeius comes forward to answer when she says, 'Lord Cardinal'. James Ballantyne best describes what followed:

> We feel it impossible to describe the majestic self-correction of the petulance and vexation which, in her perturbed state of mind, she feels at the misapprehension of *Campeius*, and the intelligent expression of countenance and gracious dignity of gesture with which she intimates to him his mistake, and dismisses him again to his seat. And no language can possibly convey a picture of her immediate re-assumption of the fullness of majesty, glowing with scorn, contempt, anger and the terrific pride of innocence, when she turns round to *Wolsey*, and exclaims, 'To you I speak!' Her form seems to expand, and her eye to burn with a fire beyond human.[106]

The dying scene was, of course, entirely different, played with melancholy and infinitely touching pathos, full of a gentle grief and restless bodily pain, but also of consideration for others. It also exhibited a courageous faith and a beautiful prospect of heaven before her. Bell's notes on the scene state that Mrs Siddons was 'admirable in simplicity and pathos . . . The voice subdued to softness, humility, and sweet calmness. The soul too much exhausted to endure or risk great emotion.'[107] A spectator at a private reading of scenes from *Henry VIII* in 1822 observed that 'in the farewell dying scene the very pillow seemed sick'.[108] In Queen Katharine Siddons displayed two contrasting powers: the ability to move sweepingly and majestically through a scene of high passion, of pride, contempt, and noble sorrow; and also the ability to achieve, by the utmost economy and richness of detail, a visible and pitiable progress to decay and dissolution. Something of the same contrast, between the Lady Macbeth who compels her husband to murder and the Lady Macbeth of the sleep-walking scene, preceded the playing of Katharine at Drury Lane by three years. Mrs Siddons grew into Katharine (she claimed she improved in all her parts), and her performance of the role late in her career seems to have been transcendent; many declared it was her most moving portrayal.

By now it must be clear that Sarah Siddons did not play her characters by concentrating on the emotional peaks of a role and treating the rest of it with a minimum of care and energy. The central idea of preserving unity of character would never have permitted this approach from her, and she was renowned for the patient building of a role and the most scrupulous attention to detail. The gradations and transitions in her performance of a part were known for being natural and unforced, even though sudden and violent transitions in mood were a feature of contemporary tragic writing and acting. Her powers of facial expression and pantomime were sufficient to develop and extend an emotional reaction either simultaneously conveyed by speech or registered in a silent reaction to an unfolding narrative. In the second act of *Douglas*, for instance, Lady Randolph listens with joy to the story of Young Norval's rescue of Lord Randolph from his foes: 'her countenance, through the whole scene, was so expressive of her feelings, that one could almost trace the passions as they rose, and succeeded one another in her soul; even her silence was eloquent'.[109]

The 'Lady of Distinction' whose letters about Mrs Siddons' acting in Dublin are published in *The Beauties of Mrs Siddons* records her performances in considerable detail and is a useful source of information about the fine points of the actress' repertoire. The final parting between Jaffeir and Belvidera in *Venice Preserved* (v.ii) is fraught with pity and agony; the letter-writer describes the descent into madness after Jaffeir departs, illustrating Siddons' attention to detail and the careful building of emotional effect:

> The composed melancholy, the anxious love, expressed in her countenance during Jaffeir's blessing, implored for in their last interview; the horror, the increase of horror, as she repeats his last word, 'parting', so expressive of her despair, all her strenuous affecting efforts to detain him – and when all failed – the grief in her voice and looks while she uttered these words;
>
> > 'Oh, my poor heart, when wilt thou break! –'
>
> I could have joined her. – The kiss begged with such affecting earnestness for her infant son, while with a piteous tone, and a voice interrupted with sobs, she uttered – 'I'll give't him, truly!' – the speechless horror she stood transfixed in at the departure of Jaffeir; the growing madness she finely

marked by the increasing wildness of her eyes, and the complete distraction manifested by striking her forehead as she exclaims –

'The air's too thin – it pierces my weak brain!'

Her wan countenance, her fine eyes fixed in a vacant stare, her shrieks of horror at the account delivered of Jaffeir's death – her smile and the imaginary embrace – were horrid in the extreme, and it was a relief to see her at last sink under miseries.[110]

In another example of careful gradation and a wealth of illuminating detail, Mrs Siddons' selection of business on the deathbed of Queen Katharine and 'the astonishing nicety with which her powers are made gradually to decay from the beginning to the end of the scene' impressed James Ballantyne, and show how in a much lower key and with entirely different emotional objectives she was equally effective:

Mrs Siddons, with a curious perception of truth and nature, peculiarly her own, displayed through her feeble and falling frame, and death-stricken expression of features, that morbid fretfulness of look, that restless desire of changing place and position, which frequently attends our last decay – with impatient solicitude, she sought relief from the irritability of illness by the often shifting her situation in her chair, having the pillows on which she reposed her head, every now and then removed and adjusted – bending forward, and sustaining herself, while speaking, by the pressure of her hands upon her knees, and playing, during discourse, among her drapery with restless and uneasy fingers, and all this with such delicacy and such effect combined, as gave a most beautiful, as well as most affecting portraiture of nature fast approaching to its exit.[111]

In case it would appear that contemporary response to Sarah Siddons consisted entirely of paeans of praise, she had her detractors. There were those, as we have seen, who thought her acting consisted of too much study and art and too little nature, those who complained that she was too deliberate, those who believed Mrs Crawford the better actress, those who objected to her voice, those who declared that she was deficient in pathos and amatory tenderness, and, on the personal level, those who accused her of being grasping and miserly. Those who objected in such ways constituted, however, a small minority of critical reaction. Upon one thing almost everybody could agree: that Mrs Siddons was not much good at comedy. Although before her first appearance at Drury Lane she had obviously considered herself just as much a comic as a tragic actress, she never really succeeded in a comic role in London; Rosalind in 1785 was her chief attempt. Unlike Garrick, who was a superb comedian, she was not versatile enough to encompass both tragedy and comedy. The difficulty seems to have been that she was simply too dignified, too magnificent, too habituated to the mournful, too eminently suited for tragedy to play comedy well. Anna Seward, a great admirer, said of the Rosalind that though it had estimable features, 'the playful scintillations of colloquial wit, which most strongly mark that character, suit not the dignity of the Siddonian form and countenance'.[112] (The word 'Siddonian' entered the English language about this time to denote a person with Mrs Siddons' stage characteristics.) Or, as the wickedly irrepressible Anthony Pasquin remarked of her Rosalind,

> Her hoarse awful accents were never design'd
> To lighten those cares which obtrude on the mind.

He concluded that

> The dimples of Pleasure must *Siddons* resign;
> Who's wedded cold Horror, and bow'd at her shrine.[113]

Concerning her strengths as an actress there was, except on a few of the points listed above, a general, even massive accord. She was, all agreed, completely attentive to the business of the scene and always stayed in character, even when she was not speaking, or, as Holcroft put it, 'her passions are as active while she is silent as when she is speaking, she is not Belvidera one moment and Mrs Siddons the next'.[114] Today we take this for granted, but eighteenth-century theatrical commentary was full of complaints about actors whose eyes wandered over the auditorium when they were not speaking, who greeted friends in the audience from the stage (Kemble did this), or who stood withdrawn and vacant until their cue came. Mrs Siddons never seemed to know that there was an audience in the theatre, and concentrated entirely on what her character was doing. 'When Mrs Siddons left her dressing-room', said Boaden, 'I believe she left there the last thought about herself.'[115] Even *in* her dressing-room, as we have seen with her Constance in *King John*, she was getting into character by leaving the door open so that she could hear what was happening on stage.

Although dissenters were heard on the subject of her voice – not strong enough or varied enough at the beginning – nobody complained, until very late in her career, of her remarkable articulation or her elocutionary powers. In acting the passions, she was notably impressive in the portrayal of pride, scorn, grief, disdain, indignation, and – most would concur – the pitiable. A dissenting critic writing in 1802 thought her representations 'imperfect' in 'the gentle and pathetic parts', but said that she excelled 'in scenes of convulsive anguish, terrific agitation, or vindictive jealousy'.[116] These tremendous emotions were true to nature, commentators agreed, because they arose naturally from the character played and the emotional situation of that character; they were true to the feelings of the character and not merely theatrical displays. We know that Siddons identified with characters and was even possessed by them; their feelings depicted on stage were not artificial exercises in the acting of the passions. The always useful and observant Holcroft was aware of this when he wrote in 1783, 'It is not the declamation of study, the display of attitudes, or the stride of assumed dignity by which we are charmed, but those exact and forcible expressions of feeling that stamp reality on fiction, and make it no longer an imitation but a truth.'[117]

Of all Sarah Siddons' stage attributes, critics and spectators were most struck with what one could justly term her monumentality, her elevation, statue-like, above the common run of players. Adjectives like 'grand', 'majestic', 'regal', 'awful', 'sublime', and 'superhuman' commonly occur in the contemporary lexicon descriptive of her acting. Boaden believed that though she was always feminine, she 'seemed to tower beyond her sex'.[118] Tate Wilkinson declared that if he were asked 'What was like a queen?' he would have pointed to 'Mrs Siddons in her great chair, in the first act of "Henry VIII"'.[119] Mrs Piozzi said that the Earl of Errol in his coronation robes and Mrs Siddons as Euphrasia were 'the noblest specimens of the human race I ever saw'.[120] She also noticed 'a sort of Radiance which comes round her in Scenes where strong heroic Virtues are displayed'.[121]

The aura of heroic and sublime majesty grew brighter as Siddons matured, and by the early nineteenth century the process of deification, which had begun with Reynolds' painting *The Tragic Muse* in 1784, was complete. It was not a coincidence that the same period witnessed a new interest in the heroic in British history painting and in the Shakespearean paintings of the Boydell Gallery, an unsuccessful venture launched in 1789 that commissioned scores of paintings of scenes and characters in Shakespeare from the leading and the lesser artists of the day. A propensity for the heroic can sometimes be seen in the attitudes struck in these paint-ings, such as Benjamin West's *Lear in the Storm,* Romney's *Cassandra Raving,* and John Francis Rigaud's *The Death of Hotspur.* It can also be seen in Thomas Lawrence's paintings of Kemble as Hamlet and Rolla in *Pizarro,* and William Hamilton's two paintings of Siddons as Euphrasia. One of the reasons for her success was that she incarnated this taste for the heroic on stage, and the approved values of dignity, grandeur, and majesty were embodied for many years in the acting style of the Siddons–Kemble school. A new taste for the sublime was also strong, especially in the land-scape and in landscape painting. The grand, the lofty, the 'terrific', the awe-inspiring, and the exalted were all subsumed in the 'sublime'; they were also deemed to be part of the essential nature of Mrs Siddons' acting.

The elevation, enthronement, and enshrining of Sarah Siddons, a goddess far above mortality, is nowhere more strikingly illustrated than by Hazlitt's reverent and splendid apostrophe:

> The homage she has received is greater than that which is paid to queens. The enthusiasm she excited had something idolatrous about it; she was regarded less with admiration than with wonder, as if a being of a superior order had dropped from another sphere, to awe the world with the majesty of her appearance. She raised tragedy to the skies, or brought it down from thence. It was something above nature. We can conceive of nothing grander. She embodied to our imagination the fables of mythology, of the heroic and deified mortals of elder time. She was not less than a goddess, or than a prophetess inspired by the gods. Power was seated on her brow, passion emanated from her breast as from a shrine. She was Tragedy personified. She was the stateliest ornament of the public mind. She was not only the idol of the people, she not only hushed the tumultuous shouts of the pit in breathless expectation, and quenched the blaze of surrounding beauty in silent tears, but to the retired and lonely student, through long years of solitude, her face has shone as if an eye had appeared from heaven; her name has been as if a voice had opened the chambers of the human heart, or as if a trumpet had awakened the sleeping and the dead. To have seen Mrs Siddons was an event in every one's life.[122]

This kind of language was used for no other actor or actress, not even Mrs Siddons' respectably heroic brother John. The phrase 'the divine Sarah' refers to Bernhardt; it could just as well have been applied to Siddons a hundred years earlier. No previous performer on the English stage, Garrick included, had been accorded the adoration of such worship, and certainly none since. The actress as goddess is a cultural phenomenon unique in the English theatre; Sarah Siddons remains the only divinity of the English stage.

She may have been the queen or goddess of tragedy, but in her own home she was Mrs William Siddons. The contrast between her stage career and her domestic situation could not have been more extreme. On the one hand, she was at the head of her profession, earning large sums of money, famous, and almost everywhere honoured and exalted. On the other, she was legally inferior to her husband, who had the right to her income, the disposition of her children, and the ordering of their marital affairs. The adored William of their courtship had grown into a mediocrity with a mean streak. He never proved to be much of an actor, and was soon over-awed and reduced to a nullity by his wife's reputation and immense success. It would have been an understandably difficult position for any husband, and William Siddons did not cope with it very well. At his best he was, evidently, pleasant and affable, at his worst a bossy fusspot, jealous of his wife's standing and determined to assert himself in the home. They had their differences, and there was a great deal of tension in the Siddons household. Until he died in 1808 he managed her business affairs – not very well, it seems – dealing with managers, arranging tours, demanding fees, and making investments. His wife accepted all this (legally she had to) and was submissive rather than recalcitrant. She turned over her large income to him and received in return a quarterly allowance; we do not know how much. Raising and worrying about her children occupied most of her time away from the stage: her professional and domestic responsibilities together were crushing. She looked up to her younger brother John, by all accounts the inferior performer, and even accepted suggestions about interpretation and staging from him. In a domestic and professional world run by men, there was little rebellion in her nature.

There is no doubt, however, that her domestic life and personal situation were related to and affected her art. Most obviously her image off-stage as the good wife and mother won her audience respect and was transferred to the tragic roles like Isabella, Constance, and Lady Randolph, in which she depicted strong maternal feelings. This respect was admiringly expressed by Thomas Young:

But well may *she assume* sensations here,
Who dignifies her state in PRIVATE sphere,
The WIFE unblemish'd, and the MOTHER dear.
'Tis FICTION which commands our stage applause,
Practice in private life adorns the cause.[123]

Mrs Siddons outlived five of her seven children; one of them died in infancy, one at the age of six. In private life her own maternal feelings dominated all other emotions; she doted on her children, agonising over their health and their future. She must have used such feelings in playing mothers proud and protective of their children.

Other private feelings also provided material for her stage life. In 1828 the poet Thomas Moore talked to Mrs Siddons and made the following entry in his diary: 'Among other reasons for her regret in leaving the stage was, that she always found it a vent for her private sorrows, which enabled her to bear them better; and often she has got credit for the truth and feeling of her acting when she was doing nothing more than relieving her own heart of its grief.'[124] The precise nature of this grief and these private sorrows are left unspecified, but we can guess that they had a lot to do with her frustrating and limiting marital and domestic life. Here she was, a great star by any definition of the word, famous throughout the length and breadth of the theatrical land, treated with respect and awe by managers and her fellow players and with idolatry by the public, courted by the nobility and the cultural elite, earning entirely on her own account very substantial sums of money year after year, the sole support of her large family — and yet severely constricted in the home, unable to be independent, and subordinate to the dictates of a petty, small-minded, often cantankerous husband. No wonder there were 'private sorrows'.

The theatre, then, and the opportunities offered by the public expression of tragic woe, was the only satisfactory compensation available. At home she had little outlet for her emotions; in the theatre they could be fully indulged and grandly elaborated. The extraordinary and superhuman Euphrasia, towering over tyrant-ridden Syracuse, defiant and successfully rebellious, must have been rich recompense for Sarah Siddons, housewife of Gower Street. And was her Drury Lane Lady Macbeth, a powerful, ambitious, and resolute woman who completely controlled her lesser husband — at least before John Kemble took over the part of Macbeth from Gentleman

Smith – not only deeply satisfying to her female audience but also to her personally? Indeed, as an actress Siddons far outshone any actor on the stage, and her acting was more heroic than any male acting. In the great public world of the eighteenth-century theatre no woman could have achieved more. In her circumscribed private life, that, at least, made up for a lot.

Sarah Siddons was the first English stage performer to affect audience behaviour so powerfully, and by the nature and style of her characterisations of suffering women the first to reach out and arouse, in an almost uncontrollable outflow of feeling, the sympathetic emotions of the female part of her audience. Her reputation comprehended her performance in tragedy but went further than that. She was an actress, but she was much more. She was also a muse, a goddess, a presiding deity. She was a myth in her own time, an art object, the priestess of a worshipping cult.[125] The rich and famous in all spheres of life sought her acquaintance and fought for seats when she acted. On the stage, from the point of view of the sheer power and mastery of tragic art, nobody could come near her. Perhaps the last word can be left to Sir Walter Scott, by no means an unqualified admirer. He was doubtful about her taste, suspicious of her vanity, and wished she had read more widely. 'And yet', he wrote in 1819, 'take her altogether and where shall we see I do not say her match but any thing within a hundred degrees of what she was in her zenith'[126] – a fitting metaphor of the heavens with which to conclude a study of Sarah Siddons.

RACHEL FELIX

JOHN STOKES

To reclaim tragedy for the female performer, Rachel Félix had first to occupy a theatrical space identified with the male presence. It was this paradoxical assault that initially made her art so startling, and so different from the recent run of French *tragédiennes*. Vehement in roles that had become the repositories of pathos, Rachel seemed able to dominate the stage entirely by herself, without masculine support or masculine competition.

Jules Janin, an admirer of the Romantic writers, and Rachel's first great champion among critics, recognised this aspect of her art almost at once, writing later that,

> Whatever the merit or the talent of tragic actresses before Rachel, the actor was the absolute master of tragedy and, as far as we were concerned, an actress always took second place. Then, suddenly, we were both astonished and charmed by a young woman who represented all by herself the whole of Shakespeare.[1]

The anonymous comparison here is with Harriet Smithson whose conquest of Paris had begun in 1827 when, opposite Charles Kemble, she had played Ophelia, Juliet, and Desdemona to a delirious response.[2] Janin's point was not that French tragedy offered no great parts for women – which would have been absurd – but that these roles were often subjugated to a central male character who was given the burden, and the distinction, of tragic suffering, and that, in comparison with the emotional distraction whipped up by Smithson, the feelings conveyed by the female characters in French plays seemed tame and overcontrolled. Smithson, in other words, had prepared for Rachel's effect upon French audiences by teaching them that they could expect great things of actresses as well as of actors.

9 Photograph of Rachel as Phèdre by Nadar.

Rachel may have begun with female heroics, later she discovered the drama in erotic desire, and, later still, she pioneered a style of acting based on Romantic emotion. But she also experimented with types of theatre in which fixed ideas of gender are questioned, and sometimes overcome. And all along, from the very start, her representation of the variety and depth of female experience was thought to be complicated by her own racial and social origins.

Born in 1821, she was the daughter of an itinerant Jewish pedlar and had an arduous, even brutal, childhood. But membership of the Jewish community – her family became involved with the Jewish colony who lived in the Marais[3] – gave her an identifying tradition that she could always invoke, as well as a political present she would have to confront. Her racial background conditioned the way in which she was seen by others, both Jewish and non-Jewish,[4] and to some extent the repertoire she chose. The most obvious example is *Judith* by Madame Girardin, introduced in 1843 as a bid to create a modern tragedy on a biblical theme, but there were others, such as Racine's Old Testament drama *Athalie* (1847), and Rachel even managed to bring a racial implication to plays set in classical Greece or Rome. In Napoleonic times, in spite of some relaxing of barriers, the legal rights of Jews had still been debated in terms of where their ultimate loyalty might lie[5] – with the state or with their own people – and signs of that legacy can be found in Rachel's relationship with her Paris audience in the late 1830s which is said to have included a Jewish claque, though she was undoubtedly subjected to harsh anti-Semitic attacks as well. In her tragic roles Rachel addressed this factional audience as if it were one, and by refusing to be appropriated, yet retaining her racial identity, held it in thrall.

She went on to demonstrate the same power on an unprecedently international scale. Between 1841 and 1856 she appeared in cities throughout France and Great Britain; in the Low Countries, Italy and Switzerland; in Warsaw, St Petersburg, Berlin, and Vienna; in New York, Boston, and, her very last performance, Charleston, North Carolina; and always in a language that many in her audience couldn't understand. It was beyond all doubt that here was an extraordinary phenomenon, a performer able to touch a huge and variegated audience at some deep and instinctive level of recognition.

Like many great Romantic talents Rachel may in part have succeeded by breaking rules she didn't even know to exist. Her spell at the Conservatoire – where she was brusquely criticised by Provost, a celebrated Professor – had been brief and unhappy. True, she had then been taken up by Joseph Isidore Samson, another formidable teacher who instructed her according to his own principles of declamation.[6] Nevertheless, however important Samson's contribution, the Romantic aura of an untutored 'genius' continued to surround her, all her life.

Rachel's relations with institutional authority were always fraught. In 1838 she joined the Comédie-Française, having first made a stir with her performance in *La Vendéenne*, a melodrama derived from Sir Walter Scott's *The Heart of Midlothian*, at the Gymnase in April of the previous year. It was at the Comédie-Française that she was to create, in rapid succession, her most famous roles: among them, Camille in *Horace*, Emile in *Cinna*, Pauline in *Polyeucte*, all by Corneille, Hermione in Racine's *Andromaque*, Roxane in his *Bajazet*, and eventually Phèdre. Although at first the receipts failed to reflect her talent, by October 1838 Rachel was demanding, and getting, a considerably increased salary that was raised yet again early in 1839. The instrument behind this rapid advance was Rachel's father, Jacob Félix, who now not only insisted that his daughter should be made a *sociétaire* and receive substantial payment, but that she be granted four months' annual leave. This allowed the actress to perform away from Paris, a profitable custom that she inaugurated first with performances in provincial France, and then with a sensational season in London in May 1841.

By 1846 Rachel's relations with the Comédie-Française, dogged by absence and ill health, had reached such a point that she submitted her resignation. But this gesture appears not to have been ratified and, with interruptions partly brought on by pregnancy, she was still appearing at the rue de Richelieu when revolution broke out in 1848. It was at the Comédie-Française that she was able to introduce in 1849 *Adrienne Lecouvreur* by Scribe and Legouvé, a play that required a quite new style of acting. In the autumn of that year the threat of resignation again became serious, resolved only by the appointment of Arsène Houssaye, Rachel's favourite, as Director, and by a new contract that, although reducing her status to that of *pensionnaire*, allowed her six months' annual leave. Rachel took considerable advantage of these arrangements: there were several

long engagements abroad between 1850 and 1854, matched by great antag-
onism at home culminating in a major quarrel at the time of Samson's
retirement in 1853. In 1854 Rachel's resignation was again declared, but
that autumn she returned to the Comédie-Française for what was, as it
turned out, to be her last season, its achievements somewhat overshadowed
by the continuing row over Legouvé's *Médée*, a role she had finally refused.

By now Rachel's state of health was exacting an ever greater toll.
Periods of extended leave from the Comédie-Française enabled a last visit
to London, and, starting in 1855, the fateful American tour. Long before her
death in 1858 it was apparent to all that the days of glory were over.

Rachel had the most extraordinary and complicated career. She set a
pattern for professional endeavour that actresses all around the world were
to inherit. The temptation to attribute the scale of her financial success primarily to her fondness for tough negotiation or, for that matter, to her
apparently scandalous private life with its series of influential lovers and
mentors, should be resisted. Whatever her strengths as an independent
woman, her acting style alone was felt as the expression of large-scale
struggles. She lived in an age of revolution, and the fact that her own political allegiances sometimes appear to have been guided largely by
opportunism does not affect the rebellious significance of her art. The idea
that creativity should be autonomous, self-generating, was itself historically based and, although in France it could be linked to conservative ten-
dencies on individualistic grounds, faith in the power of pure inspiration
always enlivened the present. Rachel drew much of her potency from the
complex intellectual climate in which she worked, and she gave back
energy in return.

In fact it was heated engagement with tradition that made the French
theatre of the 1830s such a fertile forcing ground, and so very demanding
on the performer. An actress who was able to persuade the French
Romantics, let alone an international public, that there was life to be found
in the stiff formality of neo-classical tragedy, certainly never lacked
courage. And it is courage that is always said to be one of the bases of
Rachel's theatre – courage and intelligence.

Rachel's most recent biographer, Rachel M. Brownstein, insists that
'Rachel and her life were embedded in legends', and announces her own
aim as wanting to 'map that fantastic forest, to suggest that the interlocking

10 Portrait photograph of Rachel. Photographer unknown.

branches of fact and fiction there cannot be disentangled'.[7] The aim of this essay is at once more modest and more risky: to recapture Rachel in performance through the processes of scholarly reconstruction, the traditional means of the theatre historian.

The material is certainly to hand. Modern biographies are exceptionally well-researched, and Rachel is mentioned in countless memoirs. There are several works entirely given over to recording her presence. Janin's *Rachel et la tragédie* (1859) includes a remarkable sequence of photographs by Henri de la Blanchère. Samson's long poem *L'Art Théâtral* (1863–5) describes many of Rachel's roles and implies, not unexpectedly, that in her interpretations she was, by and large, following his edicts.[8]

Janin, the modern journalist, whose development of a loosely rhetorical prose style paralleled Rachel's progress as an actress, tends to explain her art as the result of instinct. Samson, her teacher, prefers to see it as the product of a closely guided talent. The divergence reflects a much wider debate about the nature of acting, but read together their accounts do create a useful frame through which to focus her impact.

As for contemporary reviews, those by foreign spectators are in some ways the most useful because they spell out in detail what might be overfamiliar to a French readership. English critics can be extraordinarily meticulous in this respect, matching their intimate knowledge of French prosody with precise attention to Rachel's delivery. The best-known English records of her performances, which are by G. H. Lewes, are invaluable, but far from unique.[9]

In truth, the wealth of material accumulated over the fifteen years when Rachel was touring should act as a caution as much as an invitation. Performances vary and audiences differ, so no reconstruction can ever provide a complete account of an interpretation, while composites are, by definition, occasions that never occurred. Still, with these provisos in mind, it can be rewarding to re-create a role from a range of sources, to select some of the effects that were sometimes achieved. In the case of Rachel, because so much of the documentation is to do with her use of her body and with the kind of rhetorical stresses she developed, the underlying principles of her acting do emerge. These, in turn, can bring us closer to an understanding of an important phase in the changing relation between tragedy, gender, history.

Rachel M. Brownstein makes an essential point when she writes that by opting for classical tragedy in the 1840s the actress:

> revived multiple pasts and superimposed them on one another: an idealized Greco-Roman world that seemed nearly legendary, and the differently, dubiously glorious periods of the *ancien régime* and Napoleon. And by figuring high tragedy and heroism in female form, she subtly redefined and undercut them.[10]

This is all true: what remains to be determined is what exactly Rachel did on stage.

LE REGARD

The most famous image of Rachel is a posthumous portrait by Jean-Léon Gérôme, dated 1859, which hangs in the Comédie-Française. Entitled *Rachel personnifiant la Tragédie* it shows her expression very much as it was universally remembered and described. By Fanny Kemble, for instance:

> Mademoiselle Rachel's face is very expressive and dramatically fine, though not absolutely beautiful. It is a long oval, with a head of classical and very graceful contour, the forehead rather narrow, and not very high; the eyes small, dark, deep-set, and terribly powerful; the brow straight, noble, and fine in form, though not very flexible.[11]

In Gérôme's academic painting Rachel is surrounded, correctly, by the attributes of Melpomene: pillar, dagger, and mask, and she leans against a plinth upon which are listed the roles with which she was most famously associated: Phèdre, Hermione, Camille, Roxane, Pauline. On a sarcophagus to one side the names of the great tragic playwrights, Aeschylus, Sophocles, Euripides, Corneille, Racine, are all listed.

Melpomene is a conventional enough identification for a great French actress. The Comédie-Française houses a bust of Clairon as Melpomene;[12] Voltaire's elegy for Adrienne Lecouvreur laments that 'Melpomene is no more!'[13] Rachel herself was often hailed as 'the Jewish Melpomene', the tragic muse incarnate, during her own lifetime: by Janin, for instance, when he wrote that 'she had the arms of Melpomene', or that 'in the disguise of Melpomene she achieved the dignity of an heroic marble statue'.[14]

11 Engraving of 'Rachel personnifiant la Tragédie' by Jean-Léon Gérôme.

In Gérôme's picture Rachel has unmistakable suggestions of 'an heroic marble statue': her arms are almost vertical columns and the set of her head seems fixed, though whether she is settling into marmoreal stasis or emerging out of it, remains, even in this commemorative study, uncertain. Which is as it should be since, although Rachel's ability to evoke the statuesque was undoubtedly celebrated, it was seen as only a part of the complex process of her acting style. As Théophile Gautier wrote of her,

> This frail girl with her stern gaze, her pale face, her nervous febrile bearing, with her gestures both restrained and violent, her bitter smile, her nostrils flaring with disdain, with her ferocious diction and her explosions of rage, who seemed like an ancient marble mask of Melpomene, had such a splendid, noble appearance that she never allowed suffering to alter its beauty, and even when plunging a dagger into her heart worried about the fine folds of her tunic, preserving the purity of her outline until her final convulsion.[15]

The same image of breathing statuary is relied upon by Arsène Houssaye, once a Romantic poet, in a verse that places Rachel in the line of great *tragédiennes* at the same time as it indicates her difference:

> Champmeslé, Lecouvreur and Clairon have destroyed themselves,
> But you reign, Rachel, with your beating heart and your wise brow;
> Your great soul gives life to a race of statues,
> Passionate muse, heart of gold, living marble.[16]

What the Romantics saw in Rachel was not just the technical skill that allowed her to stand as still as stone, but, rather more than that, an ability to convey the sense of gestation. After all, it was 'time to show that tragedy is something more than just a declaiming statue', as another great admirer of Rachel, Alfred de Musset, pronounced in his symptomatic essay of 1838 entitled 'On Tragedy'.[17]

All this is apparent in a portrait that was, in fact, painted from photographs, certainly from a study by Nadar. While a biographer might reasonably protest that Gérôme show us a female figure so dwarfed by the surrounding paraphernalia that she 'seems to be its sick, apprehensive victim, a woman who dreads becoming her own monument',[18] the portrait, which became widely distributed as a print, does conform to Rachel's Phèdre, at least in some of her moods. More importantly its origin in the Nadar photograph is a significant reminder that Rachel was among the very first performers to be systematically recorded by the camera.

At the same time as it evokes a transitional breaking into movement, so Gérôme's painting preserves, in the living detail of her gaze, something of the physical intensity of some (admittedly not all) of these photographic studies. The head is foregrounded in the overall composition, the look direct yet slightly oblique, compelling the spectator to imagine the ways in which that inner concentration must have been answered by the response of her audience.

In the middle of the nineteenth century the relation between photography and theatrical realism was reciprocal. Early photographers, tied to long exposure times, were more interested in recording a significant pose than the instants of arrested motion that preoccupied their successors, and the codified gestures of nineteenth-century acting provided suitable subject matter. Performance, in due course, had to match the new means of representation with a display of the living body that possessed all the tension, the human intelligence, that an acutely detailed photographic portrait might convey. This is why the photographs of Rachel, while disappointingly muzzy, are significant. Their very staginess is the point.

When Rachel left for America in 1855 an English newspaper consoled itself with this thought:

> To us in the meantime there will remain, not only the vivid recollection of her wonderful creations, but a new and very life-like portrait to remind us of them. Copies have been multiplied of a full-length photograph of Mdlle Rachel in the character of Phèdre, which is curious for its exact resemblance. Indeed it enables the distinctive features to be seen more accurately than when we look at the real Phèdre or Camille from before the footlights . . .[19]

It is clear from this alone that Rachel's acting was subjected to an attention every bit as intense as that directed at an eighteenth-century actress such as Siddons, but with a new, technological yardstick. After Rachel to be a performing woman was always to be subjected to a particularly severe form of scrutiny, and, if successful, to become a widely distributed image.

Nevertheless, in Gérôme's picture the unavoidable proximity of Rachel's gaze and the precisely rendered vertical drop of her draped body are countered by mysterious distance: in the background a series of classical columns recede into shadow, and are mirrored or matched by another set of pillars, even further behind, which are, for the most part, lost in gloom. These upright parallel lines, which seem at some points to sway as if on a painted backcloth, suggest both the classical themes with which Rachel was associated and the theatrical means necessary to bring them to life. They also mark the hymeneal boundary between the stage world and whatever lies behind and beyond, the dark, creative matrix from which theatre emerges, where no mere spectator can ever go.

Because she can represent both stasis and flux, because she is both ancient and modern, origin and artifice, masculine force and feminine poise, the most revelatory aspects of her acting are the moments of transition that reveal the workings of change itself, the process of coming into being that could be both inspirational and terrifying.

ROLES

HORACE

It was in 1838 when she was seventeen years old that Rachel made her first great impact, as Camille in Corneille's tragedy *Horace*, a performance that inspired Janin's most lavish tributes. 'Nothing is greater than this untamed Camille', he was to write,

> She is as Roman as a woman could ever be, and yet she is still too much of a woman, a lover, to rejoice when the man she loves dies in the middle of those famous struggles for and against the might of the emerging republic.[20]

Unusually for a seventeenth-century tragedy, *Horace* is based upon an actual historical incident. In the war between Rome and the Albains in the seventh century BC two of the three Horatii brothers are killed by their rivals, the Curiace family. The surviving brother murders his sister Camille in a fit of rage when he discovers her grieving over her murdered lover, a member of the enemy family, Curiace himself.

Despite its characteristically Corneillien theme of patriotic and familial duty at catastrophic odds with personal desire, *Horace* had had a chequered history at the Comédie-Française: only 122 performances between 1720 and 1800, but 110 performances between 1801 and 1820.[21] The reason for the revival of interest is clear: in the Napoleonic period there was greater call for a play about national honour, and Corneille had been, after all, the Emperor's preferred playwright.

Even in immediately pre-Revolutionary times the story of the Horatii offered a useful vehicle for contemporary allegory. The most famous example is David's painting of *The Oath of the Horatii* (1784) which anticipated the Tennis Court Oath and subsequently provided a powerful touchstone for Republican sympathies. Although originally inspired by a performance of Corneille's *Horace* in 1782, the painter had eventually settled on a situation of his own devising. His picture shows Old Horace extracting an oath from his three sons that they will save Rome or die: their bunched swords and upraised arms, which occupy the central position, denote a dominant masculinity, while, in the lower right-hand third of the composition, a group made up of Old Horace's wife and a young child, together with Camille and Sabine (a Curiace married to one of the Horace brothers), sink down in graceful postures of grief. In this respect at least David's picture is faithful to the text of Corneille's play, which announces the theme of sexual roles in its very first speech with the remark of Sabine that, 'Commander à ses pleurs en cette extrémité, / C'est montrer pour le sexe assez de fermeté.' ['To weep at these desperate events / Is the only strength our sex can show.']

It's hardly surprising, then, that for much of its previous stage history, the play had been seen as more important for its male than its female characters. In particular the role of the elder Horace had been judged the dramatic pivot of the play, somewhat at the expense of Camille. Voltaire, for all he thought that Camille's imprecations were fine pieces to declaim which always showed an actress off to her best advantage, also found at least one of her soliloquies to be tedious, complaining that 'real misery doesn't reason, doesn't recapitulate so much'.[22]

Not the least of Rachel's innovations was to accentuate the role of Camille, to turn *Horace* into a woman's tragedy. The transformation was effected in a number of ways: by making sure that audience attention was focused on Camille at all times, even when she was not actually speaking; by frequently dropping the last act, which takes place after Camille's death and is mainly concerned with political justice; and, most brilliantly, by the subtle redeployment of emphasis in the delivery of celebrated speeches so that the turning points of the play clearly became Camille's moments of decision. Each change was duly noted and explicated by Rachel's critics.

The first key moment came in I.ii, the 'dream' scene, in which Camille foresees the bloodbath to come. Rachel imbued the lines with an overwhelming sense of foreboding:

Qu'elle a tort de vouloir je vous entretienne!
Croit-elle ma douleur moins vivre que la sienne . . .

[How wrong she is to want me to talk to you! / Does she believe that my grief is less alive than hers . . .]

Delivered with a cold solemnity from a drooping body, eyes downcast, with a 'nervous, feverish action of the facial muscles',[23] these opening words hinted at the warnings of the oracle, of yet deeper forebodings. There was an especial emphasis on *'Tout ce que je voyais me semblait Curiace'* ['Every face I saw seemed to be that of Curiace'], and on the terrible dream described at the end of this first great speech:

J'ai vu du sang, des morts et n'ai rien vu de suite:
Un spectre en paraissant prenoit soudain la fuite,
Ils s'effaçaient l'un l'autre, et chaque illusion,
Redoublait mon effroi par sa confusion.

[I have seen blood and corpses and nothing else: / A vision no sooner come than it had gone, / One blotted out another, and each delusion / Redoubled my fright by its confusion.]

Later, in II.vi, when Camille observes Sabine trying to persuade Horace to relent, Rachel capitalised on the slightest of lines. 'Courage! Ils s'amollissent' ['Courage! They are softening'], prompted by Old Horace's apparent surrender to Sabine's sorrow, became a cry of sheer exultation.[24]

For III.iii there are three women on stage. Camille's most famous line is very brief and comes right at the end: 'Moi, je n'espère rien' ['As for myself, I hope for nothing'], delivered fittingly with 'unobtrusive grace'.[25] In III.iv, with almost equally potent brevity, she admits the power of love:

Je le vois bien, ma sœur, vous n'aimâtes jamais.

[It is clear, sister, that you have never loved.]

In effect these cryptic comments acted as nervous preparation for the tumultuous release that occupied two scenes of the fourth act: in IV.ii Camille learns of the death of her lover, Curiace, and in IV.iv she delivers the tremendous speech of some fifty-five lines beginning 'Oui, je lui ferai voir...' ['Yes, I will make him see...'] This great passage of emotion is prepared for by Camille's prolonged silence throughout IV.ii – a scene in which Rachel resisted all opportunities for premature point-making. Nevertheless, as the truth sank in so Rachel slowly began to tremble, until on the single 'hélas' that comes half-way through the scene she collapsed into a chair, her hands making a last attempt to grasp its arms before she finally fell back.

This extended sequence was in several parts. At first her stern Roman will tried to combat the inevitable and she remained erect. Then she tottered, reeled: 'her features lose their elasticity, her limbs their power, a trembling seizes the entire frame, and it is with the sickening sensation of an overwhelming grief that she falls back into the chair, where she remains in a state of insensibility'.[26] Now she was fragile, graceful, 'her head thrown back pale as Parian marble, her lips half open, and her arms loosely hanging down, like the drooping boughs of the willow'.[27] Next came an attempt at reassertion:

> The returning animation and the quivering of the limbs, and the spasmodic movement of the hands as they catch at vacancy, and the vacant gaze and shuddering of the entire frame, and the quick and restless action of the eyelids, as recovering from some dreadful dream, are terrible in their reality.[28]

She passed her hand across her brow, and there was further silence before the opening lines, spoken from a sitting position, of the long, complex speech that occupies IV.iv. The pacing was slow at first, and broken, but rapidly picked up:

> ... the first lowly uttered word, the silent vibration of which rings on our ears still, like the knell of a broken heart – the rapid and hysterical thought – the quick, lightning-like cry – the agony – the scorn – the reproach – the despair – her suppressed feeling at the entrance of her brother reeking from the slaughter of her lover – her quietude while he demands her congratulation – and the passionate, maddened, withered wrath and fury of her reproach.[29]

Rachel's delivery was marked first by indignation, then by despair, 'De joie et de douleur, d'espérance et de crainte' ['By joy and sorrow, hope and fear'], then by more indignation at the exulting manner in which the death

of her lover had been related. With 'Un oracle m'assure, un songe me tra-
vaille' ['An oracle reassures me; a dream disturbs me'], Camille's confusion
was expressed by a contrast between the two halves of the line: the confidence of the first implicitly rejected by the scornful delivery of the
second.[30] Outraged at what she took to be her father's demand that she hail
her brother's victory, Rachel produced 'a mixture of contempt and anguish
that is electrifying in it effect':[31]

> Il me fait applaudir aux exploits du vainqueur,
> Et baiser une main qui me perce le cœur.
>
> [I am made to applaud the exploits of the conqueror / And to kiss the hand
> that pierces me to the heart.]

Grief continued to build up beneath the surface, breaking out with,

> Leur brutale vertu veut qu'on s'estime heureux,
> Et si l'on n'est barbare, on n'est point généreux.
>
> [Their barbarous virtue would have everyone consider themselves happy; /
> and if one is not barbarous one lacks feeling.]

Finally, some forty-four lines into the speech came the resolution:

> Dégénérons, mon cœur, d'un si vertueux père;[32]
>
> [Let me be the degenerate daughter of such a virtuous father.]

It was now that Rachel started from the chair and began to stalk the stage.
The technical challenge (which she may not always have overcome) was to
maintain verbal intensity and intelligent stresses whilst in continual movement:

> Eclatez, mes douleurs: à quoi bon vous contraindre?
> *Quand on a tout perdu, que saurait-on plus craindre?*
> Pour ce cruel vainqueur n'ayez point de respect;
> Loin d'éviter ses yeux, crossez à son aspect;
> *Offensez sa victoire: irritez sa colère,*
> Et prenez, s'il se peut, plaisir à lui déplaire.
> Il vient: préparons-nous à montrer constamment
> *Ce que doit une amante à la mort d'un amant!*[33]
>
> [Burst out, my grief! why should you be restrained? / When all is lost, what
> more is there to fear? / Let us have no respect for this cruel conqueror; /

Let us not avoid his eyes; let us confront his gaze / Denounce his victory, stir up his anger / And take whatever possible pleasure in offending him. / He comes: let us continually show him / How a woman should behave at the death of the man she loved.]

Driven on by 'suppressed malice' (according to *The Times* in 1842),[34] she spat out the lines. Her brother entered with the sword that had slain her lover. Her response, 'O mon cher Curiace!' was grief-ridden, with rage breaking through.[35]

The imprecations that follow, beginning 'Rome, l'unique objet de mon ressentiment!' ['Rome, the sole object of my resentment!'], provided one of the great defining moments of Rachel's young career. Early on she would deliver the initial line with the utmost force, but in later years she tended to begin as if the very word 'Rome' was loathsome to her, as if she was trying to suppress her own feelings.[36] An English notation of 1841 places the stresses like this:

Rome, l'unique objet de mon ressentiment!
Rome, à qui vient ton bras d'immoler mon amant!
Rome, qui t'a vu naître, et que ton cœur adore!
Rome enfin QUE JE HAIS parce qu'elle t'honore!
Puissent tous ses voisins ensemble conjurés,
Saper ses fondements encor mal assurés! . . .
Puissé-je de mes yeux y voir tomber la foudre,
Voir ses maisons en cendre, et les lauriers en poudre,
Voir le dernier Romain à son dernier soupir,
Moi seule en être cause, ET MOURIR DE PLAISIR![37]

[Rome, the sole object of my resentment! / Rome, for whose sake you have killed my lover! / Rome, which gave you birth, which you adore! / Rome, which I hate for honouring you! / May all her neighbours come together / To undermine her foundations even more . . . May I with my own eyes see the thunderbolt fall, / See your homes burned down, your laurels turned to dust / See the last Roman give his last sigh / Let me alone be the cause of all this, and die with pleasure!]

Extraordinary gestures accompanied the visionary outbursts:

We might have believed . . . that we saw a Pythian priestess, filled with the frenzy of a god, cursing a disbeliever in him, so terrifically maniacal was the rage and agony of the girl as she tossed her arms aloft in the whirlwind of her passion.[38]

The effect is often described as one of 'triumphant fury',[39] but other accounts say that by 'Rome enfin, que je hais parce qu'elle t'honore' her voice had lost its force, her body its control. Certainly by the later line, 'Et de ses propres mains déchire ses entrailles!' ['And with her own hands tear out her entrails'], it did seem that, in an ultimate spasm of rage, she might even snatch the sword from her brother's scabbard and use it against him.[40]

But it is, of course, Camille's own death that follows, which Rachel performed in Paris off-stage according to neo-classical custom; in London, to appeal to local tastes, in full view. The final curtain, and she reappeared for the first of many calls. There was no need for the last act: 'It would not have been listened to, if it had been played.'[41]

Throughout Rachel's rendering of *Horace* the political battle was counterpointed by the sexual: Camille, quite literally, because physically, rose to the occasion. A woman was revealed as the true hero of this drama of political struggle and the Corneillian value of passionate honour was shown to belong to one who may have appeared to be frail and ill-equipped, but who was, in fact, possesssed of unusual strength.[42] Heroic tragedy was as available to women as it was to men.

ANDROMAQUE

In some ways Racine presented a greater challenge to Rachel than Corneille because Racine's female characters have a more obvious complexity and importance. This is certainly true of *Andromaque*, which owed some of its popularity to the fact that it offered two contrasting lead parts for women, though the objection was already being heard in the 1820s that this diffused the female presence.[43] Rachel performed the role of Andromaque very early on, and it was an appearance in that part in 1836 which first aroused the interest of Védel of the Comédie-Française, but she soon turned to Hermione, the preferred role of a powerful line of actresses including Adrienne Lecouvreur and Mademoiselle Clairon. The most recent precedent, Mademoiselle Dumesnil, provided a useful contrast to Rachel in that she was known for her 'tearfulness' and had been criticised by Mademoiselle Georges for being too pitiful.[44] The comment could hardly be made about Rachel who contrasted the youth of the role with an inner strength revealed in blinding flashes. Whereas other actresses and critics had complained that the divisions within the character of Hermione

12 Rachel as Camille in *Horace.*

required two actresses to do them justice, Rachel, rather as with Camille, found ways to make the contrasts between Hermione's private passion and her racial pride speak directly to her contemporary audience.

When Rachel first performed the role of Hermione on 9 July 1838 there was no doubt that, as with Camille, she had gone to considerable lengths to make her own part central. First of all she capitalised on Hermione's delayed entrance, ending the predominantly male atmosphere of the first act not with a curtain, but a few bars of music so that, 'It was altogether a different thing when Hermione entered in the second act, like a burst of sunshine after a dreary fog.'[45] The moment was accentuated by a quietly dignified costume: 'draped in the Royal *murex*, her hair knotted under the plain gold *filet*, Racine's "fière Hermione", flashing from her dark eyes, as if it only needed a strong passion to give them the energy and spell of the basilisk'.[46] Her first four lines were delivered so carefully that it made them seem deliberate statements of intention:

> Je fais ce que tu veux. Je consens qu'il me voie:
> Je lui veux bien encore accorder cette joie.
> Pylade va bientôt conduire ici ses pas;
> Mais si je m'en croyois, je ne le verrois pas.
>
> [I'll do what you want. I agree to receive him: / I am willing to give him
> that pleasure at least. / Soon Pylades will bring him here to me; / And
> yet if I were to listen to myself, I would not see him.]

Rachel continued to demonstrate Hermione's dramatic importance with a display of *déblayage* notable for its subtlety and persistence. First with her confidante, Cléone, and then with Orestes she brought out the unique dignity of the character by stressing particular words, continually varying the volume and pace of her delivery.

The immediate situation is that Hermione must confront Orestes. As she does so she comes to an ever-deepening realisation of her own plight. Even with Cléone, Rachel's controlled articulation was interspersed by sudden interventions: an involuntary exclamation, 'Ah dieux'; sudden rage when she thought of Pyrrhus: 'Je l'ai trop aimé, pour ne le point haïr' ['I've loved him too much not to hate him now']; agonised stress on the final word 'infidèle' (describing Pyrrhus) in 'Il n'y travaillera que trop bien, infidèle!'[47] ['He will work at it too well, the unfaithful one']; the abrupt self-description of 'fière Hermione' suggesting a difficult, ambiguous level of self-knowledge:

> Est-ce là, dira-t-il, cette fière Hermione?
> Elle me dédaignoit; un autre l'abandonne.
>
> [Is this, he'll say, the proud Hermione? / She scorned me once; another abandoned her.]

By stressing short words, as in '*fais-le moi croire aussi*' ['make me believe it too'], and by incompletely disguising her heartfelt sighs as in '*Hé bien*, rien ne m'arrête' ['Well, nothing stops me'] Rachel conveyed the underlying passion of the situation. The line 'Fuyons – mais si l'ingrat rentrait dans son devoir . . .' ['Let's flee – yet if the ungrateful one felt the call / Of duty once again . . .'], which comes in the middle of a twenty-two-line speech, is sometimes described as having been delivered abstractly, as if to herself,[48] an inner thought signalled by 'the change of countenance, and the effect of the lightning-flash of hope and joy that for a passing moment illumined the countenance of the actress'.[49] Vehemence reappeared when she thought of the son of Andromaque:

> Rendons-lui les tourments qu'elle me fait souffrir;
> Qu'elle le perde, ou bien qu'il la fasse périr.[50]
>
> [I'll pay her back for all the torments she has made me suffer; / Let her be his ruin, or he be hers.]

At the very end of the scene the same message of suppressed feeling was conveyed by a sigh of reminiscence: 'ses feux, *que je croyais plus ardens que les miens*' ['His passion that I believed to be stronger than mine'], coupled with an apparently resigned attitude to a future in which Orestes might already be trapped:

> Et quel que soit Pyrrhus
> Hermione est sensible, Oreste a des vertues.
>
> [Be Pyrrhus as he is, / Hermione is aware, Orestes has his virtues.]

In the scene immediately following (II.ii) Hermione is joined by Orestes. Rachel made use of elaborate courtesy:

> Enfin qui vous a dit que malgré mon devoir
> Je n'ai pas quelquefois souhaité de vous voir?[51]

[In short, who has told you that, despite my duty, / I did not sometimes want to see you?]

Passion still flashed out; in a repetition of the same single word 'L'Infidèle!' which interupted Orestes' account of his failed meeting with Pyrrhus,[52] and in Hermione's two-line response to Orestes' suggestion that despite the claims of reason her heart was still bound up with her betrothed:

Ah, ne souhaitez pas le destin de Pyrrhus
Je vous hairais trop.[53]

[Do not long for Pyrrhus' fate. / I'd hate you too much.]

At the very end of the scene, when Hermione deputes Orestes to get the truth, the weight of suppressed emotion caused Rachel's voice to falter precisely at the antitheses, at the moments when balanced language encapsulates the awful alternatives.

Je n'en puis partir
Que mon père *ou Pyrrhus* ne m'en fasse sortir.
De la part de mon père allez lui faire entendre,
Que l'ennemi des grecs ne peut être son gendre.
Du troyen, *ou de moi* faites-le décider
Qu'il songe qui des deux il veut *rendre ou garder*?[54]

[I can only depart / If my father or Pyrrhus make me leave. / Go in my father's name to Pyrrhus. Say / No enemy of Greece can be his son-in-law. / Make him choose either the Trojan or me. / Which one does he want to keep, which one give up?]

In 11.ii and 11.iii, with Orestes and with Cléone, Rachel sustained the impression of power by seeming to involve Orestes in Hermione's plans whilst at the same time conveying her duplicity. Initially there was firm controlled instruction:

Allez contre un rebelle armer toute la Grèce;
Rapportez-lui le prix de sa rébellion,
Qu'on fasse de l'Epire un second Ilion.
Allez. *Après cela direz-vous que je l'aime?*[55]

[Go. Arm all the Greeks against a rebel; / Bring him the reward of his revolt, / Make another Troy out of Epirus. / Go. Will you say I love him after that?]

But in the very last line of the scene, the stern 'Adieu! *S'il y consent*, je suis prête à vous suivre' ['Farewell. If he agrees, I'll be ready to follow you'] was accompanied by an effect entirely convincing because it was seemingly so unconscious: a 'sunny smile which suddenly shot across her features while listening to the complainings of Orestes that she is beloved by Pyrrhus'.[56]

Hermione's next appearance is in III.iv, the famous confrontation with Andromaque. For lines such as

> Vos yeux assez longtemps ont régné sur son âme,
> Faites-le prononcer; j'y souscrirai, Madame.
>
> [Your eyes have reigned over his soul for a long time, / Make him declare himself. I will subscribe.]

Rachel produced 'disdain, the cold cruelty, and bitter raillery of a triumphant rival'.[57] English reviewers often refer to this mood as one of 'withering sarcasm', or of 'scorn'. It was certainly enough to warrant Andromaque's bitter exit line: 'Quel mépris la cruelle attache à ses refus!'[58] ['How much loathing the cruel woman brings to her refusal!'] Once again Hermione's unconscious gesture told an accompanying story of single-minded purpose:

> The bye-play, which consisted in the attitude, the carriage of the person, the eyes fixed upon the embroidery, which they saw not, and the hand carefully occupied in the precise arrangement of the folds of the drapery, which it felt not, was no whit less effective, or less perfect and true to nature, than the spoken words and altered tone that dashed the hopes and chilled the heart of Andromaque.[59]

In two subsequent scenes Rachel's Hermione underwent crucial transformation from victimised alien to vengeful heroine. Her four word command to Cléone, 'Fais tu venir Oreste' ['Bring Orestes'], was delivered as to 'express the sudden resolve, suggested by despair, that opens to the attentive auditor the *dénouement* of the tragedy'.[60] Neverthless IV.iii, in which Hermione enjoins Orestes to murder Pyrrhus, was long and densely argued, a continuous build-up of thought, of predetermined ideas and sudden impulse, the intellectual sequence puntuated with stops and starts. Half-lines such as 'Vengez moi, je crois tout' ['Revenge me, I believe everything'] or a single word 'Pyrrhus', in reply to Orestes' horrified 'Qui?', were delivered with sudden savage fury.[61] There was a moment of self-betraying doubt in

> Tant qu'il vivra, craignez que je ne lui pardonne.
> Doutez jusqu'à sa mort d'un courroux incertain:
> *S'il ne meurt aujourd'hui, je puis l'aimer demain.*[62]
>
> [As long as he lives, fear that I might pardon him. / Until his death, beware
> of my uncertain anger: / If he doesn't die today, I may love him tomorrow.]

But then she finally rose to the line 'Je percerais le cœur *que je n'ai pu toucher*' ['I will pierce the heart that I could never touch'], clutching her hand as if she grasped a dagger,[63] her voice 'a wail so low, so musical, piercing down into the very depths of pathos'.[64]

A brief transitional moment with Cléone – 'Que je me perde ou non, je songe à me venger' ['If I am ruined or not, I will dream of revenging myself'] – and then the great scene with Pyrrhus in which the 'scorn' was carried over into 'grief'. In her first long speech Rachel stressed the phrase 'en criminal' ['like a criminal'] in the fourth line, and filled with varying forceful accents the remaining lines:

> *Est-il juste, après tout,* qu'une conquérant s'abaisse
> Sous la servile loi de tenir sa promesse?
> *Non, non,* la perfidie *a de quoi vous tenter*;
> Et vous ne me cherchez que pour vous en vanter . . .
> Couronner tour à tour l'esclave et la princesse;
> Immoler Troie aux Grecs, au fils d'Hector la Grèce?
> Tout cela part d'un cœur *toujours maître de soi,*
> D'un héros qui n'est point *esclave de sa foi.*
>
> [After all, why should a conqueror stoop / To keep his word, according to
> the laws of servility? / No, treachery appeals to you / And you only sought
> me out to extol it . . . To crown a princess and a slave in turn, / Sacrifice
> Troy to Greece and Greece to the son of Hector / That shows a heart that
> is always its own master, / A hero who is no slave to his word.]

A shattering change was announced with the famous 'Je ne t'ai point aimé, cruel? Qu'ai-je donc fait?' ['I did not love you, cruel man? So what have I done?'], preceding the crucial modulation from rage to regret some nine lines later:

> Je t'aimois inconstant; *qu'aurois-je fait fidèle?*
> Et même, en ce moment, où ta bouche cruelle

Vient si tranquillement m'annoncer le trépas,
Ingrat, je doute encor si je ne t'aime pas.[65]

[I loved you inconstant. What would I have done if you had been faithful? /
Even at this moment when your cruel mouth / so calmly announces my
death / Ingrate, I wonder if I don't still love you.]

At the London prèmiere there were spontaneous shouts of approval at this
point.[66] Five years later *The Times* praised

> the display of grief forcing itself through the restraint so assiduously
> imposed . . . Every syllable is held down with a strong effort, as though the
> wronged beauty had as strong an enemy to contend with in her own
> utterance, but the feeling of her heart rises up in spite of her, with all its
> desolate mournfulness. It is this grief which she makes the moral substance
> of the character; the indignation, the scorn, the irony are the accidents.[67]

In London in 1841 applause had been renewed when Rachel returned to the
stage in v.i to deliver the magnificent soliloquy which begins 'Où suis-je?
Qu'ai-je fait? Que dois-je faire encore?' ['Where am I? What have I done?
What should I do next?'] and then to dismiss Orestes with a mixture of
unconscious wonder: 'Qu'ont-ils faits?' ['What have they done?'], and
uncontrolled hate: 'Tais-toi, perfide', 'monstre'[68] ['Be quiet traitor',
'monster'], the effect of solitary tragic grandeur guaranteed by judicious
cutting of the surrounding roles and, in particular, of Orestes' final
moments.

Rachel's Hermione was a study in psychological development, the
process made all the more convincing by the ways in which the audience
was given the chance to pick up on significant details, signs of an inner life
of which the other characters remained, for the most part, oblivious.
Samson's reading of the role certainly stresses 'bitter irony', and 'increased
irony',[69] but Hermione's 'irony' was only the most obvious indication of
this technique of personal revelation. Beneath a distracted exterior, sometimes dreamy, sometimes bitter, an iron project was being forged. As the
tragic heroine developed, grew in resolution, so the audience learnt how to
decode the stages in her personal journey.

BAJAZET

When Rachel first performed the role of Roxane in Racine's *Bajazet* on 23
November 1838 the play had not been seen at the Comédie-Française for

13 Double portrait of Rachel in London in 1841.

some twelve years. There was noisy curiosity among the audience in general and, according to some reports, among a voluble group of Rachel's Jewish supporters in particular. An ancient cultural association between the Jewish community and the Orient, still very current, probably played its part in the reception of the play. This was certainly stressed in some of the reviews, and Gautier even commented upon the way that

> . . . her whole bearing at one and the same time fragile yet tense, elegant yet primitive, sickly yet full of breeding, ancient oriental blood running through Jewish veins, hasn't the slightest connection with the ideas of the sensitive poet whose idol was Champmeslé.[70]

Bajazet is unusual among neo-classical tragedies in that it is based on real history, on an event that allegedly took place in the 1630s. In the absence of her master, the Sultan Amaranth, Roxane, mistress of the seraglio, conspires with Acomat, the court vizier, to put Bajazet, whom she loves, in power. Bajazet, though, is repelled by Roxane and loves Atalide. Much of the ensuing drama is taken up with the various stages in Roxane's process of discovery and disillusionment, culminating in acts of vengeful violence and multiple deaths.

Even Racine's own prefaces, the second in particular, suggest a defensive uncertainty about how the drama should be approached, and rely on the rather unconvincing argument that modern Turkey offers a suitable field for tragedy because, in spirit at least, it is as far away from France as the pagan world of the ancients:

> Tragic personages must be regarded in a different light from that in which we ordinarily see those whom we have known close to. One could say that the respect we have for heroes increases in proportion to their remoteness from us: *major e longinquo reverentia*.[71]

Not surprisingly the role of the vindictive Roxane, the putative tragic heroine, had a difficult and intermittent theatrical history. Indeed, until Adrienne Lecouvreur and Clairon in the eighteenth century, it was Atalide that was usually considered the more appropriate role for an ambitious actress.

Estimations of Rachel's development, however, often claim Roxane as the one part in which she could demonstrate to the utmost her natural talent for the 'unfeminine', although, of course, this quality often served to signify its exact ideological counter: erotic strength. Certainly, at a time when the Orient was beginning to figure prominently among Romantic writers and painters, the role of Roxane, in comparison with those of Hermione or Camille, was significantly alien simply by virtue of its cultural, geographical setting.[72] Rachel contributed to this cultivation of the symbolic 'other' by making her appearance wonderfully exotic, as well as by making the maximum use of passionate 'points', of melodramatic 'tokens' and of unpredictable outbursts.

Costume, a dress 'literally studded with diamonds and other precious gems',[73] and a bold stance announced Roxane's character even before she had uttered a word. Here, obviously, was a harsh, unyielding personality, and when she did speak, to Atalide (1.iii), it was in entirely uncompromising terms:

> Dès le même moment, sans songer si je l'aime . . .
> *Sa perte ou son salut dépend de sa réponse.*[74]

> [All at once, without thinking whether I am in love with him . . . His ruin or his salvation depends on his reply.]

11.i continued in similar vein, at least at first. Bajazet's question 'Ah! que proposez-vous, Madame?' ['What are you suggesting, Madame?'] precipitated first pride,

> Ce Soliman jeta les yeux sur Roxelane.
> Malgré tout son orgueil, ce monarque si fier
> A son trône, à son lit daigna l'associer.

> [This Suleiman set his eyes upon Roxane. / Despite his arrogance, this king so proud / Deigned to share his throne and his bed with her.]

and then a rapid series of observations and proposals delivered with cutting irony:

> Hé quoi, Seigneur?
> Quel obstacle secret trouble notre bonheur?

> [What now, my lord? / What secret problem troubles our happiness?]

When Bajazet at first replied in a non-committal way, Roxane turned bitter:

> Je vous entends, Seigneur. Je vois mon imprudence.
> Je vois que rien n'échappe à votre prévoyance . . .

14 Rachel as Roxane in *Bajazet*.

Pour vous, pour votre honneur, vous en craignez les suites,
Et je le crois, seigneur, *puisque vous me le dites.*

[I understand my Lord. I see I have been imprudent. / I see that nothing
escapes your foresight . . . / You fear the consequences for yourself, for your
honour, / And I believe you, since it is you who tell me so.]

She then threatened him:

Mais avez vous prévu, si vous ne m'épousez
Les périls plus certains ou vous vous exposez!

[But have you thought ahead, if you do not marry me, / Of the more certain
risks that you will be exposed to!]

Next she reminded him of the limits of her power:

Songez vous que je tiens les portes du Palais
Que je puis vous l'ouvrir ou fermer pour jamais.

[Do you think that I control the palace gates, / That I can open or close
them for you for ever?]

A warning followed:

Et sans ce même amour qu'offensent vos refus,
Songez vous, en un mot, que vous ne seriez plus!

[And without this same love which you refuse / Do you think that you
would any more – in a word – exist?]

Finally, banishment:

Rentre dans le néant dont je t'ai fait sortir.

[Go back into the emptiness from which I brought you.]

She had seen through him:

Ah! je vois tes desseins.

[I see your plans.]

At this point Roxane's habit of ambiguous speech gave Rachel a chance to
take her famously ironical delivery to greater extremes than ever.[75] Her old
teacher Samson said that Roxane should be characterised throughout by
absolute self-control:

Her movements are quick, her delivery abrupt.
Her eyes, fearful of not pleasing, weep tears
That immediately exhaust her anger.[76]

Yet the most celebrated moment in the scene 11.i comes as a complete contrast to all that has gone before. On

N'en doute point, j'y cours, et dès ce moment même.

[Don't doubt it; I will start now, from this very moment.]

Rachel rushed upstage, suddenly paused, seemed to lose all consciousness of what she was about, only to break out in a whisper:

Bajazet, écoutez, je sens que je vous aime.

[Bajazet, listen, I feel that I love you.]

Her delivery here is variously described: 'the double fiend here speaks plain – the wanton and the murderess'[77] or 'infinite sweetness', 'emphatic delicious tenderness'.[78] Later came the humility of

Je te donne, cruel, des armes contre moi

[I give you, cruel one, arms against myself]

and eventually the summons to the guards prior to ordering the closing of the seraglio.

Roxane's remaining scenes are characterised by a growing awareness of her impossible situation. In 111.vi, spurned by Bajazet, she confronts Atalide and comes to the realisation that she has a rival.

De quel étonnement, o ciel! suis-je frappée!
Est-ce un songe? et mes yeux ne m'ont-ils point trompée?

[Have I been overcome with amazement! / Is this a dream? Have my eyes misled me?]

Rachel's delivery of these lines sometimes elicited applause;[79] probably because of the way she started back from Atalide, stared hard, as if divining the truth, and paused before the attack, in a movement almost universally described as 'snake-like'.[80]

There was more 'irony' in the way that Roxane calmly replied to Atalide's assurance 'Il vous aime toujours' ['He still loves you'] with 'Il y va

de sa vie au moins que je le croie'[81] ['His life depends on my believing
that'], and with the cutting *'Vous parlez mieux pour lui qu'il ne parle lui-
même'*[82] ['You speak better on his behalf than he speaks for himself']. After
that Atalide left the stage accompanied by Roxane's downward look of
contemptuous dismissal:

> J'ai, comme Bajazet, mon chagrin et mes soins,
> Et je veux un moment y penser sans témoins.[83]

> [Like Bajazet, I have my distress and my cares, / And I want to think about
> them in private for a while.]

Alone Rachel launched into her soliloquy (III.vii), marking keywords,
'une rivale' most obviously, now confining her movements to gestures of
the hand, dismissing some thoughts with a wave: 'Et pourquoi dans son
cœur redouter Atalide?' ['And why dread Atalide's place in his heart?'].
With her confidante, Zatime (III.viii), she built up a head of fury.
'Observons Bajazet, étonnons Atalide' ['We'll watch Bajazet, we'll aston-
ish Atalide']. This antithetical rhythm was repeated on the exit line itself:
'Et couronnons l'amant ou *perdons le perfide*'[84] ['Crown the lover – or
destroy the traitor'].

Two letter scenes follow. In the first (IV.iii) Roxane tests Atalide further
by showing her a letter signed by Amurat condemning Bajazet to death, an
order that she apparently is prepared to carry out. For this the two actresses
stood side by side, positioned so that Rachel's expression could reveal to
the audience all that she suspected, elicited and discovered within Atalide's
response. A mixture of thwarted jealousy and delight in the pain she was
causing her rival crossed her features. Her face fully visible, her body was
half-averted, a hand half-raised in a an expression of absolute concentration.[85]

The second letter scene comes in IV.v. This time it involves a love letter
from Bajazet to Atalide and much of the challenge lies in rendering the violence and complexity of Roxane's feelings in body language alone.

> It began with her mode of first receiving it, when, holding it with dread
> anticipation of evil yet unread, a sudden chill of terror passed through her
> whole frame. From this instant to the scene in which she confronts it with
> its writer, that letter is the one thing needful to the tumultuous passion of
> Roxane. It is all that is hateful to her, all that is precious. It is the proof of

her shame, the cherisher and sustainer of her revenge. When it is not grasped in her hand, her hand involuntarily seeks its place of concealment . . .

The letter now becomes a focus for all her confused feelings:

. . . the irritable sophistication of one dreading to be undeceived yet unable to shut her eyes to the horrible fact, crumpling up the letter, trying to despise it, yet irresistibly attracted towards it.[86]

On reading the letter Rachel exploded with 'terrible intensity' – '*Lâche, indigne du jour que je t'avais laissé*' ['Coward, unworthy of the life that I have let you have'] – laughed, turned reproachful:

Avec quelle insolence et quelle cruauté
Ils se jouaient tous deux de ma crédulité!

[With what insolence and cruelty / The two of them have played with my credulity!]

Finally she seemed entirely consumed by rage.[87]

Just how innovative these continual shifts in mood were at the time can be guessed by a comparison with the traditional illustrations of this and other moments. These show a classical poise.[88] Rachel, in contrast, was all inner turmoil: 'the tortured look and trembling frame, surcharged to bursting – the spasmodic grasp, and the continual recurrence to the hated lines, as though fearful of losing the sense of her wrongs'.[89] By v.iv the letter is twisted and torn, as the audience can clearly see when Roxane thrusts it under the eyes of Bajazet with 'Tiens, perfide, regarde, et démens cet écrit'[90] ['Take, traitor, look, and disown that writing'].

Another token, the dagger, came back into play in this scene (v.iv). In a gesture which seems to have been her own invention (for there is no reference to it in the text) Rachel at last removed the weapon from its sheath. As her final offer of love was spurned so Rachel's fingers played 'convulsively' around the hilt, and she moved towards Bajazet. Violent impulse finally became unstoppable with his plea for Atalide in the half-line 'Et si jamais je vous fus cher . . .' ['And if I was ever dear to you . . .']. This seemed to stir intolerable memories of what had been striven for, and lost. Rachel drew the dagger, held it high in the air, and then as if realising the futility of her own action, dashed it to the ground, issuing the famous injunction

'Sortez' with what some record as 'incomparable dignity',[91] others as 'womanly tenderness'.[92]

The vertical axis of her body was now re-established for Roxane's penultimate scene (v.vi) in which she looked down at the kneeling Atalide, rejected her supplications with a look of triumph, and addressed her with concentrated bitterness, stressing each word 'as if she could watch them falling on the heart of her rival like drops of molten lead, and revelled in the torture they occasioned'.[93]

When she left the stage for good in a burst of furious energy on hearing of Acomat's successful rebellion, her last words formed an enraged but still controlled couplet:

> Ah, les traîtres! Allons, et courons le confondre.
> Toi, garde ma captive, et songe à m'en répondre.
>
> [Traitors! Let's go, let's run and confound him / You, guard my prisoner, and be answerable to me.]

A French critic described Rachel's Roxane as 'a tigress', anticipating Lewes' 'panther of the stage'. 'There is in this young girl', he continued, 'something marvellous, inexplicable, the enchantment of an oriental tale, an enigma...'[94] Roxane was Rachel's most thoroughgoing representation of a threatening force who contained within herself, none the less, vestigial elements of recognisable and sympathetic emotion.

Edward Said has written in *Orientalism* of a process of cultural representation that turned the Eastern Mediterranean into 'almost a European invention'.[95] Rachel's Roxane belongs with this history, an extension of Racine's veiled act of cultural appropriation into the more racially complex and factional worlds of the nineteenth-century city. Yet the imperialistic aim of a projected otherness was thwarted, as well as confirmed, when the act of invention was represented by the 'other' herself. Rachel's Jewish Roxane may have redistributed the divided attentions of her audience, offering different messages to different sectors, yet, at the same time, she undoubtedly engaged the whole.

PHÈDRE

Rachel first performed Phèdre in Paris in 1843, in London in 1846. The immediate challenge was the recent memory of Mademoiselle Maxime, which was quite easily overcome.[96] The real battle was with theatrical history, with the legends of Champmeslé, of Clairon, and even of Duchenois.[97] Rachel triumphed because she found a Phèdre right for the times, and, as it turned out, for decades to come: a Phèdre characterised by emotional unpredictability, by an intense erotic life signalled in a series of unexpected and unforgettable moments, each one rendered with a startlingly white clarity.

For what is, after all, the most famous entrance in French drama, Rachel came on like a ghost. Gautier describes it like this:

> Rachel's entrance was truly sublime. From her very first steps out from the wings, her success was beyond doubt; never was the appearance of a role more perfectly assumed. When she advanced, as pale as an actual ghost, reddened eyes in a marble mask, arms drooping as if dead, her body inert under the beautiful drapery with its straight pleats, she appeared to us not to be Rachel at all, but Phèdre herself.[98]

And G. H. Lewes is remarkably similar:

> the unutterable mournfulness of her look . . . What a picture she was as she entered! You felt that she was wasting away under the fire within, that she was standing on the verge of the grave with pallid face, hot eyes, emaciated frame – an awful ghastly apparition.[99]

When Hippolyte's name was finally uttered – by Oenone – Rachel started back, shuddered, and confessed with a reluctance that grew ever greater over the years:[100]

> Tu vas ouïr le comble des horreurs.
> J'aime . . . A ce nom fatal, je tremble, je frissonne. J'aime.
>
> [You are going to hear the full measure of horrors / I love . . . At that fatal name I tremble, I shudder. / I love.]

The great crux. 'C'est toi qui l'as nommé' ['You have spoken his name'] was sometimes heard as deeply sad and reproachful, sometimes as an attempt to escape responsibility,[101] sometimes as a sudden burst of energy,[102] but always recognised as the trigger for the unconstrained torrent of a soliloquy in which 'by a mode of articulation which is at once rapid and impressive, she conveys the notion of a person on whom thoughts press faster than is commensurate with the power to utter them'.[103] This important early shift in pace heralded an overall pattern of change, from lassitude to fever, from passive to active, that would operate throughout the performance.

> J'adorais Hippolyte; et le voyant sans cesse,
> Même au pied des autels que je faisais fumer,
> J'offrais tout à ce Dieu que je n'osais nommer.

> [I worshipped Hippolytus; and saw him all the time / Even at the foot of the altar I had lit myself / I offered everything to the God I didn't dare name.]

By now the level of erotic passion was so great that audiences were known to break out in cheering applause.[104]

In II.v Phèdre confronts Hippolyte and declares her love. For Rachel this was the opportunity for a display of bravura acting. 'When once the barrier is overcome – when once she ventures to speak out, all is rapid – hurried – overpowering. She dares not reflect upon her words, but yields herself to the fluency dictated by the moment, as though drawn along by the mechanical power of utterance', said *The Times* when she performed the role in London in 1846.[105] This was an astute way of putting it because it was by submitting to the torrent of the tirade that Rachel, the actress, best conveyed the total identification of Phèdre, the character, with fateful desire. The verbal release and emotional ascent was prepared for by an insinuating sideways movement which took her closer to the object of her passion,[106] and which was accompanied by a raising of the head, and by a facial expression that switched from fury to tenderness, from passion to concern, but mostly from 'fear to joy',[107] and by an erotic quivering of her whole body that would in turn be soon replaced by a return to the dreamy languor of earlier on.

The rhetorical climax came, of course, with 'Ah! cruel, tu m'a trop entendue!' ['Ah, cruel one, you have understood me too well!'], but it seems likely that audiences often held back their applause until the very end of the speech.[108] Throughout Rachel's rendering there was spasmodic movement, dramatic contrasts between voice and body. In II.v she appealed to Hippolyte:

> Si la haine peut seule attirer votre haine,
> Jamais femme ne fut plus digne de pitié,
> Et moins digne, Seigneur, de votre inimitié.

15 Rachel in II.v of *Phèdre*. (From *The Illustrated London News* of 13 July 1850.)

[If hate alone could attract your hate for me, / Never did a woman deserve more pity / And less deserve, my lord, your enmity.]

This culminated with her seizing his sword, and attempting to stab herself.[109] In the scenes with Oenone, which take up act III, some thought that they heard at first the 'irony' previously employed for Hermione in *Andromaque*, but by IV.iv, the moment when Phèdre learns of her rival, a new, more powerful note was unquestionably struck. Though she uttered no more than two words: 'Quoi seigneur!'[110], Rachel's whole body responded with shock. In IV.vi the pathos of one vision, 'Tous les jours se levaient clairs et sereins pour eux!' ['For them every day began bright and serene'] preceded the terror of another, the extraordinary dream speech in which Phèdre envisages facing her father Minos:[111]

> Misérable! et je vis? et je soutiens la vue
> De ce sacré Soleil dont je suis descendue?

[Wretch! and I live? and I bear the gaze / Of the sacred sun from which I am descended?]

This 'narrative of imagined horror'[112] culminated with her sinking to her knees on the line, 'Pardonne. Un Dieu cruel a perdu ta famille' ['Forgiveness. A cruel God has condemned your family'].

Yet the moment of abasement came immediately before the ferocious attack with which Phèdre drives Oenone from the stage:

> *Va-t'en*, monstre exécrable.
> Va, laisse-moi le soin de mon sort déplorable.
> *Puisse* le juste ciel dignement te payer;
> Et puisse ton supplice à jamais effrayer
> Tous ceux qui, comme toi, par de *lâches adresses*,
> Des princes malheureux nourrissent les faiblesses,
> Les poussent *au penchant* où leur cœur est enclin,
> Et leur osent du crime *aplanir* le chemin;
> Détestables flatteurs, présent le plus funeste
> Que puisse faire aux rois la colère céleste![113]

> [Go, execrable monster / Go, leave me to my appalling lot. / May the just heavens reward you as you deserve; / And may your punishment forever frighten / All those who, like you, by cowardly addresses / Feed the weaknesses of unfortunate princes, / Encouraging them to go where their hearts incline, / And smoothing the path of crime; / Detestable flatterers, the most deadly gift / Divine anger can offer kings!]

And this preceded, in turn, Phèdre's own remorseful death, so slow and unrelenting in the demands it made upon an audience's attention, that 'you seem to hear the parting breath'.[114]

In his evocation of a miraculous performance Janin marvels at what brought Rachel 'to this amorous Phèdre, passionate and trembling at the very brink of spasm, to these tears, these sorrows, these sighs, to this ecstasy of pride and abandon'.[115] It's a familiar list of contrary elements that usually culminates, as here, with recognition of 'abandon', that state of high creative excitement which parallels the loss of consciousness brought on by absolute identification of actress with character, with the loss of self-awareness that might be achieved in sexual ecstasy. Here, surely, is the vital clue to the immense and lasting significance of Rachel's Phèdre: as a performance, it came to represent the contrary emphases that the nineteenth century was increasingly to place upon female desire. This was a force that through its very repression was to gain in disruptive power and to re-emerge as threat, in particular of 'woman's aberrant, monstrous, and fatal aspiration towards greatness',[116] but also as affirmation, finally even as salvation. Such an uncontrollable and universal, but necessarily concealed, aspect of the collective unconscious was best represented in terms of its theatricality – in a public display of the hidden imagination, in a single narrative with multiple possibilities. When spectators – Lewes, Gautier – saw Phèdre's first entrance as ghostlike they were acknowledging the return of a force that would not, could not, be buried.

ADRIENNE LECOUVREUR

As an emblem of female transgression Phèdre haunts the nineteenth century. In Flaubert's *L'Education sentimentale* the hero Frédéric begins his list of the great lovers of history with her name, and it is as Phèdre that Berma so impresses the young Marcel in Proust's *A la recherche du temps perdu. Adrienne Lecouvreur*, by Scribe and Legouvé, which Rachel introduced in 1849, is a forerunner: a calculated reworking of Racine's great drama of desire, the contrivance of its structure eventually justified by its longevity and influence. It tells of the great actress's frustrated love affair with Maurice de Saxe, her dealings with her rival, the Duchesse de Bouillon, and her tragically early death by poisoning, and it includes fragments not just of *Phèdre* but of *Bajazet, Le Cid, Cinna,* and *Andromaque.* This is a drama, designed for a bourgeois audience, that flagrantly feasts upon the classics and flatters itself with tributes to the power of theatre.[117]

While *Adrienne Lecouvreur* marked a decisive shift in dramatic history, it was an incomplete development in Rachel's career. Lecouvreur's tragic style had to be re-created and this, in some part, seems to have been the key to Rachel's rendering. At the same time she did attempt some modern effects quite removed from those she was accustomed to produce for the heroines of seventeenth-century tragedy. The play's framing devices – ancient within modern, fact within fiction (and fiction within fact), and even prose within poetry – meant that the emphasis fell upon Rachel's own renown as a public performer. By acting the part of Adrienne Lecouvreur she re-presented her own career, displayed her own tragic

power in an act of historical displacement on to a romantic or even melodramatic context:

> It seems as though having found the finest statue ever cut by Phidias, we
> were fain to deform it with the graceless rigidities of muslin and millinery,
> to transform an antique Diana to a court belle.[118]

Changefulness now has less to do with the awesome conflicts she
embraced in classical tragedy than with an organic or holistic variety of
personality:

> . . . at one moment intensely passionate, and the next melting into touching
> tenderness. Her energy has power, and her pathos sweetness, so that each
> variety of expression is perfect, while the face reflects both light and shade,
> as the cloud or sunshine of the mind passes over it. Her voice, too, is
> peculiarly effective, now deep and terrible as that of the waves, and anon
> silvery as the sounds of the rippling stream.[119]

There are three particularly memorable moments when *Adrienne Lecouvreur*
exploits this idea of female changeability. The first is an exhibition of
charm, the recitation of the poem 'La fable de deux pigeons'. Tenderness
and playfulness are required as Adrienne sets out to teach de Saxe how to
spell. The first line of the little poem – 'Deux pigeons s'aimaient d'amour
tendre' ['Two pigeons loved each other with a tender love'] – is at once a
change from the assumed carelessness of comic dialogue to the intensity of
emotion. The words 'd'amour tendre' are brought out with an emphasis of
passion which tells a whole internal history.[120]

> Can anything be more . . . delicate and lively than her dialogue with
> Maurice in the fifth scene, and her recital of 'La fable de deux pigeons', and
> how striking the exaltation of tenderness with which she exclaims 'Que je
> vous vois bien! Que je vous adresse tous mes vers! Je tâcherai d'être belle!
> Ah! oui, je serai bien!'[121] ['How splendid you are! I'd like to address all my
> verses to you! I will try to be beautiful! Oh yes, I shall be so good!']

The second moment comes when Lecouvreur uses lines from *Phèdre* to
condemn her rival. At this point Rachel really could play herself. As she
pointed to the stage rival and declaimed the famous lines,

> Qui goûtant dans le crime une tranquille paix
> Ont su se faire un front qui ne rougit jamais.

[Anyone who can accept a gentle peace / Can maintain an unblushing face.]

so the mood changed from comedy to tragedy, and Adrienne Lecouvreur reverted for a while to Rachel Félix, a transformation often marked by bursts of applause.[122]

Finally there was Adrienne's death by poison: a good example of an underlying tendency of Romantic acting since its prolonged detail was to invite, and receive, the epithet 'realistic'. Adrienne's ending also heralds a major motif in nineteenth-century theatre: the premature death of a beautiful woman, scrupulously re-enacted in its every phase for an anticipating audience.[123] Here is *The Times* in 1850:

> But the great effort of all – the one which is anticipated with a sort of fearful curiosity – is the death in the last act. The bouquet does not kill at once, but first produces a state of delirium, in which Adrienne does not recognise her lover, who is with her in the apartment, but fancies she is at the theatre and sees him in a box with her rival. The delighted vanity of the artist, the fondness of the devoted woman, and the agonies of jealousy are exhibited in rapid succession, an idiotic pause which occasionally occurs terribly denoting the aberration of the intellect. At least – when she is moved to a frenzy of rage, which she endeavours to express by a furious speech – and marvellous is the art by which she shows that as the feeling increases the physical power declines, till she breaks down in the middle of her inspiring anger – the delirium is gone, and she recovers her senses to feel the anguish of bodily pain and the grief she feels at leaving those she loves; and the torments both of mind and body are represented with the most elaborate truthfulness. When at length she expired, and remained with open eyes, with a countenance rigid with death, and with intelligence still written on the features, the effect was most appalling, and a sense of awe seemed to pervade the audience before they broke into the loud applause which once more summoned the great tragic actress.[124]

The obsessive involvement of that evocation is typical of a general fascination. Years after he had seen Rachel act the death of Adrienne Lecouvreur Dion Boucicault could still vividly recall its every stage:

> . . . the gaze of wonder with which she recognised the first symptoms of the poison, then her light struggles against the pain that she would not acknowledge. And when the conviction came that she was dying, her whole soul went out to her young lover – her eyes never left his, her arms clung to *him*, not to life, or only to life because life meant him. There was no vulgar

display of physical suffering excepting in her repression of it. And she died with her eyes in his, as though she sent her soul into him.[125]

What male spectators like *The Times* critic or Boucicault saw in these closing moments was a recapitulation, an encounter with an always known, always unknown, life-story, as if only in death did the woman display the essentially enigmatic characteristics of her being.

Rachel's experiment was not however entirely welcomed,[126] and it may even be that the actress was not happy with her new direction either. The 'well-made play', later to become one of the most depised of theatrical structures, was, from the very start, under attack for its reliance upon predictable conventions, including those of a supposedly female temperament. The contrast in *Adrienne Lecouvreur* between the strength that Adrienne represented in her parts and the vulnerability of her private life was to become increasingly important later in the nineteenth century (and perhaps even for Rachel herself) as the obvious intellectual resilience of the performer more and more belied the pathos of her romantic roles. That contradiction was to fuel the career patterns of Bernhardt and Duse, and of countless other actresses, many of whom found an opportunity for self-expression and perhaps self-discovery in the plenitude of roles, the total theatricality of *Adrienne Lecouvreur*.

RECIT

Rachel set many precedents: her classical heroines were models of female strength, her Adrienne Lecouvreur a legend against which later actresses were measured whenever they attempted the high Romantic style. Her performance in Soumet's play about Jeanne d'Arc involved yet another kind of representation, including something close to *travesti*, an area of theatre that Rachel generally avoided. Retaining her gold and silver armour, her coat of mail and gauntlets thoughout, Rachel as Jeanne appeared in a provocatively masculine guise that may none the less have belied the ultimate signification of her performance.

The play had first been performed with Mademoiselle Georges in 1825; Rachel introduced it in 1846, played it in London in August 1846 and 1851, and in the United States in 1855.[127] Normally judged a particularly dismal

16 Lithograph by Valentin of Rachel as Jeanne d'Arc.

example of where a dogged respect for the unities might lead, the play had never been very highly regarded and Rachel's decision to bring it into her repertoire is intriguing. One explanation is that contemporary interest in the figure of Jeanne was very strong, largely as a result of Michelet's inspirational portrait which had appeared in 1841 as a chapter in the fifth volume of his *Histoire de France*. As part of her preparation for the role Rachel is said to have studied Michelet. If so, she would have read the following proclamation:

> We shouldn't be surprised if the people now appear in the guise of a woman, if from patience and other sweet qualities a woman should pass on to the virile virtues of war, if the saint should become a soldier. She herself gave out the secret of this transformation, a woman's secret: 'PITY for the kingdom of France . . .'[128]

As a tribute to Jeanne d'Arc as an emblem of national salvation it could hardly be more pious, or more powerful.

Soumet's static play focuses on the closing moments of Jeanne's life. It opens in prison, moves to the Palais de Justice, and finally in the fifth act, which has the only dramatic action, to an open public square. Unlike Schiller's *Die Jungfrau von Orleans* (a standard comparison made by all commentators), there are no battle scenes, little opportunity for spectacle or secular passion, and the whole is constructed around a series of extended speeches.

There were possiblities within the role none the less. Janin, who spent much of his review making unfavourable comparisons between Soumet and Schiller, had little time for the tribunal scenes, but he did respect Rachel's performance for its statuesque qualities, achieved despite the cloudiness of the accompanying language.[129] Lewes, who did not even have much time for Schiller's version, saw that the point of Soumet's adherence to the unities was that he 'is only permitted to show us the fallen victim about to pay the penalty of defeat', and that the merit of the drama, such as it was, lay in the simplicity of its would-be tragic conclusion.[130]

In fact, the presentation of France's saviour as a tragic scapegoat enabled Rachel to extend her audience: when patriotism was this blatant it became, ironically, exportable. Queen Victoria's reaction to the play may have been that it was 'rather calculated to lull the British Lion to sleep than to lash him into indignation', but she still conceded that Rachel was always impressive 'whether the words she utters are for us or against us'.[131] Lewes admitted that lines such as 'Ma vie n'est qu'un instant; la France est immortelle' ['My life is only a moment; France is immortal'] were delivered with such passionate dignity that that they 'were responded to by every Englishman no less than every Frenchman'.[132]

In addition, by demonstrating (once again) her ability to represent a Christian martyr without compromising her own heritage, Rachel re-established Jewish ability and centrality. The point was indirectly signalled in her delivery of Jeanne's reply to the priest who urges her to confess, 'Je ne suis point coupable' and by the change she made to the text so that it was the French standard rather than a crucifix that was handed to her at her death. Though historically implausible (why should the English have honoured their enemy's flag at this point?), the device avoided an otherwise sensitive moment.

Above all, the representation of Jeanne d'Arc was consistent with the overall pattern of Rachel's career in that it allowed her to occupy an ambiguous space between her present identity as an outsider (a Jewish woman) and what she might become in performance (a national heroine), and to offer that ambiguity in an idealised form. As Marina Warner has shown, in the nineteenth century the figure of Jeanne was increasingly focused through the question of whether she was 'the instrument of an external design or . . . the actor of an internal inspiration'.[133] Rachel's appearance in male armour resolved the issue through theatrical means: here was both a self-determining woman and the agent of a larger power beyond gender, La France, the Republic itself.

It was still essential that this transcendence be represented by a female body, however disguised. Soumet's pedestrian play anticipated another kind of performance altogether, in which the living actress would embody not another woman, however mythologised, but an abstract idea, and yet, at the same time, retain her femaleness.

On 20 March 1848, at the end of a performance of *Horace* at the Comédie-Française, Rachel was recalled to the stage, and this, according to Théophile Gautier, is what happened next:

> After a few moments the curtain rose again and Camille appeared rid of her Roman robe, straight and tall in a white tunic, and advanced with slow majestic steps to the footlights. We had never seen anything as terrible and

as thrilling as that entrance and the audience was shivering with fright
before the actress had delivered a single one of her powerful words. The
pale, livid mask, the black look of suffering and revolt shining out of
bloody sockets, brows twisted like snakes, lips drooping at the corners,
holding within their superb curves a hurricane of threats, that were ready,
as Shakespeare said, to sound the trumpet of curses; nostrils flaring with
passion as if ready to breathe the free air outside a foetid fortress: all this
produced an effect like lightning. Here was a terrible gracefulness, a
sinister beauty, that inspired both terror and admiration.

When the actress, like a statue stood firm upon its base, gained her full
height, rippled her hips under the full pleat of her long tunic, and raised her
arm with a gesture of controlled violence that, with the fall of the sleeve,
revealed it bare to the shoulder, then it seemed to everyone that Nemesis,
the slow goddess, had suddenly freed herself from a block of Greek marble,
as if carved by an invisible sculptor. Then in an angry voice, both harsh
and dull like an alarm-bell, she began the first verse:

Allons, enfants de la patrie! . . .

She didn't sing, neither did she recite, it was a kind of declamation
in the style of ancient chants, in which the lines sometimes march on feet,
sometimes fly on wings, a mysterious music, alien, breaking free of the
notes of the composer, seeming like Rouget de l'Isle's song yet not
exactly reproducing it.

Mademoiselle Rachel had managed to make the hymn, already so
masculine, so fine in its musicality, even more energetic, even stronger,
wilder, more fearsome, through the biting harshness, the rancorous
snarls, the metallic outbursts of her diction.[134]

Rachel was to go on to perform *La Marseillaise* on many occasions, sometimes with an accompanying chorus of voices, bells, drums, even canon.
She was now, though briefly, 'citoyenne tragédienne'.[135]

It's remarkable how often Rachel's delivery of *La Marseillaise* at a time
of revolutionary turmoil is evoked by those who experienced it, and,
almost invariably, in rhapsodic terms. Arsène Houssaye said that 'she was
the personification, not only of the revolution, but of the tragic spirit of
suffering which resides in the hymn's immortal lines.'[136] For Louise Collet
she was 'a mighty breath of hope, that bore along with it all youthful
desires'.[137] 'All artists competing for the Statue of Liberty,' said George
Sand, 'ought to go and study the classic poses of Mademoiselle Rachel
singing the *Marseillaise*. She is an exquisite incarnation of pride, courage,

17 Lithograph by Cuisinier of Rachel singing *La Marseillaise* in 1848.

and energy.'[138] One of the most gripping descriptions of Rachel's 'incarnation' is given by the Dean of Westminster, who happened to be in Paris at the time, and it sums up a general feeling. 'She had seemed to be a woman,' he wrote, 'she became a *"being"* – sublime irony, prophetic enthusiasm, demoniacal fierceness, succeeded each other like flashes of lightning.'[139]

Struck by the overwhelming evidence of the performative power of Rachel's personification, historians have always wanted to establish its political reference. This remains disconcertingly obscure.[140] Some have said that the point of Rachel's declamation was 'to please the popularist audience the revolution had thrust upon her and to flatter the new sovereign',[141] others that it was a matter 'of a sincere if fleeting sympathy with the atmosphere felt by an artist's soul'.[142] Her version of *La Marseillaise* has been shown to derive from a tradition of 'living allegory' that goes back to 1789, and also to relate to the image of Liberty depicted in Delacroix's *Liberty on the Barricades* of 1830. Yet the meaning of Delacroix's painting has been much discussed too,[143] and it can be as difficult to establish the connection between a conservative painter's political sympathies and the image of a half-clad woman as it is to ascertain the allegiances that led an established actress to adopt the tricolour and declaim a battle-song. To interpret either we have to move into the field of the symbolic body, where the lasting significance of the gendered image may be more important than any immediate political circumstance, and in complicated ways. The relation between the figure of woman and the all-encompassing principle she is said to represent is particularly elusive because it is always circular. Whenever Rachel is said, as by the Dean of Westminster, to have become transformed from a woman into a 'sublime being', the very terms of the tribute reinforce her original femaleness: since the clear implication is that no man could have been so transformed. The convention of female transcendence is energised by its own unending negations.

The process is none the less historically specific. Rachel was able to seize upon a political occasion to move beyond sectarian politics because there were identifiable formulae available; and because she had relevant experience – she had, for one thing, already acted Jeanne d'Arc. Now, as Janin said, 'She was a Muse . . . a Fury. She came down from Helicon.'[144] Rachel's initiative seems to have combined the traditional Muse figure with that of a revolutionary goddess and with the Sibyl herself. Her means was the power of oratory, a medium that came in nineteenth-century France to be prized almost above all others.

Writing in the late 1870s Ernest Legouvé, who had spent decades observing the methods of the Comédie-Française, proclaimed that, 'Sixty years ago, a faculty for public speaking was a rarity in France; oratory, a signal exception. To-day the voice has become the great agent, the most powerful medium, in all our social relations.'[145] And he stressed the importance in the development of the national expertise not only of the legendary teachers at the Conservatoire – Samson, Regnier, Got, Delaunay – but of Rachel, who had been rejected by Provost, but then accepted by Samson, who was by far the most voluble champion of the power of the spoken word. As Legouvé puts it elsewhere: 'For M. Samson the art of theatre and the art of speech are one and the same thing. He often said the actor is essentially *there*, he displays his brain *there*, his breath *there*, and he displays his heart *there*.'[146] Legouvé, who was something of a feminist,[147] resolves the conflict between training and talent by citing the exemplary practice of a master who released a natural force. 'It is impossible completely to know M. Samson without Mademoiselle Rachel, nor Mademoiselle Rachel without M. Samson,' he writes, 'Nature made a great tragédienne, M. Samson made a Muse!'[148]

This Muse, created by a male, is validated by her female gift for an oracular speech that can express transcendent truth. Here is the most far-reaching aspect of Rachel's precedent. For the voice of the possessed prophetess, of the sibylline outpouring that only a woman's body can produce, resounds through the decades and is consistently related to Rachel.

When the American actress Eleanor Calhoun went to Paris to study French theatre at the end of the century she found herself being cared for by the daughter of Rachel's laundry-woman, who turned out to be a living record of greatness herself. 'Oh, mademoiselle, she was magnificent, superb; there are no words to say how she was,' she told Calhoun.

> Then in high exaltation: 'Oh, mademoiselle, if you could have heard her when she said –' and she began to pour out whole scenes from the tragedies, one after another, rushing on like flame or molten lava, which nothing can stop. It was comic at first. Her eyes seemed to start from her head; she gasped for breath, and floundered with her arms in an occasional gesture,

her hands on her hips. But what amazed me, beyond the enormous volume of energy and dramatic force, was that she spoke the verses correctly, and managed with all her rough speech to project to an extraordinary degree the nobility of emotion and the passion of the character she avalanched forth. At last she stopped short, the tears streaming down her face. '*Oh, pardonnez-moi – pardonnez-moi, mademoiselle*, what have I done here! But if you could have seen her! – Mon Dieu! Mon Dieu! it was beautiful!'[149]

This is a vision of transformation, of cultural change, part of that long-standing political process whereby the figure of woman, whether reduced to servitude or expelled to some external and idealised realm, repeatedly returns to lead the society that has displaced her, represents still the future.[150]

RAPPEL

When Rachel died of pulmonary consumption in 1858 she was the most celebrated actress on earth. Her achievements were not only to outlast her, they were to increase in their significance. As an essential component in the mythic figure of the great performing woman she reappears again and again in nineteenth-century literature – in poems by Matthew Arnold, in novels by Benjamin Disraeli, Charlotte Brontë, George Eliot, Edmond de Goncourt, Henry James.[151] Her posthumous influence was equally strong in the living theatre. All the great actresses of the nineteenth century paid tribute to her: from Adelaide Ristori to Aimée Desclée,[152] from Charlotte Cushman to Helen Faucit, from Helena Modjeska to Sarah Bernhardt.

Herself proudly Jewish, Bernhardt deliberately courted comparison with Rachel, selecting her roles whenever she could. But Bernhardt developed a style more obviously geared to the erotic, to melodrama, and to the kinds of the Romantic theatre with which Rachel had only begun to experiment. And Bernhardt was to exult in *travesti*.

The endless comparisons made between the two actresses in the second half of the nineteenth century, particularly of their interpretations of *Phèdre*, reflect the different styles of different eras: Bernhardt's febrile sensuality against Rachel's volatile strength. Bernhardt posed problems of sexuality, and a repertoire based on Dumas fils and Sardou coloured her performances in Racine. Much of the early criticism of her manner was due to a failure to appreciate how the approach might be more appropriate to the 1870s than Rachel's austerity; how, in the field of sexual politics, erotic self-consciousness might, paradoxically, be more challenging to the patriarchal self-confidence of the bourgeoisie than visionary heroics.

Strong memories die especially hard. All great performers articulate the conflicts of their time; Rachel had done more. For the first half of the nineteenth century, in her wild tirades, her dangerous silences and her violent transitions, she had seemed to intimate the rhythms of history itself.

ADELAIDE RISTORI

SUSAN BASSNETT

On 29 December 1899 the seventy-seven-year-old Adelaide Ristori, *grande dame* of the Italian theatre, wrote to her old fellow actor Tommaso Salvini, expressing her views on the current state of the theatre. It is a letter that does not mince words, for Ristori's opinion of the state of Italian theatre on the eve of the new century was decidedly negative:

> Would you like to know what I think about the new style of our theatre? *It is absolutely dreadful!*
>
> *Neurosis* is an illness that is devastating the human brain at the close of our century. Audiences like this horrible illness and good taste in representative Art is quite ruined.
>
> Generally speaking, a large share of the blame must go to the *unbridled politicking* that is going on which destroys minds and throws the sense into turmoil. The style of dress, the luxuriousness of clothing all make an impression on audiences and so they do not think that anything they see on a stage could be natural and right. I am of the *modest opinion* that the current style of acting is *false* and *mere acrobatics!* and that we should be proud of having been who we were, *followers of Truth and the portrayers of great Art.* [1]

Ristori's sentiments here are very clear: she deplored the emphasis on extravagant staging and the fashion for neurotic introspection on the part of actors like Eleonora Duse, whom she described as being essentially 'the Modern Woman with all her complaints of hysteria and anaemia and their consequences'.[2] Such acting, she felt, was false and artificial, and she contrasts this with her own work and that of Salvini, the followers of Truth and creators of great Art.

The strength of Ristori's feelings as expressed in this letter and others cannot be underestimated, and it would be unjust to dismiss them as being

18 Adelaide Ristori as Judith.

the result of hurt pride and advancing old age. Ristori had retired from the theatre in 1885, though she made brief reappearances in 1887, 1896, and 1898, but she continued to take a close interest in the Italian theatre, as her letters reveal. Duse's star was in the ascendant and Duse's acting style was very different from Ristori's, but Duse herself acknowledged a debt to Ristori, as did most Italian actors of the period, for Ristori had effectively put Italian theatre on the international map and established the base from which later generations of touring companies could depart.

Ristori was alarmed by new trends in acting and in staging, which seemed to her unnecessary and undesirable. She deplored the amount of money spent on spectacular theatrical effects and expensive costumes. The audience's attention should be focused on the performers, in her view, not on extravagant stage settings, and in any case, the object of creating a stage picture was to provide an illusion of something, not a perfect reproduction of a setting outside the theatre. A palace should look like a palace, but should not *be* a palace, and a king's robes should look like a king's robes but should not be made of genuinely expensive material and created by leading designers. She saw the theatre as a place where the imaginary could hold sway, where the task of the actor was to create an illusion of reality, not to bring reality into the theatre. An actress should not seek to represent herself through a part, but should rather submerge herself in the part and let it take over. The truth and honesty to which Ristori refers involved the process whereby an actor dissolved his or her own personality into a part after a period of meticulous study and attention to detail. What Ristori regarded as dishonest was for an actor to impose his or her own personality on to a role and hence to take over the character.

This is an important distinction, that needs to be made if we are to under-stand something of Ristori's extraordinary appeal to audiences in the nine-teenth century and to appreciate why she felt so disillusioned towards the end of her life. Ristori's concept of acting was, of course, pre-Stanislawski, and when she speaks about realism and truth, what she means is that it is the task of the actor to study a part (the word 'study' recurs a great deal in her *Memoirs*) and to re-create an impression of the emotional life of the character externally, rather than by searching within one's own subconscious. Ristori's chief complaint about Duse's work was that Duse sought points of reference within her own personality for all the parts she played:

> In terms of theatre, if any criticism has to be made, it is the lack of variation in her repertoire, the refusal to introduce any new work that would enable Duse's personality with all her special qualities to disappear, so that she could identify with a new character whose qualities, nature and expression should belong to the role she is portraying . . .[3]

Even her performance as Juliet, in Ristori's view, was no exception, 'because Juliet only has speeches about love'. Duse's method followed a centripetal motion; she pulled roles into the centre that was the actress herself. Throughout her life Duse was concerned to find roles that suited her, to expand her repertoire but on her own terms. Ristori's work, in contrast, followed a centrifugal motion, as she released her own personality into a range of different roles and selected parts that offered her an opportunity to try out different skills. She describes this process as an exhausting one:

> I realize that one cannot easily take a decision to undertake a detailed disembowelling of the great historical characters that one usually plays through fusing them with one's own individuality because that would be both exhausting and time-consuming, and it cost me a great deal to transpose myself into the different roles in my repertoire (some of which were totally the opposite of my own nature), making the actress herself disappear and bringing the character of the part painfully into view.[4]

An anonymous reviewer in *Il Buttafuori* (24 January 1853) the year before she embarked on the first of her overseas tours, remarked that she could, 'with the same truth and sublimity', be a nineteenth-century character one night and a thirteenth-century character the next, a reference to her portrayals of Adelaide in Cocomero's farce, *Il regno d'Adelaide* and of Pia de' Tolomei, in the title role of Carlo Marenco's play. This is what she strove to achieve, since acting for her was a public demonstration of a range of skills and professional expertise, not an expression of her own inner feelings and certainly not a neurosis.

In her *Memoirs* she describes her preparation and interpretation of two of her most successful roles, Mary Stuart, in Andrea Maffei's version of Schiller's play and the role of Elizabeth I in Paolo Giacometti's *Elisabetta Regina d'Inghilterra*. That she could choose two roles that involved such different personalities is an indication of the extent to which she saw her skill as an actress transcending any relationship of empathy. It was the difference between the two characters that appealed to her, because through two such contrasts of character she felt she had the opportunity to show her ability as a performer.

Her first step, once she decided to add the role of Elizabeth to her repertoire in 1854, was, she tells us, to make 'an exhaustive study of such historical notices of her as might serve to elucidate the character and disposition of this celebrated Queen'.[5] What her research revealed to her was a portrait of a cruel, violent woman whose character was such that it was 'utterly repugnant' to Ristori's feelings to attempt to portray her.

But here Ristori's sense of her duty as an actress takes over. Though strongly tempted to refuse the part, she insisted on playing it:

> I felt I must endeavour to overcome my own personal reluctance, and so, although the character of Elizabeth was so uncongenial to me as to take from me all desire to interpret it, I resolved to make an extra effort to enter into the spirit of the part. And I had my reward, for I believe I shall not err in saying that the public have always regarded this as one of the most elaborate and complete studies in my repertoire.[6]

In her discussion of how she played Elizabeth, Ristori highlights moments of transition that enabled her to shift between tragedy and comedy, between rage and stillness. She describes her changes of voice and physical expression in order to render the different states of mind of her character, and the various tableaux or set scenes, such as Elizabeth's hesitation before signing Essex' death warrant in act IV and her protracted death scene in act V. In a moment that doubtless owed a lot to Giacometti's melodramatic readings of Shakespeare, Ristori as Elizabeth struggles across the stage to her couch:

> I dragged myself towards it with the greatest difficulty.
>
> As I staggered along with bent body, and bowed head, I lifted my trembling hands to my aching brow, and felt the crown which still rested there,
>
> > 'Ah! a heavy weight is on it.'
>
> I moaned with a weary air.
>
> > 'And yet for forty-four years I have worn it, and it seemed so light to me.'
>
> I lifted it slowly from my head and gazed at it with deep emotion.
>
> > 'Who will wear it after me?'[7]

The success of her portrayal of Elizabeth is attested in the favourable reviews her playing received, especially on her London visit in 1858. The

19 Adelaide Ristori as Elizabeth I.

Athenaeum review of 17 July 1858 declared that 'as a display of imperious passion, stronger than death, because it is more strong than love, nothing has been seen in our time comparable to Madame Ristori's outbreak of choler in the third act'. That outbreak of choler, which involved Ristori brandishing her father's sword and defying the Spanish ambassador's threat, culminated in a tableau with Elizabeth's faithful courtiers drawing their swords and touching hers whilst swearing allegiance . The curtain came down on this tableau, fixing it in the audience's memory. *The Times* reviewer on 19 July 1858 singled out her death scene for special praise, and compared her performance to that of Edmund Kean as Louis XI, pointing out that she was 'a follower in the same track'.

The role of Mary Stuart offered Ristori other opportunities. She had, she tells us, a lot of sympathy for her and she begins her discussion of her training for the role with a brief statement refusing to enter into debates about the rights and wrongs of the historical character. Mary Stuart, she argues, 'was the victim of her own extraordinary beauty, her own personal fascination and her fervent Roman Catholicism'.[8] She claims to have been helped in her endeavours to portray Mary by the careful study she had made of the period for her role as Elizabeth I, and contrasts her performance after study with her first attempt at the role at the age of eighteen when she joined Mascherpa's company as *prima attrice assoluta* after five years with the Reale Sarda Company.

That study led her to diverge from Schiller's conception in various ways, as she imposed her own interpretation on events in Mary's life. Commenting on the stage directions which required her to wear a rich white gown, a crown, and a long black veil as she stepped up to the scaffold, Ristori argues that this is ahistorical. Mary, she notes, had spent nineteen years of her life in prisons so damp that her knees swelled in later life and she had to be helped up on to the scaffold by Melville. Moreover, permission to wear a crown would have had to be given by Elizabeth, which was unlikely, and finally she refuses to believe that Mary could have 'retained so much vanity as to try and produce an effect upon the minds of those who saw her for the last time'.[9] She insisted on wearing a costume that seemed to her 'most strictly historical', and substantiates her case by describing an exhibition of Mary Stuart relics in London in 1857 which contained a portrait of Mary's execution at Fotheringay wearing 'the ideal costume I had

20 Portrait of Adelaide Ristori, Italian actress. Artist unknown.

already imagined for the part'.[10] Ideal, that is, with one exception: Ristori had substituted a black coif and veil for the white one in the portrait, 'in the belief that by so doing I should give additional effect to the scene'.[11] Similarly, when visiting Athens in 1856 she claims to have studied the Caryatides to learn about Grecian drapery so as to be able to reproduce the effect in her portrayal of Medea.

Ristori was always aware of the importance of detail in creating stage pictures, and accounts of her invoices make interesting reading. Performances of *Elisabetta* called for twenty-five costumes for thirteen characters, quite apart from Ristori's own wardrobe, and thirteen costumes for twelve characters were required for *Maria Stuarda*. For her last London visit in 1883, she took four productions: *Macbeth, Marie Antoinette, Elisabetta,* and *Maria Stuarda* and inventories reveal the close attention to detail that included precise instructions to stage managers and bit players. For *Elisabetta* one list specifies such items as two full inkstands, one mirror for act v, one ornamental sword, seven carpets, three cushions, trophies for Elizabeth, and twelve halberds.[12]

A document choreographing opening scenes for each act of *Maria Antonietta* shows Ristori's meticulous sense of stagecraft and her determination to produce exactly the effect she wanted:

> Enter Marie Antoniette, followed by
> 6 Ladies who divide into two groups of 3 on each side
> 6 gentlemen who stand behind the Ladies
> 6 bodyguards, one of whom stands beside Varicour,
> 2 up against the columns at the rear of the stage and
> the other three along the back
> 6 Swiss Guards with halberds are ranked from front
> to back. Same arrangement in the finale.
> Act 1 – Finale

> Enter the Prince of Orleans with
> 6 Bodyguards who enter from his right
> and cross slowly to stage left then:
> 6 Swiss Guards with halberds who stand
> stage right, following the Duc de Brisac
> then the 6 Ladies and 6 gentlemen
> who enter quickly following Campan

who moves close or even in front of
the Bodyguards with muskets who stand
rear stage right.[13]

The opening moments of all five acts are detailed in this way, with precise instructions to the actors. Ristori had, as she tells us in her *Memoirs*, total control over artistic decisions once she had her own company:

> Everything relating to the artistic management rested entirely in my hands.
> I gave all orders, made all arrangements and occupied myself with all those
> great and small details which anyone who knows the stage fully will
> understand, and which are so essential to the success of the performance.
> A special administration had charge of the business department. But I am
> proud to say my husband was the soul of every enterprise.[14]

If anyone questioned her authority, Ristori knew how to impose herself. For anyone who was out of line, 'the firmness of my demeanour speedily put them in their proper place'.[15] Having known hardship as a child, Ristori was not about to relinquish anything once she held the power. Despite her refusal to portray only characters with whom she felt a sense of empathy, it is perhaps significant that she gradually narrowed down her repertoire to include only queens; besides Marie Antoinette, Elizabeth I, Mary Stuart, and Lady Macbeth she also played Medea, Phaedra, Renata di Francia, another Giacometti role, and princesses like Mirra or Lucrezia Borgia.

Through her marriage to the Marchese Capranica del Grillo, Ristori became entitled to be called Marchesa, and from the start she seems to have worked hard at being an exemplary noblewoman in life as well as in art. She combined the skills of a lifetime spent in the theatre with a good business sense and a belief in her own superior good fortune. Alessandro D'Amico refers to her period of greatest fame, from 1855 to 1885, as her 'theatre monarchy'.[16] He points out that her marriage in 1847 at the age of twenty-five placed her in a uniquely privileged situation in comparison with other actresses of her time. Because of her exceptional economic position, and the fact that her husband owned substantial properties, Ristori was able to collect and keep fairly full records of her life in the theatre, including her costumes. Her desire to be remembered, which also led her to write her *Memoirs*, a volume that includes studies of several of her major roles, has proved fortunate for theatre historians, for we have letters and other documents that give insight into how she worked and how she organised and ran her company. D'Amico points out, however, that from the documentation that remains we can see not only the conscious process of role creation but also the unconscious process of self-transformation:

> we can see that the task of the 'grande attore' in building a character went in two directions: the first towards history, that is a careful, almost fanatical study of the historical reality of the character (as for example, Maria Stuarda) and the other an investigation, a study of the behaviour (as in the case of Maria Stuarda or Marie Antoinette) of a queen; how a queen moves and talks and acts.[17]

Ristori's queenliness was frequently commented on by reviewers, both on and off stage. By the end of her life she was lady-in-waiting to Queen Margarita of Italy, as regal in life as she had endeavoured to be in art. Henry Knepler describes her as an example of the Horatio Alger tradition, a poor child who rose to the heights of success, unhindered by any moral doubts. He sees her as the archetype of nineteenth-century respectability, someone who could

> personify in the age of the great middle-class Queen Victoria the aspirations of the middle class to respectability mixed with romance. She could also inject colour into the drab existence of the lower orders. She supplied some of the gilt for the Gilded Age.[18]

Her repertoire further reflected that combination of respectability and romance, though the plays in which she starred fell out of fashion long before the end of the century and are mainly forgotten. Great noble ladies fighting against cruel fate were supplanted by women like Ellida Wangel and Nora, products of a different age and a completely different mentality.

There is an episode in Ristori's *Memoirs* that is highly significant in enabling us to understand something of her character. She describes a visit to Madrid in 1856, and the enthusiastic response to her portrayal of Medea, noting that Queen Isabella came to the theatre every night. On 21 September she was in her dressing room talking about local customs and learned that the bell she had heard being rung in the streets earlier in the day was to collect alms for the soul of a man condemned to die the next day. Further details emerged; the man had drawn his sword against a superior officer in retaliation for a blow he had received, and his sister had only learned of his impending execution when she had inquired for whom the alms bell was ringing. Ristori records her reaction to this story:

> This history touched me to the heart.
>
> 'My God!' I exclaimed, 'while we are here full of gaiety and expecting applause and success, that miserable wretch is counting the moments he has yet to live.'[19]

Unable to concentrate, Ristori was then approached in her dressing room by two relatives of the condemned man, asking her to intervene with the Queen on his behalf. Ristori relates how she demurred at doing this, despite the faith the relatives had in her, and then decided to speak to General Narvaez, Duke of Valencia and President of the Council of Ministers, despite his reputation as a hard man. She gives a long account of her interview with the General whom she invited to her dressing room before the performance and his initial refusal of her plea. Narvaez informed her that the entire municipality had asked for grace from the Queen and he had advised her not to give in, because an example needed to be made. But Ristori persisted – 'I did not lose heart . . . I recommended my attacks.' The General began to give way, and finally agreed that if she could persuade the Queen to consent, then he would permit the man to live.

Ristori asked for an audience with the Queen in the Royal box during the first interval, and as she was waiting to be admitted to the Queen's presence, the condemned man's sister was carried out in great distress. Ristori then entered, and threw herself at the Queen's feet pleading for the man's life:

> 'Calm yourself, Madame', said the Queen, without being able to dissemble her emotion. 'I would like to pardon him – but the President of the Council assures me that –' Forgetting all etiquette, and without heeding that I was interrupting her Majesty, I exclaimed:
>
> 'Only deign to give utterance once more to your clement intentions, and the Marshall, whose humane sentiments I am acquainted with, will not persist in his severity.'[20]

The Queen agrees, the General approves and the pardon is duly signed. But Ristori's version of the story continues. She describes how the news of the man's pardon spread through the theatre, and she was greeted with wild applause when she returned to the stage for the second act:

In the enthusiasm of the moment the name of the Queen was confounded
with my own. I intimated by my gestures that it was she alone who deserved
their thanks; while the Queen, graciously pointing to me, cried from her
box:

'No! no! it is she, it is she!'[21]

Later, on another visit to Madrid, Ristori recounts how she met the man she
had helped to save, and obtained a full pardon for him. Whenever she
played Madrid he would come to the theatre as her most energetic
claqueur.

What is significant about this story is, firstly, the amount of space that
Ristori devotes to it, and, secondly, the obvious pleasure it gave her to have
been equated with a reigning queen by the general public and by the Queen
herself. She remarks that 'I owe to Queen Isabella II one of the most memorable evenings of my life.'[22] Her account of the evening is obviously
embellished, and reads like a fairy story that abounds in coincidences: she
enquires about the meaning of the bell just before the relatives come to her
dressing room, the man's sister is carried out in a dead faint while she waits
for admission to the Queen's presence, she accomplishes a series of increasingly difficult tasks and succeeds every time. Finally, back on stage, the
name of the real Queen is confounded with her own. She has effectively
become a queen, with the power of life and death.

Ristori's version of the Madrid incident lends itself to an interpretation
of her behaviour as snobbish and self-complacent. But despite the delight
she obviously felt about her success, it is also important to analyse her
actions in terms of her profoundly held political convictions. For although
Ristori was an aspirant member of the middle class, a *figlia d'arte* who
turned into a Marchesa, she was also an Italian patriot, and throughout her
career her belief in the policies of the Risorgimento was a strong force. She
was asked to leave Venice by the ruling Austrian authorities in 1858, when
her performance as Judith was deemed unacceptable by the censors. (It had
been banned in Leghorn two years earlier.) She recounts in her *Memoirs*
how the students of Utrecht pulled her carriage through the streets in token
of their appreciation of her and of the 'marvellous prestige of Victor
Emmanuel and Garibaldi'.[23] This incident took place in 1860, the year
Garibaldi's Redshirts landed in Sicily and began the unification process in
earnest. Ristori notes the significance for her of that struggle:

> I delight to mention that this period of my artistic life (1860) coincided
> with the warlike feats of arms which were then attracting the notice of the
> civilized world towards Italy.[24]

As late as 1868 her performances were still controversial. The opening
night of *Marie Antoinette* in Bologna on 3 November was potentially explo-
sive. She had had to argue strongly to be allowed to perform the play, since
the subject matter was deemed undesirable, and the theatre was surrounded
by military police in the event of disturbances by anti-monarchists. As the
play unfolded, Giacometti's line was seen to be far less radical than the anti-
monarchists had hoped for, and the noise in the theatre was so bad that the
third act was drowned out completely. Ristori urged Giacometti, who was a
well-known Liberal figure, to go out on stage and speak to the audience,
but claims he was too upset to do so. She went out instead, urging the audience to be tolerant. This had the desired effect of calming the situation, and
she gives us a delightful vignette of going out for several curtain calls
'holding poor Giacometti, trembling in his excitement, tightly by the
hand'.[25] Once again Ristori had saved the day, and she notes that the
authorities came to congratulate her on her courage at facing up to the
hostile public 'as though I had saved the country'.[26]

A similar compliment was paid to her by Cavour, for whom she acted as
honorary ambassador overseas. In a letter dated 20 April 1861, replying to a
letter from Ristori of 4 April 1861, Cavour urges her to 'continue in Paris
your patriotic apostolate. You must go into the midst of heretics in order to
convert them,' though he comments that it was currently fashionable in
France to be a papist. This use of irony (the Papal States had vehemently
opposed Italian unification and the far right of the Catholic Church was
anathema to men like Cavour and Mazzini) then dissolves into congratu-
lating Ristori on her success with French audiences, which he suggests will
give her considerable authority to present the Italian case. 'Use that authority to serve our country, and I will applaud you not only as the greatest
actress in Europe, but also as a highly effective collaborator in our diplo-
matic negotiations.'[27]

Adelaide Ristori was born in Friuli, in the north of Italy on 29 January
1822. Her place of birth was determined theatrically: her parents happened

21 The young Adelaide Ristori, 1845.

to be performing in Cividale del Friuli at the time. Her father, Antonio Ristori, may have been a descendant of Tommaso or Giacomo Ristori, *commedia dell' arte* players of the seventeenth century, and certainly came from a long-standing theatre family. Antonio was the son of Teresa Ristori Canossa (1777–1842), an actress, and married another actress, Maddalena Ricci-Pomatelli, Adelaide's mother. The whole family, like Duse's family, were performers who travelled ceaselessly around Italy, and it is likely that the ease with which Ristori travelled round the world in later life, taking husband and children along with her, derives from a childhood spent on the road. She claims to have made her first stage appearance at the age of three months in *I regali di Capodanno*, a farce, which called for a baby to be concealed in a basket. She also claims to have stolen the show, by screaming so loudly that she drowned out the other actors and the audience laughed so much that she had to be removed.

Whatever the truth of this apocryphal tale, Ristori did begin her stage career in early childhood. It is significant that the tales she recounts of these early experiences are primarily comic, in stark contrast to Duse's recollections of the pain of having to perform in front of strangers, the hardships of the travelling lifestyle and the grief she suffered at watching her mother die of exhaustion. Ristori's mother lived until 1874, one year off her century, and her daughter seems to have had no grudge at all against her for putting her on the stage before she could walk. From the beginning Ristori's version of her early life in the theatre is a positive one. She even goes so far as to suggest that some people might have prophesied that she would hate the theatre after her early exposure to it, but insists that this was never the case.[28]

Her progression followed the standard pattern of a *figlia d'arte*. She started out playing child parts, both in farces and in sentimental pieces, then graduated to playing servants. At the age of twelve she began to be given soubrette roles, but by thirteen she was so well developed physically that she took on *seconda donna* roles. Her size was something that would be commented on all her life; in 1855 Delacroix noted that she was 'a large woman with a cold expression', adding that 'her little husband looks as if he were her oldest son'.[29] Her photographs show a woman with broad shoulders and large breasts, who added height and breadth to her already statuesque person with heavy draperies and regal headgear. Even the early images give an impression of considerable size: a long neck, a large head, a square jawline, pronounced eyebrows, and thick dark hair. Ristori seems to have been striking rather than classically beautiful. She moved well, had a good voice, and an aura of confidence that attracted audiences and, as will be discussed later, she had a keen sense of kinetics and knew how to place herself in space to create the most effective stage picture.

At around this time she and her parents joined the actor-manager Meneghino Moncalvo[30] and she continued to play *seconda donna* roles. At fifteen she played a leading part, the title role in Silvio Pellico's *Francesca da Rimini*. This was a role that she kept in her repertoire for some years, along with the other archetypally Italian tragedy *Pia de' Tolomei*. Both characters derive from Dante, Francesca being eternally damned for having committed adultery with her brother-in-law and Pia saved, but only after having been brutalised by a cruel and vengeful husband. In the *Divina Commedia* both women are presented with great sympathy, as victims of their own passion and of men's violence, and the episodes concerning both these characters are focal points in Dante's opus. The dramatists of the Risorgimento turned to such figures as these for inspiration, not only because of the good dramatic material their stories provided but also because of their essential Italianicity, as protagonists of Dante's great epic. Pellico was renowned as a supremely patriotic writer; as editor of a Liberal journal, he had been arrested by the Austrian authorities and imprisoned for ten years, as a result of which he wrote the great classic of the early Risorgimento, *Le mie prigioni* (1832). *Francesca da Rimini* was an early work, but was revived and brought back into the repertoire of the Reale Sarda Company in 1826, and after Pellico's release from prison in 1830 there was a renewal of public interest in his work. But the political climate made writing difficult; in 1835 Pellico announced his decision to stop writing for the theatre, on the grounds of excessive censorship and paranoia on the part of both audiences and authorities, who perceived political allusions even where none were intended. Nevertheless, although most of his plays sank into obscurity, *Francesca da Rimini* continued to enjoy popularity, and when Ristori joined the Reale Sarda Company in 1837 it became one of her principal roles. When she went to Paris with the Reale Sarda Company in 1855, the performance of *Francesca da Rimini* was prefaced by a recitation of one of Pellico's patriotic odes.

The decision to join the Reale Sarda Company seems to have been taken by Ristori's father. In her *Memoirs*, she explains that her father was concerned about her taking on prima donna roles at such a young age, and felt that she might overtask herself. What seems more likely is that Antonio Ristori saw the move from Moncalvo to the Reale Sarda Company as a good career prospect for the family. The financial situation of the company was not auspicious, but as Marvin Carlson suggests, the quality of the actors was so good, that 'even the lesser actors of this brilliant company would have stood out in one of Italy's minor companies'.[31]

Again, Ristori makes no complaint about her beginnings with the Reale Sarda Company, where she worked with such stars as Carlotta Marchionni and Luigi Vestri. She began playing young prima donna roles in 1838, and by 1840, when Marchionni retired, she moved to playing leading roles. Her contract was for four years, during which she claims to have learned a great deal about acting. Two points in particular stand out when she writes about her training with the Reale Sarda Company. She notes the importance of voice work:

> No less important is the study of elocution in order to speak distinctly.
>
> The diction ought to be clear, distinct, not too slow, well understood, in order not to fall into any mannerisms, but at the same time deliberate enough to allow the audience to grasp the meaning of every word, and there must not be any suspicion of stammering.[32]

Ristori's well-modulated, clear voice would be praised by reviewers throughout her life. Angelo Gattinelli, who performed with Ristori during the 1850s, wrote a comparative essay that appeared in *Il vessillo della libertà* in 1856, analysing Ristori's technique in contrast to that of Carlotta Marchionni. In act III of *Maria Stuarda*, he describes Marchionni and other leading actresses of her day as 'shouting at the pitch of their lungs', while Ristori did the opposite. He notes that Marchionni declaimed her lines, because that was the fashion of their time, while Ristori spoke hers, Marchionni walked about and gesticulated a lot, while Ristori 'made few gestures and walked naturally':

> Marchionni was always in tears and Ristori only wept when the dramatic situation demanded it. Marchionni's great flaw was a nasal whine in her speech . . . Marchionni was a clever actress but had all the defects of the old

school . . . Her voice was monotonous in performance, a constant whine, a voice better suited to singing than to acting . . . she was a systems actress, not a genius . . . Ristori rejected the past and threw herself brilliantly into the future, where she could have some impact and make an impression on good voice work, competing with the French, who are justly held to be masters of dramatic art.[33]

Ristori seems to have regarded good diction as crucial, in contrast to other performers of her time whose style came closer to the operatic. Time and again, reviewers praise her well-modulated speaking voice, particularly in countries where she was working in a language unknown to most of her audiences. To achieve her vocal effects, she worked hard. She points out the need for proper training, and also suggests that it is important for performers to work their way through the ranks, starting with small parts and only moving gradually to larger ones. This view was one she held throughout her life; actors needed to serve an apprenticeship in order to acquire the skills of the craft and to adjust their own personalities to whatever demands the role made upon them.

Equally significant was the need for an actor to understand how to shift between moods. These points of transition, which were a hallmark of her acting style, she compares to the chiaroscuro, or play of light and shadow in painting. Reading her accounts of roles that she took in repertoire around the world, we return again and again to this point. In her account of her playing of Medea, for example, she describes the transition from an attitude of despair to wild rage in the scene with her rival Creusa. In her preparatory work for Phaedra, she studied the character as being composed of two distinct personalities, so that she could move between two states of mind and two patterns of behaviour. Her Elizabeth I was a powerful, public stateswoman who concealed her troubled, passionate interior life beneath a mask of control. A review in *L'Arte* of 12 July 1851 describes the transitions in her performance in *Maria Stuarda*:

> At the point where Mary, who is about to burst out with bitter reproaches towards Elizabeth, tries and succeeds in controlling the interior fire that threatens to explode, abasing herself with a kiss that she, filled with heavenly resignation, presses upon the crucifix hanging from her waist, at that precise moment of unattainable sublimity because it demands an artistic beauty carried out with the simplest, most natural means, as in all the soliloquies, in all the most delicate and gracious poetic similitudes with

22 Portrait of Adelaide Ristori early in her career.

which this magnificent work by the German tragedian abounds, and from which Ristori knows how to draw the tiniest and most perfect moments, the Pistoian audience was particularly moved, carried away in their enthusiasm . . .

Taste in matters of dramatic art is improving every day under the influence of a school that is no longer exaggerated and ludicrously imitative of absurd, conventionalized forms, but is simply based on principles of simple, wise imitation of the real.[34]

Ristori argued that her ability to make these transitions derived from close study of a role, and an attention to detail that came from years of experience and willingness to take on any type of part, even one she actively disliked at first reading, like that of Medea. These skills were not acquired easily, without a great deal of hard work, for the touring schedule was exhausting and there was little money for actors. Ristori left the Reale Sarda Company when her four year contract expired and in 1841 joined Mascherpa's company as *prima attrice* where she stayed until 1846, when she joined the Domeniconi–Coltellini company. Her repertoire was fairly limited, though as she notes there was little demand from audiences for innovation. Again, this is another point of major contrast between Ristori and Duse, for whilst the former was content to work on a smallish number of roles, which diminished gradually throughout her lifetime, Duse was forever anxiously searching for new roles to add to what she saw as a restricted repertoire that reflected the dire state of the Italian theatre of her day. In the late 1840s Ristori toured with *Francesca da Rimini* and *Pia de' Tolomei*, a version of *Romeo and Juliet*, several tragedies by Alfieri, including *Antigone*, *Ottavia*, and *Rosmunda*, comedies by Goldoni, *Adriane Lecouvreur*, and a range of other plays by French writers such as Scribe and Giraud. Gherardi wrote *Une folle ambizione* for her in 1844, which launched him on his career as a successful dramatist, whilst Vincenzo Martini wrote *Una donna di quarant'anni* and *Il misantropo in società* for her, both of which were first performed in 1853. The impact of the revolutions across Europe of 1848, which led to the resignation of Metternich, the abdication of the Emperor Ferdinand of Hapsburg, and in Italy resulted in the abdication of the King in 1849, was felt in the theatre through a gradual relaxation of censorship which allowed greater possibilities to comic writers in particular. In her early years of fame as one of Italy's leading players, Ristori toured a balanced programme of tragedy, comedy, and drama, catering to the taste for French theatre but also introducing new Italian work alongside classics.

Nevertheless, Ristori had strong views about the desirability of certain roles. She would not play Marguerite Gautier, and had a clause written into her contract with the Reale Sarda Company in 1853 that allowed her to refuse any role she considered to be immoral. She had misgivings about Mirra, the protagonist of Alfieri's tragedy who incestuously loves her own father, but once the play was no longer prohibited by the Papal censor after 1848, she agreed to take it on, though claims she was forced into it by Domeniconi and Coltellini. Ironically, when she first went to London, in 1856, with *Mirra* by then established in her repertoire, the British censors refused to allow its performance.

Maintaining the respectability of her public image was important to Ristori throughout her life, and increased in intensity after her marriage. In 1846, at the age of twenty-four, Ristori met the man who was to become her husband, the Marchese Giuliano Capranica del Grillo. The occasion of their meeting, when she was performing at the Teatro Capranica in Rome, and the story of their elopement in the teeth of his family's bitter opposition to a match they saw as a *mésalliance* is played down in Ristori's *Memoirs*. Having become a member of the aristocracy, a friend of the nobility both on stage and off, Ristori did not seek to dwell on the days when she had been considered beneath her husband's family and the two had been forbidden to meet.

The story of Ristori's marriage is significant, because it marked a watershed in her career as an actress and in her life. She and her husband-to-be fled across central Italy in disguise, and married secretly in a village in Romagna. Later, once her father-in-law had adjusted to the news, they went through a second, public ceremony and Ristori was welcomed into the Capranica del Grillo family. There is a wonderful account of the elopement in *Il Diavoletto*, the Triestine paper, which gives a résumé of Ristori's biography up to 1856 and transforms the story of her runaway marriage into a theatrical plot:

> Her biographers have told us the dozens of strange adventures that befell them! They relate how a stern father recalled his besotted son back to Florence and ordered him off to a castle in the heart of the Romagna, how

that chaste, courageous young woman sailed from Leghorn and landed, after
a terrible storm, at Civitavecchia; how she learned there that her Giuliano
had been locked away in another castle in the insanitary climate of the
maremma; how she tried in vain to see him again; how finally they did
meet, how they went into a village church and knelt before a priest at the
altar who blessed their union. They even relate how Adelaide and her
husband were attacked by a band of miscreants at Porretta; how they tied
the marquis to a tree; how the actress' desperation gave her enough strength
to disarm those savage souls; how Giuliano's mother and then his father also
blessed the couple who had been enriched by the dear gift of two precious
children . . .[35]

In this version, it is Ristori who plays the starring role, seeking out her
imprisoned husband, fighting off a gang of bandits, finally winning the
hearts of her in-laws. It is the story of a woman triumphing over all the
odds, and it is significant that Giuliano is imprisoned in a castle in the
maremma, the same place where the tragedy of Francesca da Rimini
unfolded. The author of this biographical account attacks the class
consciousness that led Giuliano's parents to repudiate his choice of an
actress, and sees the success of the marriage as a sign of important democra-
tic changes in the new Italy.

Marriage to a Marchese gave Ristori respectability and social status; it
also gave her a degree of economic security that she had never enjoyed
before. Her relationship with her husband seems to have been happy; he travelled with her, acting as her business manager, whilst she stayed firmly out of
any alternative relationships and avoided scandal throughout her life. They
had four children, but only two survived, Giorgio and Bianca, and Ristori
kept her children close to her, travelling with them as she had travelled with
her parents, though in totally different economic and social circumstances.
There seems to have been some pressure on her to retire from the theatre after
her marriage, but she returned to the stage to do benefit performances and
then in 1853 rejoined the Reale Sarda Company, setting up tough financial
terms that ensured her a decent income. Her contract specified that the
Marchesa Adelaide Capranica del Grillo née Ristori, as *prima attrice* of the
company should, for a three-year period starting on the first day of Lent 1853
and ending on Shrove Tuesday 1856, be entitled to receive 20,000 new
Piedmontese lire and one-third of the profits of the company, to be paid in
gold or silver napoleons, and in Austrian currency outside Piedmont.

23 Adelaide Ristori as Mirra.

Despite this contract and her husband's property, Ristori appears to have needed more money. Paola Bignami draws attention to letters from this time suggesting that all was not well financially, and notes that she rented her Rome apartment to the actress Teresa de Giuli Borsi for a season in 1854.[36] There was a cholera epidemic in 1854 which led to theatres being closed, and the situation for actors at all levels in Italy was problematic. Ristori's favourable contract depended on her being able to perform regularly and attract good-sized audiences.

Her *Memoirs* give a different picture. She cites grief for the death of two of her children and her passionate love for the remaining two as principal reasons for a decline in her interest in the theatre. Having discovered motherhood, which she obviously enjoyed, and remained close to her children throughout her life, she found herself less concerned with her public. But she also complains about the state of the Italian theatre, claiming that opera was given preferential treatment over dramatic theatre. Everything was sacrificed to the opera, she claims, and budgets that could be stretched to cover the demands of operatic staging were severely restricted the rest of the time. Moreover, the problems of censorship at a highly sensitive moment in the history of Italian unification in the Papal States made working difficult. She lists some of the more extreme examples of the absurdity of the censors – changing the lines spoken by the witches in *Macbeth*, even altering the title of Bellini's *Norma* because of the allusions that might be contained in the word. Nor was this kind of ludicrous nit-picking limited only to the Papal States; it also went on in those parts of Italy still under Austrian domination. All these factors contributed to Ristori's depression, and she claims to have decided as late as in 1855 to retire from the theatre altogether to devote herself to her family.

What she did instead was to go abroad. In 1855 she set off on the first of her overseas tours, and for the next thirty years, until her final tour in 1885, she travelled the world. Marvin Carlson sees this decision as inaugurating a new era in the Italian theatre, and certainly the visit to Paris in 1855, with Ristori and Rossi as the stars of the Reale Sarda Company, established a precedent from which future generations of Italian actors could benefit. Ristori claims that the decision to go to Paris was a sudden whim, a last grand gesture before her final retirement:

> One idea incessantly occupied my mind. This was to vindicate, before
> leaving the stage, the artistic worth of my country in foreign lands, to show
> that, in spite of all, Italy was not the land of the dead. But how was I to do
> this? All of a sudden I made up my mind to go to France.[37]

This version of Ristori's decision to go abroad ignores the facts of her
financial difficulties, though she does refer to the unsuccessful Internari
company tour of 1830, when Luigi Taddei and Carolina Internari had been
ruined by the bad timing of their visit which clashed with the revolution
that overthrew Louis Philippe. She comments, however, that the timing of
the Reale Sarda tour was more auspicious, and certainly there seems to have
been some support for the tour from Cavour, who obviously wanted to
raise the profile of Italy in Europe generally. Ristori does appear to have
genuinely believed in the Italian cause, and it may be that her motives were
not entirely financial. Alessandro D'Amico points out that Ristori's move
on to the international stage coincided with a shift within Italy that marked
an increase in status for the dramatic theatre as a whole. The new Italy
dreamed of by the patriots of the Risorgimento also had an artistic dimension; political unification was only part of an agenda, which also included
the need to revitalize the arts and restore the Italian language and culture to
its place within the rest of Europe. Commenting on Ristori's support for
the cause, D'Amico notes

> Ristori often used to remark 'patriotism yes, politics no'. Seen from this
> point of view, Ristori is the most emblematic character of the Italian theatre
> world. She was genuinely the incarnation of the soul of Italian moderation
> against the republican, democratic ideal personified in Gustavo Modena.
> Ristori lived out that monarchist, moderate Italian position as a woman, as a
> member of the nobility, as a mother and as an actress, in every aspect of her
> life. You may note that Ristori's patriotism came out in ways that had never
> been open to an actor before. Ristori even undertook diplomatic missions
> abroad on behalf of Cavour.[38]

Ristori and the Reale Sarda Company, which included Ernesto Rossi and
Bellotti Bon, left for Paris on 1 May 1855. The repertoire was a standard
one, and included *Francesca da Rimini*, *I gelosi fortunati*, *Mirra*, *Oreste*, *Pia de'*
Tolomei and comedies by Goldoni, including *La Locandiera*, *Il curioso acci-*
dente, and *Il burbero benefico*. The great success of the tour was undoubtably
Mirra, which provided Ristori with a vehicle through which she could

mount a challenge to the great Rachel. Lamartine wrote a poem to her, suggesting 'tu donnes de ton sang aux ombres de ces drames'; de Vigny wrote how 'Myrra nous a pris tous dans sa large ceinture / sanglante et dénouée', while de Musset equated Ristori with the spirit of the newly emerging nation state of Italy:

> Quelqu'un m'avait dit que malgré la misère,
> La peur, l'oppression, l'orgeuil humilié,
> D'un grand peuple vaincu le genou jusqu'à terre
> N'avait pas encore plié.
> Que ces dieux de porphyre et de marbre et d'albâtre
> Dont le monde romain autrefois fut peuplé,
> Étaient vivants encore, et que dans un théâtre
> Une statue antique, un soir avait parlé . . .[39]

> I have been told that despite the misery, the fear, the oppression, the
> humbled pride of a great defeated people, bowed down almost to the earth,
> they were yet not vanquished. And that those gods of porphyry, of marble
> and of alabaster which once peopled the Roman world were still alive, and
> that in a theatre, one evening, an ancient statue spoke . . .

Ristori's Paris visit was carefully planned, down to the smallest detail. She needed to make an impact on French audiences both as a political and personal statement. In her *Memoirs* she claims that the representation of nature in a living, truthful way was the hallmark of what she terms the Italian school of acting, and there was clearly a conscious determination on the part of the company to serve as representatives of their country at a moment of historical transition. But in terms of Ristori's own career, going to Paris meant performing in the city where Rachel, arguably the greatest actress in Europe, held sway, and the younger woman needed her acting skills to be seen as at least on a similar level of excellence.

The Ristori–Rachel contest, which prefigures the Duse–Bernhardt contest a few decades later, provided fodder for the male-dominated press and helped bring audiences into the theatres. It is a story that follows the typical sexist myth that views women as inherently competitive with other women, vying for favour with the predominantly male world of critics and reviewers, unable to coexist except in a state of disharmony with one another. It is a titillatory myth, for it assumes that the passion generated in the clash between female rivals is directed exclusively towards winning male approval. The most extreme example of this myth is provided in the representations of life in the harem, that all-female locus of the imagination apparently filled with sexually frustrated women yearning for male favour and seeking to annihilate their rivals in the quest for that favour. In a European context, the next best thing to a battle between oriental beauties was a battle between actresses, also judged to be sexually less inhibited than other women, because their movements were so obviously less constrained. The woman exposed to the male gaze on a stage was public property, a public woman about whom fantasies could be woven, an object of desire. That Ristori was a happily married women with small children who travelled with her on tour, a woman about whom there was never any hint of scandal throughout her life, a woman who prized respectability so highly did not deter the speculation about her encounter with Rachel.

Henry Knepler notes that Jules Janin appears to have been the principal engineer of the story of the conflict between Ristori and Rachel, and endeavours to find an explanation for this phenomenon.[40] Proceeding rationally, he tries to account for Janin's deliberately loaded review in favour of Ristori, that effectively marked the end of his support for Rachel. His suggestion that there may have been old submerged rivalries, sexual jealousy, and other factors is certainly not improbable, but what he misses is the reality of the power of the myth of female conflict in the middle of the nineteenth century. The alternative to the image of the Angel of the House was a passionate, sexually voracious creature, and the actress, a woman who sold herself to her public, was one more example of this subversive and disquieting figure. As Tracy Davis puts it,

> No matter how consummate the artist, pre-eminent the favourite, and modest the woman, the actress could not supersede the fact that she lived a public life and consented to be 'hired' for amusement by all who could command the price. For a large section of society, the similarities between the actress's life and the prostitute's or *demi-mondaine*'s were unforgettable, and overruled all other evidence about respectability.[41]

Ristori's own version of her Paris tour plays down the rivalry between herself and Rachel. She takes some pains to refute the idea that there was any hostility between them, and states that she disliked the press attention given to her at Rachel's expense. Her *Memoirs* add credence to the suggestion that the whole thing was deliberately engineered, and that she and

Rachel were caught up in a media circus beyond their control. Her recognition of Rachel's talent is unequivocal; she admires her skills, she accords her recognition as a great artist.

Despite her self-admitted admiration for Rachel, Ristori also notes the points of difference between their two acting styles, which she sees as representative of their national differences. Rachel, she maintains, follows the French school of acting that laid stress on control and self-possession, while she follows the Italian way, that insisted upon truthful representation of states of mind. When someone is overcome by joy or sorrow, she asks, do they not automatically move their hand to their head and disarrange their hair? That such a gesture might be itself conventionalised never occurred to her; acting required the studied representation of signs of a state of mind, and just as the crown signified kingship, so the hand to the head signified a sudden rush of emotion. Gestures that today would be regarded as absurdly histrionic were interpreted in terms of realism, according to the convention that established norms of realistic performance.

In her comments on Rachel's work, Ristori stresses her appearance and the skill with which she used costume to disguise her thinness. Describing the first time she saw Rachel on stage, as Camille in *Horace*, Ristori writes:

> I seemed to see before me a Roman statue: her bearing was majestic; her step royal, the draping of her mantle, the folds of her tunic, everything was studied with wonderful artistic talent.[42]

She too studied everything with meticulous care. In a letter to her husband, who had gone ahead of the company to Paris to ensure that everything was suitably organised, Ristori sets out minute details of her costume requirements for Pia de' Tolomei. She describes colours, materials, trimmings, gives him detailed instructions on what to select, and reminds him several times to be careful about the cost.[43] Ristori worked in the tradition of the actor-managers of the travelling companies, and the Paris visit marked her increased involvement in company finances.

Her attention to detail reflects her two principal artistic concerns. She believed in precise historical reconstruction of characters in period and she drew her inspiration from a range of sources, in particular from contemporary paintings. In this respect, she reflects the prevailing taste of the middle of the nineteenth century which perceived history in very visual terms. She was also concerned to create powerful stage effects, strong visual images that would have an almost photographic impact on the spectators. One of the key concepts in her idea of acting was the notion of study, and for each character she portrayed she endeavoured to locate the role visually in its historical context. Her second key concept was the idea of the pose, the stage picture, the image that would be retained in the imagination after the performance had ended. A review in *The Musical World* on 11 July 1857 praised her picture-acting and noted that

> She shines the most in the parts that afford her a statuesque exhibition. She loves to drop into a pose at the conclusion of an act and to let the curtain fall on a sculptural epigram.

Her account of her choice of roles stresses this visual dimension. Of *Medea*, she wrote:

> The second act abounds in fine situations and marvellous scenic effects, which offer the actress a large scope for the display of her dramatic capacity.[44]

For her performance as Phaedra, she describes how she constructed stage pictures that were held a long time, to maximise their impact:

> In order to increase the scenic effect, I had arranged that after a *long pause* Oenone should fall on her knees beside me, and with kindly and persuasive words raise my inanimate form, until it rested partially upon her knees, while I slowly and gradually recovered my scattered senses and broke out into reproaches against her.[45]

Dying, Ristori's Phaedra offers a very nineteenth-century stage picture, with attendants grouped around her:

> As my agony increased I was placed in my easy-chair and I breathed my last with my body half-falling from the grasp of one attendant, while all the other people were kneeling around me, in sign of their deep grief and reverent respect.[46]

It should, of course, be noted that the nineteenth-century translator of this text has added an additional fillip to Victorian propriety by giving Ristori an 'easy-chair' on which to recline, rather than a couch.

Ristori's style was described as 'picture-acting'[47] and along with her own accounts of how she created these pictures, contemporary photographs serve to give some idea of the effects she sought to create. As Judith she is bare-armed, wielding a sword above her head, as Marie Antoinette she sits centre stage, clasping a small child in her arms with attendants strategically placed to direct attention on her face. In all these photographic images it is her face that dominates. Her body is statuesque, draped, exquisitely costumed, but her face and head capture the gaze of the spectator. The *Times* reviewer on 9 June 1857 declared that 'Madame Ristori's impersonation is of the purely ideal kind . . . in the art of giving each motion a statuesque grandeur she is unique'. Many images of her show her hands carefully placed alongside her cheek, on her breast, beside her lips, in gestures that direct attention to her mouth and eyes. Most of her photographs show her gazing upwards, away from the spectator and from other characters on stage, a further indication of the upward mobility of her expression. She had a large head and strong features, and in an age when the female body was constrained by corsets and by conventions of decorum, she used her face to express the passion that in terms of body language remained caparisoned in splendid costumes that served not so much to facilitate movement but rather to inhibit. Later in the century, as female clothing both on stage and off became less constraining, so the use of the face as prime vehicle for the expression of feeling declined, but Ristori had been trained to use the eyes and other facial features with as much care as a Kabuki performer trains today.

Perhaps the best-known photographic images of Ristori show her as Medea, clasping her children in her arms from the very first moment of her appearance. She describes how she planned this first stage picture of the devoted mother who will ultimately be driven to commit infanticide:

> At last the moment of my appearance arrived and I stood already prepared on the platform of the shaking piece which represented the base of the mountain I was slowly and with difficulty to ascend. I carried my little Melanthe in my arms, while his tiny head rested on my shoulder, and the part of my ample mantle, which was afterwards to hang down my back, and the arrangement of which had so preoccupied Ary Schefster, now covered half my head and almost the whole of my child's. I had placed the other boy, Lycaon, at my left side, making him put one hand within my girdle, as he leant against me in an attitude of utter exhaustion . . . Arrived at the summit of the mountain, I stood for a moment in the attitude of a woman utterly exhausted. I was indebted for this '*pose*', and for many others in my

24 Adelaide Ristori as Medea – the entrance with the children. 1857.

studies of tragedy, to the famous group of the Niobe, which occupies the Sala della Niobe in the famous Uffizi Gallery at Florence.[48]

Achieving such an effect had its difficulties. In a letter to her mother, dated 21 September 1866, Ristori describes the problems she had had with her children on the occasion of her opening night in New York. She tells her mother about the success of the evening, the impressive box-office receipts, the flowers she received afterwards, but also provides her with details of how close she came to disaster:

> I was covered in icy sweat and my breathing nearly choked me because they had built me such a narrow pathway up such a steep mountain.
>
> I had to try and stop Ninì sliding out from under my arm, to mind I did not miss my footing because of the palpitations and keep the child over my shoulder quiet, because he was wailing 'I want my papa, I want my papa' in a voice like a lovesick cat that set my teeth on edge. Just imagine how terrified I was that he might not want to go on and finish the act! In the end, in Act III I went on with a different one, and the finale was a success.[49]

The role of Medea was one of Ristori's great triumphs, and she toured with it for decades. Her version was an idiosyncratic one, which she arrived at after her initial displeasure with the role. Legouvé's reading of the story of Medea, the woman who kills her children in an act of revenge against her husband, Jason, the man who has abandoned her for a younger woman despite her having helped him to power, shifted the emphasis significantly. Legouvé's Medea is not so much a demonic character bent on bloody revenge, but an abandoned wife and mother, an archetypal representative of the dozens of wretched women who also committed infanticide in the nineteenth century when deserted by their lovers and left to starve. This version of the story offered Ristori a means of approaching the taboo subject with a view to arousing some degree of sympathy and her careful staging accentuates that process. As Elaine Aston points out,

> Ristori's entire performance was therefore based on a series of images delivered in a fearful and imposing manner, and designed to highlight the plight of the seduced and abandoned woman, and outraged mother.[50]

Even in such an extreme role, Ristori sought to combine the respectable with the political. That she managed to carry this off so successfully is clearly an indication of the power she brought to the role. Even Queen Victoria was impressed, and noted that Madame Ristori was 'a magnificent looking person . . . Her voice is most beautiful . . . Every attitude and action is like that of an antique statue.'[51] The ending of *Medea* was indeed reminiscent of an antique statue: Ristori describes how she fled with her children to the altar of Saturn, away from the fury of Jason whose bride Creusa is dying. Jason wants to take her children from her and have her executed, but in a final act of desperate love she kills them. The tableau showed the dead children and their desperate mother standing with her arm outstretched towards Jason in a gesture of accusation:

> Jason now hurried in, asking desperately –
>
> 'Murdered? Who has murdered them?'
>
> 'Thou!'
>
> exclaimed Medea, drawing herself up in an imposing and ferocious attitude and extending her arm towards Jason like an image of inexorable destiny!
>
> And here the curtain fell.[52]

In her *Memoirs*, Ristori claims that Medea was the role she preferred above all others, and from which she learned the most. In the making of her Medea, she sought to develop the portrayal of two emotions, jealousy and hatred, which she describes as contrasting but from which ultimately revenge is born. Her Medea was a wronged woman, not a savage, a noble mother and wife driven over the edge of reason by the callous indifference of Jason, the man in whom she had placed her trust. She is, quite simply, overwhelmed by passions that she cannot control. In this respect, her Medea is a post-Romantic construction, an individual struggling to retain control over forces that destroy her from within.

Aldo Gennari, writing in the *Gazzetta di Ferrara*, on 26 November 1852, describes Ristori as a highly intelligent actor, a performer who combined a strong physical presence with 'an exceptional mind . . . a unique sense of intuition'. Ristori, he claims, 'may be said to have abandoned classicism in the art of theatre', since she refused to contain her acting within a framework of predetermined physical and vocal systems, 'trusting instead in her own strength and in the power of her own genius'. Although a believer in the importance of training and convinced that only close and detailed study of a role could qualify her to take it on, Ristori was also searching for a new mode of acting, ideally one that would reflect the new reality of an Italy moving rapidly towards unification.

Again and again, we find reviewers praising the way in which Ristori unleashed her emotions after a desperate struggle to keep them under control. The success of her portrayal of Medea reflects that technique, as does her Mirra, and there is a significant passage in her *Memoirs* where she discusses why she felt Alfieri's *Mirra* to be so important as a vehicle for what she calls 'our Italian school':

> This tragedy, written in pure and severe Italian style, and with many distinctly Greek forms, gave me an opportunity of showing my artistic feeling, the profound psychological study I had bestowed on the part, and the ability of our Italian school to unite national spontaneity to Greek plasticity, detaching itself entirely from academical conventionalisms, not because academical conventionalisms are devoid of everything praiseworthy, but because we argue that in the whirl and fury of the passions, it is not possible to give full attention to the greater or lesser elevation of the arms, or hands. Provided the gestures are noble and not discordant with the sentiments expressed, the actor must be left to his own impulse. Constraint and conventionalism, in my opinion, obscure the truth.[53]

Ristori here defines the new Italian school as being the combination of what she calls 'Greek plasticity' with 'national spontaneity'. By her use of the term 'national', she signals her intent to create a specifically Italian style, and she draws upon the stereotype of Mediterranean spontaneity to make a statement about art. By spontaneity she appears to mean two things: the Italian characteristic of immediate expression of emotion, and the representation of emotion in such a way as to convey a sense of the reality of feeling. Earlier generations of Italian actors had been trained from manuals, which gave precise choreographic indications of how to express emotions, indicating how the body should be placed, where the hands should be in relation to the face, and so on. Ristori defines this form of acting as 'conventionalism', adding also that it constrains the actor who is compelled to use fixed forms through which to represent feeling, at the expense of his or her own impulse.

As an example of the new Italian style of acting, she cites her co-star, Tommaso Salvini. She insists that the hallmarks of Salvini's technique were spontaneity through close study of nature, and describes him as the living incarnation of Italian inspiration. Clearly, what Ristori means by Italian spontaneity, however, is not the same thing as the reviewer in *The Athenaeum* on 7 June 1856, who declared that 'never was actress more earnestly, passionately, gracefully Southern than Madame Ristori'. The attribution of 'Southern' as a quality to Ristori owes more to the way in which Anglo-Saxon audiences constructed an image of exotic Mediterranean 'otherness' than to any understanding of the ways in which Ristori was endeavouring to build a new national acting style.

In her discussion of Mirra, as with Medea, Ristori again emphasises the problem for an actor of representing the contrasts within the character. She writes about the problems she had with the role, explaining that her first attempt at it was not successful, noting that it made demands upon her that 'seemed to paralyse my intellectual powers'.[54] Her explanation of the difficulty is interesting: Mirra is a young girl doomed by Venus to love her own father, a punishment against Mirra's mother who boasted of her daughter's beauty. She is therefore, as Ristori sees her, 'a pure soul', an innocent who is afflicted with incestuous passion almost like a disease, and who is appalled by what is taking place within her. It is this sense of conflict, the clash between the natural purity of the maiden and the unnatural lust that is visited upon her, that Alfieri manipulates to arouse the compassion of the audience.

Ristori's interpretation stressed the contrasting states of mind of the character, deriving from her inner struggle to understand and overcome the raging passion that ultimately devours her and leads her to suicide. She was able to balance the two states of mind by the device of playing Mirra as two people, as a woman in control of her own life part of the time, and as a woman out of control whenever she is in her father's presence. This must have enabled Ristori to play contrast against another actor, giving her the opportunity to raise the emotional level whenever her father, played on her first Paris visit by Ernesto Rossi, was on stage with her. Her account of her appearance in act v gives some indication of how she and Rossi must have worked the scene:

> I presented myself, arrayed in a most simple Greek dress of the finest white wool, with my hair plainly arranged, an ashy paleness on my face, my eyes fixed, my looks bent on the ground, my steps tottering and uncertain. My whole appearance at once made the spectators aware of the terrible conflict

that raged within me, and prepared them for the final catastrophe. At the sight of my father I remained as if petrified, and with my head bent awaited my condemnation.

Without speaking a word, by negations, by interrupted and hardly expressed monosyllables, by gestures expressive of my grief, and by my unutterable anguish, I produced a by-play which formed, as it were, a dialogue with my father.[55]

Writing about her Medea at the Lyceum, on her second British tour in 1857, the *Morning Post* review of 9 June, comments on her 'flexibility of counte-nance, which catches the instantaneous transitions of passion with such a variety of effect as never to fatigue'. Ristori's flexibility, as demonstrated by her ability to effect transitions of mood very quickly and her dialogic style of acting that enabled her to play alongside fellow actors, rather than over-whelming them, was the key to her success in many roles, most particularly in the years of her first foreign tours.

Ristori's versions of both Medea and Mirra were premised on the same concept: a virtuous woman is destroyed by an excess of passion that is visited upon her through no fault of her own. The cause of Medea's down-fall is her love for the faithless Jason, the cause of Mirra's wretchedness and early death is the arrogance of her own mother and the vindictiveness of the goddess. What Ristori, a pillar of respectability in her own private life, wanted to depict in her portrayal of these two characters was the conflict that raged within each of them as the fabric of their lives was gradually destroyed.

Reconsidering Ristori's work from a late twentieth-century per-spective, what appears most striking is the clash of values that her career in the theatre exposes. On the one hand, she seems to have been a performer of genuine talent, who worked hard on each of her roles and who took the Italian theatre beyond the classical actor's manual into areas of great originality of expression. As a woman, she took an active part in managing her company and held the reins of power for years. But on the other hand, in her search for balance between conflicting states of mind and her insis-tence on the inherent nobility of all her characters, she reflects the bour-geois tastes of her age. Her Mirra and her Medea are victims, decent women from good families whose lives are destroyed by hostile forces.

In her *Memoirs*, Ristori compares the role of Mirra to that of Phaedra, another character overwhelmed by incestuous passion. She agrees that the contrasts in Phaedra were difficult to achieve, but makes out a strong case for the difference between the two women. Mirra, she argues, dies because her youthful innocence was not strong enough to help her contain her guilty secret. Phaedra, on the other hand, has the self-knowledge to stop herself and yet chooses not to do so. She discusses the variations in the character of Phaedra as depicted by Euripides, Seneca, and Racine, but notes that the significance of Racine's version is that he shifted the emphasis on to the female character, away from Hippolytus.

The contrast between the characters of Mirra and Phaedra, however, is only part of the story. The principal contrast is between a classical French play, albeit in a new translation, and a play by the great Italian Romantic dramatist, Alfieri. Ristori writes about her preparation for the roles with great sensitivity and intelligence, but the demands placed on her by the two differing styles of theatre also affected her way of working. Racine's play is all about the containing of passion, and his adherence to the three unities kept violent action off the stage. Alfieri, in contrast, has Mirra kill herself on stage, and his creation of great histrionic scenes offered Ristori an ideal vehicle for her acting style. In her *Memoirs* Ristori gives an account of her performance of *Fedra* at the Teatro del Fondo in Naples in 1857. She claims to have been so caught up in her role that she fell into the footlights at the end of the fourth act, injuring her arm and narrowly escaping serious burns. This is a curious anecdote, and suggests that she was trying too hard to adapt the framework of the play to her own style. Significantly, as she grew older she toured fewer and fewer plays, selecting only those in which she felt completely confident and which reflected her own highly individual interpretation.

During the 1850s and 1860s she built up her repertoire. She performed other plays by Alfieri, including *Rosmunda* and *Ottavia*, added *Macbeth*, translated by Giulio Carcano as *Macbetto* in 1857, Montanelli's *Camma* in the same year, Giacometti's *Giuditta* in 1859, a play by Legouvé written especially for her, *Béatrix*, in 1860, and a host of lesser-known historical dramas including *Brunechilde*, *Anna Bolena*, and *Noema, or la figlia di Caino*, performed for the first time in Naples in 1859. She took Dall'Ongaro's new play, *Etra, or l'ultima Sibilla*, to St Petersburg in 1861, although it had been commissioned for the 1859 Naples season, which is indicative of some of the problems she had with her Italian repertoire. After her triumphal Paris visits in 1855 and 1856, and her first British tour, also in 1856, she began to encounter more obstacles as she travelled round Italy. The fact that Italy was a collection of separate states with their own individualistic regulations and, in places like the Kingdom of Naples and the Two Sicilies, Venice, and the Papal States, an extremely repressive censorship made working conditions far from easy. In 1859, for example, the Neapolitan censors banned three plays she was planning to tour, including *Macbeth*. Compelled to opt at short notice for a more conservative repertoire, Ristori wrote desperately to Carlo Balboni on 12 January 1859:

> Just imagine, I simply did not know *where* to turn to find anything new, so great are the difficulties of setting up both new and old productions . . . so I am doing Metastasio's *Didone abbandonata* and *Romolo* and *Ersilia!!!* I am a queen and I am a lover, and I want to hold sway over my own house and my own heart – la de da – whoever would have thought that I should have ended up playing Dido abandoned by Signore Aeneas![56]

Teresa Viziano, who has documented Ristori's three visits to Naples, in 1857, 1859, and 1863, suggests that her tours were less than successful, despite the enthusiasm that surrounded her initial tour, fresh from her Parisian triumph:

> How could an actress who came from Italy (which is how Naples described the rest of the peninsula in those days) and had just returned from her Parisian successes fit into such a climate of jealous conservatism? Very badly, as demonstrated during the three tours that Adelaide Ristori made to the Teatro del Fondo in a six year period.[57]

During her first tour, most of her repertoire was banned, including *Mirra*, *Maria Stuarda*, *Elisabetta regina d'Inghilterra*, *Francesca da Rimini*, *Ottavia*, and *Fedra*. She finally managed to persuade the censors to allow her to perform modified versions of *Fedra* and *Ottavia*, but problems continued to plague the company. Fêted abroad, at home Ristori was controversial, often heavily criticised and regarded in some quarters as a subversive, touring a repertoire full of politically suspect pieces. From the late 1850s onwards Ristori began to tour abroad, where she could be more sure of unconditional public acclaim, receive better box-office figures, and not have to deal with censorship on the same scale as in Italy. She also increasingly took over the management of her company, along with her husband, carefully handling press-releases, and working towards the creation of an image of herself as an internationally acclaimed figure. Paola Bignami sees the years from the middle of the 1850s to the middle of the 1870s as the period when Ristori and her husband transformed their company into a highly successful theatrical publicity machine, increasingly geared for their commercial advantage. By 1873, she argues, 'the Company now seemed like an industrial microsociety', in which the finished product, that is, the performance, relied on a clear division of labour and the assigning of very precise tasks.[58] Ristori employed members of her own extended family by preference, following the old tradition, but insisted that they had properly worded contracts. In 1855 she had taken on her cousin, Luigi Bellotti Bon, as administrator; in 1873 this job went to her sister's ex-husband, Luigi Trojani.

In the late 1850s, Ristori travelled across Europe, performing from Poland to Portugal, from Amsterdam to Vienna. She was back in Paris in 1860 to rehearse the play Legouvé had written for her, *Béatrix*, the story of a noble heroine who sacrifices herself for love. She performed this play in French, taking lessons in French pronunciation to accomplish this feat, which she claims was requested by Legouvé, though the character of Béatrix was meant to be Italian and so a foreign accent was admissible. In her *Memoirs* she describes this period as one of the happiest times of her life. She was fêted all over Europe, she mixed with royalty, she was at the height of her powers, and in 1860 the unification of Italy became a reality.

She was also beginning to tour outside Europe. In 1864 she went to Egypt, and performed at Smyrna and Constantinople in Turkey. Then in 1865 she began preparations for an American tour the following year. Parmenio Bettoli, in his tribute to Ristori of 1906, credits her with single-handedly putting Italian theatre on the international map:

> She alone initiated a new period in the history of our dramatic art; she it was who forced her way through and opened up the pathway to other lands, along which the Rossis, the Salvinis, the Emanuels, the Novellis, the Zacconis, the Pezzanas, the Duses, the Di Lorenzos, the Reiters, and so on and so forth could all usher forth to be fêted.[59]

The myth of Ristori as the great pioneer, the first woman to venture outside Italy and reveal the greatness of Italian theatrical talent, was consolidated by her visits to the English-speaking world. She was by no means the first, nor was her company the only Italian company to tour extensively, but her publicity machine was superb and her organisation left nothing to chance. So successful was she at manipulating public opinion that the great Republican actor Gustavo Modena declined an offer to go with her to the United States, writing to Dall'Ongaro that 'Italian theatre outside Italy is called Ristori, and one cannot act at all if one does not act with her.'[60]

The advance publicity for Ristori's United States tour was engineered by her own people and by the American impresario Jacob Grau. Ristori's aristocratic connections were vaunted, as was the sumptuousness of her costumes. The whole enterprise was billed around Ristori herself, a matter of necessity since she had not been able to persuade any leading actor to join her company as leading man. Although she performed at times with Salvini and Rossi, the difficulty of finding a leading man was one which troubled her for decades, and her repertoire increasingly came to be structured around roles that gave her single-handedly the opportunity to take over the stage for most of the performance. Performing with Ristori was obviously not an inviting prospect to an up-and-coming actor, and it took a Modena or a Salvini to hold his own against her. Eventually Achille Cottin and Ludovico Mancini were taken on for the United States tour.

Eugenio Buonaccorsi describes the tour in terms of a three-act drama:

> Adelaide Ristori's expedition was carefully orchestrated, which involved a precise division of the whole operation into separate acts, offered to the public as a one-off performance.
>
> Act one consisted of the agreements and preparations for the tour.
>
> Act two consisted of Ristori's departure from Europe, her journey by sea and her arrival in New York.
>
> Act three continued with her stay in New York whilst waiting to make her debut.
>
> The Epilogue consisted of the actual performance and the appearance of the reviews.
>
> Everything else, which involved a colossal organisational effort, depended in one way or another on the successful reception of all the above. The gamble was taken in New York, where the first impact of that as yet untried reality would be felt. The rest of the tour, which passed through a number of cities with absolute efficiency, basically consolidated the profit made in that first

encounter and was essentially a repeat of the first success.[61]

Ristori's United States tour was a great success. The timing was obviously right, and a country recovering from the ravages of civil war was doubtless in the frame of mind to be charmed by a European actress with a title and a repertoire of great women characters from the past. The company opened in New York, and among the cities they played were Washington, Boston, Baltimore, and Philadelphia on the east coast, then out west through Detroit, Cincinnati, and Chicago, and down to St Louis, Memphis, and New Orleans. Henry Knepler gives some figures for the tour, claiming that each performance took in more than $2,000 and that *The New York Times* estimated her overall profits at $270,000.[62]

Besides the box-office receipts was the money earned from marketing Ristori, who was packaged in a way similar to that of twentieth-century rock superstars. Already in 1857 in Naples hairstyles and hats *à la Ristori* had been seen, and a letter from Ristori's mother to her daughter of 12 July 1855 asked whether it was true that Parisian ladies were wearing their hair *à la Ristori*, adding that in Italy there was now Ristori ice-cream and clothes in Ristori colours.[63] In the United States, besides the hairstyles and dresses, there was Ristori eau de cologne on sale, Ristori eyelash cosmetic and a range of Ristori foodstuffs. Ristori was the woman of the moment, the Madonna of her age.

Ristori returned to the United States in the autumn of 1867, bringing with her a new performance, Giacometti's *Maria Antonietta*. The success of this play ensured it a place in Ristori's international repertoire, and one interesting aspect of the tours to the Anglo-Saxon world was the way in which she came to tailor her repertoire to accommodate her audience's demands. The roles she came to regard as her 'war-horses' were the three figures from classical mythology, Medea, Mirra, and Phaedra, her one Shakespearean character, Lady Macbeth, and the three queens, Mary Stuart, Elizabeth I, and Marie Antoinette. As she grew older, the repertoire that she had sought to expand at the height of her success became increasingly restricted and she rarely performed anything apart from these roles, which were the ones her audiences demanded.

In 1869 she toured South America, and then in 1874 embarked on a tour round the world. She began this tour in Rio de Janeiro, performing in

Argentina, Chile, Peru, Mexico, and the west Coast of the United States, before sailing to the Sandwich Islands, New Zealand, Australia, and returning to Europe via Ceylon, Aden, and Egypt. Her *Memoirs* depict this tour as a kind of royal progress, with Ristori and her extended family being entertained by foreign potentates around the world. She is constantly 'charmed' by delightful sights, but has little to relate of what she saw other than the anecdotal. Significantly, she summarises the tour in numerical terms, an indication perhaps of the extent to which she was by now concerned with figures and sums, rather than with developing her performance skills:

> I closed my series of 212 performances on the 14th of December with the tragedy of *Mary Stuart*. During this artistic tour I traversed 35,283 miles of sea and 8,365 of land (I kept the figures out of curiosity.) I spent 170 days upon the water, and seventeen days eight hours in railway trains. In a word, I left Rome on the 15th of April 1874, and returned there by way of India and Brindisi on the 14th of January 1876, after an absence of twenty months and nineteen days.[64]

In 1880, when she was fifty-eight, she attempted something new. She began to learn English. Her popularity in Britain and in the United States ensured her a following in both countries, and her publicity machine had carefully crafted different versions of the Ristori story to appeal to different cultures. For the United States audiences, Ristori was presented as an embodiment of the American dream: a beautiful, talented woman from humble beginnings who, through her own efforts and hard work had become a Marchesa, invited to dine with the crowned heads of Europe. This image appealed greatly to her public, and her performances of queenly roles such as Marie Antoinette and Elizabeth I were favourites with audiences.

For London this kind of publicity was understandably adjusted. Ristori was not packaged as an *arriviste*, but as a lady who also engaged in acting. Moreover, whereas in the United States the publicity campaign could focus exclusively upon her visit, in Britain Ristori had much more competition, from English and from Continental actors, and Rachel was still a major figure against whom she was often unfavourably contrasted when she first played London in 1855. On that occasion, the *Athenaeum* reviewer of 14 June 1856 commented enthusiastically that

25 Adelaide Ristori later in her career as Lady Macbeth – the letter scene.

we are disposed to rate Madame Ristori's *Medea* in its unity of beauty, force,
terror, tenderness, and intense passion higher than any single tragical
presentment we have yet seen.

Ristori's British image was constructed out of a combination of fantasies
about Southern passion, ideals of womanhood, and good taste. She
appeared as a lady and mother first, as an actress second. E. Peron
Hingston's hagiography published in 1856 was entitled *The Siddons of
Modern Italy. Adelaide Ristori, a Sketch of Her Life and Twenty Words Relative to
Her Genius*, and described her as deriving greater satisfaction from the
smiling faces of her delightful children than from any amount of audience
applause.[65] Reviewers praised her capacity to create powerful and striking
stage effects, but always within the boundaries of respectable good taste.
Her sensibility and 'wholesomeness', a revealing adjective in the review of
5 July 1856 in *The Illustrated London News* were admired. Eight years after
her first London appearance, on her fourth British tour, *The Illustrated
London News* of 20 June 1863 compared her playing of Medea with previous
occasions and noted that

> Time, which has matured the genius of the *artiste*, has also ripened, as
> it were, her manner of presenting this particular character . . . now we
> recognise a repose, an intensity, a subtlety in the developments of every
> phase at which the actress had not previously arrived.

What is significant about this somewhat pompous statement is the suggestion that Ristori's playing was becoming more subtle and intense, the
vibrancy of what reviewers had previously seen as Mediterranean passion
and spontaneity now more refined, we might almost say, more Anglicised.
Her style of performance was becoming in some respects more familiar, less
exotic, and critics admired her grandeur and magnificence. On that same
tour in 1863, *The Evening Standard* of 16 June compared her work to that of
Macready, noting that

> Madame Ristori is a *melodramatic* actor, and one of the grandest and most
> 'terribly in earnest' ever witnessed, reminding us frequently, and sometimes
> vividly, of Macready.

On her first British tour, when she played the Lyceum in London and then
went on to Manchester and Liverpool, Ristori performed *Mirra, Medea, Pia
de' Tolomei, Francesca da Rimini, Maria Stuarda, Rosmunda*, and two comedies,

La Locandiera and *I Gelosi Fortunati.* Critics rated her tragic playing much higher than her performance of comedy, and in later tours she dropped the comic plays. On her second tour, in 1857, she added *Macbeth.* The addition of this play to her repertoire was to give her the last of her great war-horse roles, and offer her an opportunity to try something new: performing the role of Lady Macbeth in English.

Carcano's translation had first appeared in 1848. Ristori used a stage version that, as Giovanna Buonanno points out, freely followed Carcano's translation and bore 'more than an incidental resemblance' to the libretto of Verdi's *Macbeth,* which had premiered in Rome in 1847.[66] She had requested a number of changes to the text, which was considerably short-ened and restructured so that the emphasis was wholly on the character of Lady Macbeth. After the opening scene on the blasted heath, the play proper began with the scene of Lady Macbeth reading the letter, and ended effectively with the sleep-walking scene. The death of Macbeth was rushed through as a kind of epilogue. *The Atlas* on 11 July 1857 complained that 'In the Italian version everything has been sacrificed for the part of Lady Macbeth. We protest against the scandal.' It was a feeble protest, since most other critics went to see Ristori in one of her finest virtuoso roles. *The Times* on 6 July 1857 commented enthusiastically on the innovations she brought to the playing of Lady Macbeth:

> She gains a great advantage by her non-observance of the old law of the English stage, according to which Lady Macbeth must take up her candle and retire by the centre door through which she entered. Entering at the centre door, retiring at the wing and not resuming her candle, Madame Ristori obtains a variety of positions and freedom of movement that she turns to the best account. Her acting of this scene is her great triumph.

In her notes on the character of Lady Macbeth, Ristori says that she found the part difficult. She seems to have struggled to find a way into the charac-ter, and concluded that the motivating force behind Lady Macbeth was personal ambition, rather than ambition for her husband or affection for him:

> She was well aware of his mental inferiority to herself, of his innate weakness of character and indolence of disposition, that was not to be stimulated into action, even by the thirst for power that was consuming him, and she therefore made use of him as a means for attaining her own ends,

and took advantage of the unbounded influence her strong masculine nature and extraordinary personal fascination enabled her to exercise over him. . . . It is difficult to credit a woman of this kind with any of the feelings of ordinary humanity.[67]

If this sounds like Mrs Siddons, it is hardly surprising. Ristori acknowledges her debt to Siddons, and claims that her version was probably quite similar to that of the English actress. She cites the letter scene as an example of their shared perception of the role, and offers an interpretation of how Shakespeare may have intended the scene to be played. She suggests that the reading of the letter serves a different purpose than simply to inform the audience about events and about Lady Macbeth's own mental struggle. She foregrounds the immediacy of the reading:

> The intention of the author certainly seems to have been to represent Lady Macbeth as receiving the note at the moment she appears upon the scene, and such a representation must be most simple and natural. Presenting herself, anxious and agitated, she makes the public understand that, by means of the writing she holds in her hands, she would probably be able to reveal to them events which would change her whole future existence and raise her to the summit of greatness . . . 'They met me in the day of success . . .' These words are not likely to have been the beginning of such an important letter, and it is very probable that Macbeth had begun the letter by telling of the victory, and of the existence of these three fatal sisters.[68]

Ristori's analysis of this scene offers insights into how she went about building a character. Her insistence on studying detail led her to ask questions not only about the role, the personality that she was seeking to represent, but also the textual strategies employed by the playwright in the creation of that character. That her readings were idiosyncratic is also the case; for example, she dismisses the second act of *Macbeth* as being perfectly clear, with everything arising 'naturally' out of the progress of the action. The banquet scene, on the other hand, offered her an ideal opportunity to demonstrate her ability to move between moods, to play what she did best, that is the interchange between states of mind, between the need to conceal and the force of repressed emotion. 'I found it necessary and opportune to engage in a kind of double by-play', is how she explains her performance.[69] This scene concluded with another of her famous stage pictures, with a timorous Macbeth being calmed by his wife, using tactics of 'gentle violence'.[70]

Her *tour de force* was the sleep-walking scene, which she claims

> cost me long and most anxious study to represent this artificial and duplex manifestation, melting the effects one into the other, without falling into exaggeration at every change of manner, voice or expression of my face.[71]

Critics responded well to her performances. *The Sunday Times* of 5 July 1863 declared of the sleep-walking scene that 'we doubt if it has ever been equalled – if it ever could be surpassed'. Ten years later, during her fifth British tour, *The Athenaeum* of 19 July 1873 noted that 'The scene from *Macbeth* was principally noteworthy for the realistic accessories of deep breathing and drooping head.' The reviewer also pointed out that although such a display was ingenious and original, it was 'scarcely correct'. Ristori explains in her *Memoirs* how she used her breathing to create an effect of mental illness in the sleep-walking scene, keeping her eyes fixed and staring and sniffing at her hands as she rubbed at them to wash off the blood.

During that tour, Ristori made her first attempt to use English on stage. On 28 October 1873 at the Drury Lane Theatre, she performed part of the sleep-walking scene in English. Critics and public alike were enthusiastic. *The Illustrated London News* on 8 November 1873 noted that her pronunciation was correct, although a little overemphatic. The review in *The Athenaeum* of 18 October commented that the 'effect on the audience was electrical', and described Ristori's delivery as slow and measured, with some wrong emphases and the stress being placed on the final syllable. But overall, her efforts met with success, and she persisted in her study of English, with the assistance of Mrs Ward, mother of the actress Genevieve Ward, and then with a certain Miss Clayton. Genevieve Ward records her method of studying English, first copying out the text, then listening to it being read and copying it down in Italian orthography. When she had this basic phonetic text, she would mark it with her own notation system to ensure that the stress patterns were accurate.[72]

In her *Memoirs*, she relates how she had been considering retirement in 1880 (she was by then fifty-eight years old) and suggests that the prospect of performing in another language was a major reason for continuing to tour. In 1882 she returned to Drury Lane to play *Macbeth* entirely in

English, with an English cast. Macbeth was played by William Rignold, Duncan by Arthur Matthison, and Macduff by J. H. Barnes. The gesture of performing in English was appreciated, as indicated by the good box office receipts, but on the whole critics preferred her work in Italian. She went on to add the role of Elizabeth I to her English repertoire, and her final performance in Britain, in Manchester in 1883 at the end of her seventh tour, was Elizabeth in English. On her fourth United States tour, in 1885, she played Lady Macbeth opposite Edwin Booth, and then on 12 May 1885 played Mary Stuart in English with the permanent company who worked in German at the Thalia Theatre, New York.

By the end of her career Ristori was working very much as a virtuoso performer, and her acting had become out of date. Reviews became increasingly unkind, though her box-office takings stayed high. Her contract for the last United States tour gave her forty per cent of the gross income, a huge sum for a single performer. In Britain, *The North British Daily Mail* on 9 October 1883 commented that she could do nothing without pantomime, adding, 'Time has robbed Madame Ristori greatly of the power by which these efforts were characterised in former years.' *The Saturday Review* of 13 July 1882 criticised her transformation of Lady Macbeth into a star role, leaving the part of Macbeth to 'doubtless well-meaning but very incapable hands'. The age of the Grand Actor was giving way to another kind of theatre, and an ageing star with a tiny repertoire of queens was hardly in the theatrical vanguard. Photographs of Ristori from this period show her looking much older than her sixty years, heavy-jowled and inclining to fat. After her retirement in 1885 she concentrated on her social and family life, moving in court circles, fêted and celebrated until her death on 9 October 1906.

In his essay on how to study nineteenth-century theatre, Fernando Taviani comments on the availability of material evidence and on the problem of how we interpret that evidence. Discussing nineteenth-century actors, he points out that

> We can watch them travelling, we can watch them going into theatres, we can watch them being applauded and occasionally coping with failures, we can watch them setting off again, but we cannot actually see them performing.[73]

This is the fundamental problem for the theatre historian; however carefully we try to reconstruct performance from documentary evidence – playbills, prompt books, photographs, reviews, and so forth – we are still left outside, struggling to imagine what a performance must have been like. In Ristori's case, we have the evidence of her own account of her work to add to the other materials available, though given her propensity for self-publicity, her *Memoirs* need to be treated with caution. As her career progressed, she seems to have become more and more megalomaniac, insisting on almost Royal status and demanding to be the centre of attention. An example of how she dominated the company may be seen from one extraordinary publicity announcement probably from 1873, where the Compagnia Drammatica Italiana announces eight forthcoming productions. Ristori's name is on the first line, immediately after that of the company, and the announcement of the eight productions specificies that in all of them the famous actress ADELAIDE RISTORI will take part. Four other Ristoris are in the company list. Significantly, Ristori is credited as having done most of the writing. *Medea* by Legouvé is billed as translated by Ristori, as are Racine's *Fedra* and Victor Hugo's *Lucrezia Borgia. Giuditta, Elisabetta Regina d'Inghilterra*, and *Maria Antonietta* are billed as *written* by Adelaide Ristori *through* Paolo Giacometti. Not content with being the star performer, and taking a close interest in company finance, Ristori here takes over the role of writer as well. Giacometti, Racine, and Legouvé are relegated to the position of providers of a preliminary text, which Ristori rewrites to suit her own needs.

During her penultimate British tour, *The Liverpool Daily Post* of 21 November 1882 commented that

> We see in Madame Ristori one of the last remaining examples of the truly grand old style, when roundness, melody, grace, and flowing majesty were deemed . . . essential to the highest flights and fiercest throes of tragedy.

This rather gentle put-down places Ristori firmly into a period, and acknowledges the qualities that she brought to the roles she played. Ristori was obviously a professional who for many years sought to push the frontiers of her own technique forward. She seems to have had an imposing presence and a very good voice, and given the fact that in the Italian theatre the prompter read the text aloud from the wings, an actor had to have a good voice in order to overcome what to many audiences outside Italy was a constant irritation. In her early years, she was by all accounts a gifted performer who began to develop her own style of acting that was based on meticulous individualistic study of a character, not on conventional notions of good acting within the Italian tradition. She sought out roles that were very demanding, because they often required her to move a long way away from her own personality, away from the respectability of her everyday very privileged lifestyle and contented domestic arrangements. Her preparation for a role was painstaking, and she seems to have studied the words in the text with as much care as she studied the details of costume, props, and staging. The parts in which she excelled were those that required shifts of mood and balance, and it is the playing of the transitions, the abrupt moves from violence to stillness, that seems to have been most greatly admired by audiences and critics alike. For her choice of roles, she opted for the exceptional woman character, the larger-than-life figure from mythology, history, or romantic fiction.

Was she the greatest nineteenth-century Italian actress? Such a question is unanswerable, because however good she may have been, Ristori also had other factors working in her favour. Her marriage and subsequent partnership with her husband helped to stabilise her economic position, and the couple's canny financial arrangements, their insistence on carefully devised contracts and attention to detail on expenditure, ensured that they did not collapse, as so many companies did, under the weight of debt. When she began to tour outside Italy it seems clear, despite her denials, that financial problems were at the root of their original decision to go abroad, for the company needed the assurance of box-office successes overseas in order to survive. It is also likely that money rather than artistic idealism lay behind her decision to keep on working until the middle of the 1880s. She oversaw the marketing of Ristoriana, and there was even an attempt, which came to nothing, in 1857, to set up a Ristori journal.

But the other crucial factor in understanding Ristori's success is the timing of her career. She began as a *figlia d'arte* in a disunited Italy, and by early adulthood had aligned herself with the monarchist forces of the House of Savoy and the struggle for a united Italy led by Cavour. She saw herself as an ambassador for the new Italy, and certainly in the 1850s she was treated by the authorities in many parts of Italy as a potentially subversive figure, touring an ideologically loaded repertoire of plays by known patriots and plays with a message that could be interpreted as revolutionary. She was, however, always a respectable revolutionary, a monarchist with a strong sense of class superiority, never a Republican. As Italian society ossified into the dull years of the *fin de siècle*, when the loss of revolutionary idealism and the rise of the middle classes created the kind of discontent that was to lead to the emergence of Mussolini and Italian fascism, Ristori lived regally, a queen of the stage and a member of Queen Margarita's inner circle. But at the high point of her career, through her touring in the 1850s and 1860s, she came to be associated with the patriotic cause, an emblem of the new Italy that became a political reality after 1860. For audiences all over the world she was the incarnation of Italy, the passion of her acting mirroring the dignity of her suffering under the yoke of foreign oppressors. When Garibaldi and his Redshirts began the unification process in 1860, audiences rejoiced with their heroine.

Nevertheless, despite the favourable reviews, the bouquets, the encores, the Ristori souvenir industry, and all her admirers, perhaps the greatest tribute to her skills came in the end from the woman who was to take over her mantle as international Italian superstar, Eleonora Duse. Ristori admired Duse, but was extremely critical of her, seeing her as mannered and neurotic on stage, gullible and profligate off the stage. Her comments on the huge sums of money that Duse spent on her lover D'Annunzio's *Francesca da Rimini* reveal the tough, shrewd voice of Ristori the astute businesswoman, a persona that emerges from time to time in her intimate letters. Writing to her son, Giorgio, on 14 December 1901 she comments tartly:

> Nobody would be surprised if it ended with a revolver. But keep that between ourselves. The *famous* Francesca cost her *two hundred thousand francs!!* Costumes, music, (that was so bad they had to cut it out), sets, everything paid for by her! They tell me she is ruined! Poor soul!! Last night the show did not go on because one of the actors was ill. I believe they are going to perform tonight. But fortunately she did not send me a box. I prefer to stay at home.[74]

But Duse, recalling Ristori's Lady Macbeth, was kinder. Interviewed by Silvio D'Amico in 1921, Duse talked about the only time she saw Ristori perform, when she was quite young, possibly some time in the 1870s:

> She played the sleep-walking scene with classic dignity, combined with a
> particularly curious realism; composed, clear, wearing a crown on her head,
> her eyes staring fixedly at the footlights, and in between sentences she was
> breathing heavily as though still asleep, she was actually snoring.[75]

When asked what impression Ristori had made on her, Duse replied
simply: 'An image of regal composure. When I got home, I felt compelled to
tidy up my little room.' Such was the power of Adelaide Ristori's acting,
that Duse carried something with her away from the theatre, a desire to go
home and tidy up. We can interpret this very domestic image in two ways:
what she had seen was, on some level, so disturbing that Duse felt compelled to tidy up her life and out of the new sense of order to follow in the
footsteps of her meticulously well-prepared predecessor. The alternative
reading is that Ristori's immaculate representation of the woman who
would be queen was so domestic in its detail, that Duse, whose mother had
died when she was still in her teens, felt a sense of guilt that could only be
translated into the banalities of everyday action. Ristori the phantom
mother would not have approved of untidy rooms; Ristori the great actress
did not approve of unstudied, erratic acting. Either way, the power of
Ristori reached out and affected Duse's life, and it took considerable efforts
on her part, lasting several years, to shake off that legacy. Duse in her
heyday was quite unlike Ristori had been, she was a product of another
time and another mentality. Ristori's work, like her life, belonged to the
middle of the nineteenth century. The roles she created were queenly
figures, tormented by passions beyond their control, driven to despair and
often to death. However great the power wielded by those characters, ultimately they were prisoners of their own feelings. Lady Macbeth, Elizabeth
I, Marie Antoinette, Mary Stuart, all her great parts depict women who are
rendered powerless despite their social status, beauty, or intelligence. Such
roles reflected the status of women in society as a whole, but by the end of
the century, as women began to demand the vote, to be educated and to
organise in trades unions, the new roles for women in the theatre reflected
that changing awareness, and new roles called for new performance techniques. The sound of the end of the age of the Grand Actress was Nora
slamming the doll's house door.

Notes

INTRODUCTION

[1] Recent scholars – among them Elaine Aston, Nina Auerbach, Susan Bennett, Tracy Davis, Christine Dymkowski, Lesley Ferris, Viv Garner, Julie Hankey, Sheila Stowell, and Claire Tomalin – have, of course, been at pains to rediscover the contribution made by women to every aspect of theatrical production, particularly in the nineteenth century.

[2] John Hill, *The Actor: A Treatise on the Art of Playing* (London: R. Griffiths, 1750), p. 141.

[3] The standard account is still Joseph Donohue, *Dramatic Character in the English Romantic Age* (Princeton: Princeton University Press, 1970), although also see Joseph Roach, *The Player's Passion* (Newark: University of Delaware Press, 1985).

[4] *Realities* (London: Saunders and Otley, 1851), vol. ii, p. 303.

[5] *Illustrated London News*, 18 July 1846.

[6] 11 June.

[7] 15 July 1842.

[8] William Charles Macready, *Reminiscences* (London: Macmillan, 1875), vol. ii, p. 291.

[9] Constant Coquelin, 'Actors and Acting', in *Papers on Acting* (New York: Hill and Wang, 1969), p. 199.

[10] *Daily News*, 4 July 1857.

[11] *Corinna or Italy* (London: printed for Samuel Tipper, 1807), vol. iii, pp. 197–8.

[12] *The Morning Post*, 5 June 1841.

[13] *The George Eliot Letters*, ed. Gordon S. Haight (London: Oxford University Press; New Haven: Yale University Press, 1956), vol. v, p. 24.

[14] *The Times*, 11 May 1841.

[15] *Morning Post*, 23 July 1846.

[16] Edward Mangin, *Piozziana* (London: Edward Moxon, 1833), p. 85.

[17] *Morning Post*, 27 July 1850.

[18] *Morning Post*, 18 July 1850.

[19] *Morning Post*, 9 June 1857.

[20] *Athenaeum*, 27 June 1857.

[21] The burlesque was described by Dickens. See George Taylor, *Players and Performances in the Victorian Theatre* (Manchester and New York: Manchester University Press, 1991), p. 77. There was also *The Golden Fleece*, an extravaganza adapted from Euripides by Planché in 1845 with Madame Vestris and Charles Mathews. See Taylor, *Players and Performances*, pp. 71–2 and Michael R. Booth, *Theatre in the Victorian Age* (Cambridge: Cambridge University Press, 1991), p. 195.

[22] Sir Theodore Martin, *Monographs: Garrick, Macready, Rachel and Baron Stockman* (London: John Murray, 1906), p. 255. Also see Sylvie Chevalley, *Rachel* (Paris: Calmann-Lévy, 1989), pp. 293, 301–5, 325; and Rachel M. Brownstein, *Tragic Muse. Rachel of the Comédie-Française* (New York: Alfred Knopf, 1993), pp. 214–17.

[23] *Dramatic Reminiscences; or Actors and Actresses in England and America* (London: Thomas W. Cooper, John Camden Hotten, 1860), p. 41. The comparison was endlessly made. See, for instance, Sébastien Rhéal (de Cesena): *Les Deux Phèdres: Mme Ristori and Mademoiselle Rachel* (Paris: L. Dentu, 1858); G. H. Lewes, *Actors and the Art of Acting* (London: Smith, Elder and Co. 1875); Henry Morley, *The Journal of a London Playgoer, 1851–1866*, with an introduction by Michael R. Booth (Leicester: Leicester University Press, 1974).

[24] See Elaine Aston, 'Ristori's Medea and Her Nineteenth Century Successors', *Women and Theatre: Occasional Papers*, 1 (1992), pp. 38–47.

[25] Adelaide Ristori, *Memoirs and Artistic Studies* (New York: Doubleday, 1888), p. 205.

SARAH SIDDONS

[1] There is disagreement as to the number of mourning coaches. Thomas Campbell, Mrs Siddons' biographer, gives thirteen, but the *Morning Post* for 16 June 1831 says sixteen.

[2] *Examiner*, 16 June 1816.

[3] *Macready's Reminiscences*, ed. Sir Frederick Pollock (London: Macmillan, 1875), vol. 1, p. 180.

[4] Thomas Gilliland, *The Dramatic Mirror* (London: C. Chapple, 1808), vol. II, p. 978.

[5] Quoted in Roger Manvell, *Sarah Siddons* (London: G. P. Putnam's Sons, 1970), p. 23.

[6] *Ibid.*, pp. 25–6.

[7] *The Reminiscences of Sarah Kemble Siddons 1773–1785*, ed. William Van Lennep (Cambridge, Mass.: Widener Library, 1942), p. 16. Mrs Siddons' spelling has been preserved.

[8] *Ibid.*, pp. 6–8.

[9] It was actually William Siddons who negotiated her contracts. This point will be discussed below.

[10] John Jackson, *The History of the Scottish Stage* (Edinburgh: P. Hill, 1793), pp. 126–30.

[11] Tate Wilkinson, *The Wandering Patentee* (York, 1795), vol. III, p. 6.

[12] Quoted in *The Swan of Lichfield*, ed. Hesketh Pearson (London: Hamish Hamilton, 1936), p. 68.

[13] James Boaden, *Memoirs of Mrs Siddons* (London: Gibbings, 1893), p. 178.

[14] *Ibid.*, p. 195.

[15] *Horace Walpole's Correspondence*, ed. W. S. Lewis (New Haven: Yale University Press, 1955), vol. XXIX, p. 282.

[16] Quoted in John Alexander Kelly, *German Visitors to English Theatres in the Eighteenth Century* (New York: Octagon, 1978), pp. 112–13.

[17] *Ibid.*, p. 146.

[18] *Ibid.*, p. 95.

[19] *The Beauties of Mrs Siddons* (London, 1786), pp. 2–3.

[20] *Ibid.*, p. 29.

[21] *The Piozzi Letters*, eds. Edward A. Bloom and Lillian D. Bloom (Newark, Del.: University of Delaware Press, 1989), vol. I, p. 292.

[22] *Ibid.*, vol. I, p. 342.

[23] *Diary, Reminiscences, and Correspondence of Henry Crabb Robinson*, ed. Thomas Sadler (London: Macmillan, 1869), vol. I, p. 39.

[24] Charles Robert Leslie, *Autobiographical Recollections*, ed. Tom Taylor (London: J. Murray, 1860), vol. II, p. 4.

[25] This happens off-stage, of course. Such a situation is depicted in more than one painting, in Caravaggio's *Seven Acts of Mercy* and in Poussin's *The Israelites Gathering Manna*, in which a woman suckles her starving father. The Poussin was widely known, and Murphy may have used it for his play.

26 Thomas Gilliland, *A Dramatic Synopsis* (London: Lackington, Allen, 1804), p. 87. Although 'pompous' in the eighteenth century had its modern pejorative meaning, it also meant 'stately', 'magnificent', and 'splendid.'

27 *The Swan of Lichfield*, p. 70.

28 Campbell, *Life of Mrs Siddons* (London: Edward Moxon, 1834), vol. I, p. 180.

29 *English Review*, March 1783, p. 264. All subsequent references are to this issue.

30 Boaden, *Memoirs of Mrs Siddons*, p. 202.

31 James Boaden, *Memoirs of the Life of John Philip Kemble* (London: Longman, Hurst, Rees, Orme, Brown, and Green, 1825), vol. I, p. 136.

32 Campbell, *Life of Mrs Siddons*, vol. I, p. 206.

33 Jacques Henri Meister, *Letters Written during a Residence in England* (London: Longman, 1799), p. 215.

34 *Ibid.*, pp. 219–20.

35 C. A. G. Goede, *The Stranger in England* (London: Matthew and Leigh, 1807), vol. II, pp. 226–7.

36 So did Crabb Robinson, but I have not come across another recorded case of male hysterics at a Siddons performance, which does not imply that they did not occur.

37 Mrs Siddons played Alicia in the 1786–7 season, which surprised many. Campbell's explanation is probably correct: 'Wretch as she is, *Alicia* is an impassioned being; and none but players can duly estimate the craving of the public for new impressions from performers, or the difficulty of satisfying that avidity. A meritorious actor once told me that no risk in a new part was so formidable as cloying the public with over-frequency in an old one' (*Life of Mrs Siddons*, vol. II, p. 114). This was a problem that faced Mrs Siddons through most of her career, since her best parts were not numerous and had to be given repeatedly.

38 'A woman's courage is always a virtue,' said Anna Jameson, 'because it is not required of us.' (*Characteristics of Women* (London: Saunders and Otley, 1832), vol. I, p. liv).

39 *The Spectator*, no. 342, 2 April 1712.

40 Her relationship with her husband will be considered below, but at least one piece of information relevant to these comments can be given here. When in 1817 John Kemble was honoured by a public dinner and the usual complimentary speeches upon his retirement, Mrs Siddons said – having received no such honours on her own – 'Well, perhaps

in the next world women will be more valued than they are in this.'
(*Recollections of the Table-Talk of Samuel Rogers*, 2nd edn. (London:
Edward Moxon, 1856), p. 188.)

[41] Quotations from Shakespeare in this chapter are taken from *The
Complete Works*, eds. Stanley Wells and Gary Taylor (Oxford: Oxford
University Press, 1988).

[42] *The Beauties of Mrs Siddons*, p. 52.

[43] Quoted in H. Fleeming Jenkin, 'Mrs Siddons as Lady Macbeth and
Queen Katharine', *Papers on Acting*, ed. Brander Matthews (New York:
Hill and Wang, 1958), p. 98.

[44] *Monthly Mirror*, 10, July 1800, p. 41.

[45] Julian Charles Young, *A Memoir of Charles Mayne Young* (London:
Macmillan, 1871), vol. I, pp. 40–1.

[46] *English Review*, p. 265.

[47] John Taylor, 'Sonnet to Mrs Siddons', *Poems on Various Subjects*
(London: Payne and Foss, 1827), vol. I, p. 160.

[48] Taylor, 'To Mrs Siddons, On Hearing That She Intended To Perform
the Character of Millwood', *Poems on Various Subjects*, vol. I, p. 303.

[49] Anthony Pasquin, *The Children of Thespis* (London: Denew and Grant,
1786), p. 17.

[50] *The Reminiscences of Sarah Kemble Siddons*, p. 13.

[51] *A Biographical Dictionary of Actors, Actresses, Musicians, Dancers, Managers,
& Other Stage Personnel in London, 1660–1800*, eds. Philip Highfill Jr,
Kalman A. Burnim, and Edward A. Langhans (Carbondale, Ill.:
Southern Illinois University Press, 1991), vol. XIV, pp. 37–67.

[52] John Adolphus declared that when Mrs Siddons acted the effect was as
if 'one of the sublimest conceptions of Michael Angelo had been
animated and inspired for the occasion'. (John Adolphus, *Memoirs of
John Bannister, Comedian* (London: Richard Bentley, 1839), vol. II,
pp. 243–4.)

[53] *Papers on Acting*, p. 108.

[54] In painting Mrs Siddons, Gainsborough did complain that there was
no end to her nose.

[55] Boaden, *Memoirs of . . . Kemble*, vol. I, p. 131.

[56] Taylor, 'The Stage', *Poems on Various Subjects*, vol. I, p. 33.

[57] William Hazlitt, *Characters of Shakespeare's Plays*, Everyman edn.
(London: J. M. Dent, 1960), p. 108.

[58] Campbell, *Life of Mrs Siddons*, vol. II, p. 265.

[59] Boaden, *Memoirs of . . . Kemble*, vol. III, p. 450.

[60] Campbell, *Life of Mrs Siddons*, vol. II, pp. 10–34.

[61] This question, and other aspects of their partnership in the play, are discussed in a thorough and illuminating article by Joseph Donohue, 'Kemble and Mrs Siddons in *Macbeth*: the Romantic Approach to Tragic Character', *Theatre Notebook*, 22 (Winter 1967–8), pp. 65–85.

[62] *Macready's Reminiscences*, vol. I, p. 55.

[63] In *Papers Literary, Scientific, Etc.* (London, 1887).

[64] *Papers on Acting*, pp. 79–80.

[65] *Ibid.*, p. 82.

[66] Boaden, *Memoirs of Mrs Siddons*, p. 308.

[67] *Papers on Acting*, p. 83.

[68] *Ibid.*, p. 85. A quick transition from one passion to the next, especially in facial expression, was an important aspect of contemporary tragic acting.

[69] *Ibid.*, p. 89.

[70] *Examiner*, 16 June 1816.

[71] *Examiner*, 5 July 1812.

[72] *Papers on Acting*, p. 96.

[73] These readings, like her stage performances, were well attended by the social, literary, and artistic elite.

[74] Boaden, *Memoirs of Mrs Siddons*, p. 462.

[75] Edward Mangin, *Piozziana* (London: Edward Moxon, 1833), p. 118.

[76] John Genest, *Some Account of the English Stage* (London: Richard Bentley, 1832), vol. VIII, p. 306.

[77] Frances Ann Kemble, *Record of a Girlhood*, 2nd edn. (London, 1879), vol. II, p. 21.

[78] The list of performances and dates appears in Genest, *Some Account of the English Stage*, vol. VIII, p. 312.

[79] Crabb Robinson, *Diary*, vol. I, p. 326.

[80] *Macready's Reminiscences*, vol. I, p. 57.

[81] Campbell, *Life of Mrs Siddons*, vol. I, p. 208.

[82] *Ibid.*, vol. I, p. 140.

[83] *Diaries of a Lady of Quality*, ed. A. Hayward (London: Longman, Roberts, and Greer, 1864), p. 102.

[84] Campbell, *Life of Mrs Siddons*, vol. I, pp. 215–16.

[85] *True Briton*, 4 February 1797.

[86] Campbell, *Life of Mrs Siddons*, vol. II, p. 209.

[87] *English Review*, p. 259.

[88] Mangin, *Piozziana*, p. 85.

[89] William Russell, *The Tragic Muse* (London, 1783), p. 9.

[90] Mangin, *Piozziana*, p. 85.

[91] Campbell, *Life of Mrs Siddons*, vol. I, p. 287.

[92] Thomas Davies, *Dramatic Miscellanies* (Dublin: S. Price, 1784), vol. III, p. 147.

[93] Gilliland, *The Dramatic Mirror*, vol. II, pp. 977–8.

[94] Meister, *Letters*, p. 198.

[95] *Horace Walpole's Correspondence*, vol. XXXIII, p. 359.

[96] *English Review*, p. 260.

[97] *The Diary of Benjamin Haydon*, ed. Willard Bissell Pope (Cambridge, Mass.: Harvard University Press, 1963), vol. III, p. 369.

[98] Davies, *Dramatic Miscellanies*, vol. I, p. 148.

[99] *English Review*, p. 265. Hazlitt declared that 'it was in bursts of indignation, or grief, in sudden exclamations, in apostrophes and inarticulate sounds, that she raised the soul of passion to its height, or sunk it in despair'. (*Champion*, 16 October 1814.)

[100] Goede, *The Stranger in England*, vol. II, pp. 213–14.

[101] Boaden, *Memoirs of Mrs Siddons*, p. 402.

[102] Meister, *Letters*, p. 209.

[103] Quoted in Kelly, *German Visitors to English Theatres*, p. 95.

[104] *English Review*, p. 261.

[105] Pasquin, *The Children of Thespis*, 13th edn. (London: Kirby, 1792), p. 35. One critic complained ironically of modern tragedy and Mrs Siddons' dominant position in it that 'there is no striking *situation* unless the lady loses her wits' and that every author who writes for her knows that she must run mad in the last act. (*The Devil's Pocket-Book*, no. 2 (1786), p. 26.)

[106] James Ballantyne, *Characters of Mrs Siddons* (Edinburgh, 1812), quoted in Genest, *Some Account of the English Stage*, vol. VIII, pp. 303–4.

[107] *Papers on Acting*, p. 107.

[108] *Maria Edgworth: Letters from England 1813–1844*, ed. Christina Calvin (Oxford: Oxford University Press, 1971), p. 392.

[109] *The Beauties of Mrs Siddons*, p. 57.

[110] *Ibid.*, pp. 9–10.

[111] Ballantyne, *Characters of Mrs Siddons*, quoted in Genest, *Some Account of the English Stage*, vol. VIII, p. 304.

[112] Quoted in Campbell, *Life of Mrs Siddons*, vol. II, p. 70.

[113] Pasquin, *The Children of Thespis*, 1st edn. (1786), pp. 18–19.

[114] *English Review*, p. 267.

[115] Boaden, *Memoirs of Mrs Siddons*, p. 401.

[116] *The Thespian Dictionary* (London: T. Hurst, 1802). Zara in Congreve's *The Mourning Bride* would have been her leading role for 'vindictive jealousy'.

[117] *English Review*, p. 262. Rage, Distraction, Grief, Despair are 'drawn so true / That Beauty's self with terror strikes the view'. (Russell, *The Tragic Muse*, p. 10.)

[118] Boaden, *Memoirs of Mrs Siddons*, p. 186.

[119] Wilkinson, *The Wandering Patentee*, vol. IV, p. 23.

[120] *Boswell's Life of Johnson*, ed. George Birkbeck Hill (Oxford, 1887), vol. V, p. 103.

[121] *Thraliana*, ed. Katharine C. Balderston (Oxford: Oxford University Press, 1951), vol. II, p. 715.

[122] *Examiner*, 15 June 1816. Elsewhere, Hazlitt said that 'she appeared to belong to a superior order of beings, like some prophetess of old'. (*Champion*, 16 October 1814.) Ballantyne's description of her playing of Queen Katharine's anger at Wolsey has already been quoted: 'Her form seems to expand, and her eyes burn with a fire beyond human.' This is nothing less than god-like; at least that is what the language says.

[123] Thomas Young, *The Siddoniad* (Dublin, 1884) p. 15.

[124] Quoted in Mrs Clement Parsons, *The Incomparable Siddons* (London: Methuen, 1909), p. 24.

[125] Upon hearing of her aunt's death, Fanny Kemble wrote in her journal, 'I wonder if she is gone where Milton and Shakespeare have gone – whose thoughts were her familiar thoughts, whose words were her familiar words.' (*Record of a Girlhood*, vol. III, p. 43.)

[126] *The Letters of Sir Walter Scott*, ed. H. J. C. Grierson (London: Constable, 1932–7), vol. V, p. 358.

RACHEL FELIX

[1] Jules Janin, *Rachel et la tragédie* (Paris: Amyot, 1859), p. 69. Unless otherwise stated all the translations are mine and are intended to be literal.

[2] Peter Raby, *'Fair Ophelia': A Life of Harriet Smithson Berlioz* (Cambridge:

Cambridge University Press, 1982), pp. 69–70, 109; and F. W. J. Hemmings, *Culture and Society in France, 1789–1848* (Leicester: Leicester University Press, 1987), p. 277.

[3] Sylvie Chevalley, *Rachel* (Paris: Calmann-Lévy, 1989), p. 14. An appendix lists all her roles.

[4] Bernard Falk, *Rachel the Immortal* (London: Hutchinson, 1933), p. 96, quotes Franz Liszt: 'Hers is the resounding and acrid voice of a hunted and degraded people . . . She cannot – she should not – portray love. Her vocation is for curses, imprecation, bitter and hate-saturated irony.'

[5] See Albert Lemoine, *Napoleon Ier et les Juifs* (Paris: Fayard Frères, 1900).

[6] See F. W. J. Hemmings, 'The Training of Actors at the Paris Conservatoire During the Nineteenth Century', *Theatre Research International*, no. 3, vol. 12 (Autumn 1987), pp. 240–53.

[7] Rachel M. Brownstein, *Tragic Muse. Rachel of the Comédie-Française* (New York: Alfred Knopf, 1993; Durham and London: Duke University Press, 1995), p. 69. All future references to this book are given as Brownstein.

[8] *L'Art théâtrale* (Paris: E. Dentu, 1863–5). Also see Samson, *Lettre à Monsieur Jules Janin* (Paris: chez tous les librairies, 1859), the pamphlet in which he claims that he taught Rachel 'la grammaire' and in which he takes Janin to task: 'M. Janin always uses the word *inspiration*: but inspiration is scarcely art' (p. 33). Samson's ideas are considered in Ann Raitière, *L'Art de l'acteur. Etudes de philologie et d'histoire* (Paris: Librairie Droz-Genève, 1969).

[9] I have discussed Lewes' treatment of Rachel in 'Rachel's "Terrible Beauty": An Actress Among the Novelists', *English Literary History* (Winter 1984), pp. 771–93.

[10] Brownstein, p. 111.

[11] Frances Anne Kemble, *Records of Later Life* (London: Richard Bentley, 1882), vol. ii, p. 100. For more on Gérôme's painting see Adeline R. Tintner, 'Miriam as the English Rachel: Gérôme's Portrait of the Tragic Muse', in *Critical Essays on Henry James: The Early Novels*, ed. James W. Gargano (Boston: G. K. Hall and Co., 1987), pp. 185–97. The Musée Carnavalet in Paris has an oil-sketch for the picture and the Musée Bonnat in Bayonne has a preliminary drawing.

There are significant comparisons to be made between images of Rachel and the tradition of theatrical portraiture represented by, say, Coypel's portrait of Adrienne Lecouvreur, or Vanloo's of Clairon, or Libourd's of Mademoiselle Georges, or even Reynolds' portrait of Mrs

Siddons which was influenced by Michelangelo. Most convey a Raphaelesque sense of sacred inspiration with raised arms and uplifted eyes. Portraits of Rachel tend to eschew this vision of sublimity in favour of a direct gaze that simultaneously looks directly at the spectator and deep into the actress' own self. Also see Brownstein, pp. 27–35.

12 *La Comédie-Française. 1680–1980* (Paris: Bibliothèque Nationale, 1980), p. 57.

13 'La Mort de Mademoiselle Lecouvreur. Célèbre actrice', *Œuvres Complètes de Voltaire*, vol. IX (Paris: Garnier Frères, 1877), pp. 369–70.

14 Janin, *Rachel et la tragédie*, pp. 510, 512.

15 *Histoire de l'art dramatique* (Paris: Editions Hetzel, 1859), 2nd series, p. 246. For an extended discussion of Rachel as statue see Brownstein, pp. 172–81.

16 Houssaye quoted in Francis Gribble, *Rachel. Her Stage Life and her Real Life* (London: Chapman and Hall, 1911), p. 65.

17 Alfred de Musset, *Mélange de littérature et de critique* (Paris: Charpentier, 1867), p. 90.

18 Brownstein, p. 28.

19 *Examiner*, 4 August 1855.

20 See Janin, *Rachel et la tragédie*, p. 75.

21 See Maurice Descotes, *Les Grands Roles du théâtre de Corneille* (Paris: Presses Universitaires de France, 1962), p. 119.

22 *Œuvres complètes*, vol. XXXI (1880), p. 305.

23 *Morning Post*, 31 July 1855. A good example of close-up concentration on Rachel's face.

24 *Morning Post*, 14 July 1846.

25 *Morning Post*, 11 June 1842.

26 *The Times*, 11 June 1842.

27 *Morning Post*, 27 July 1850.

28 Ibid.

29 *Morning Post*, 11 June 1842.

30 *The Times*, 15 May 1841.

31 *The Times*, 30 June 1851.

32 *The Times*, 14 July 1846.

33 *Morning Post*, 27 July 1850. A typical example of an English critic attempting to transcribe a passage according to Rachel's stresses, with italics. In nearly all such cases I have left quotations from speeches exactly as they were originally printed in the newspaper.

34 *The Times*, 11 June.

35 *The Times*, 14 July 1846.

36 A comparison between *The Times*, 11 June 1842 and *The Times*, 14 July 1846 suggests that she changed her delivery here quite considerably over the years.

37 *Examiner*, 23 May 1841.

38 *Morning Post*, 11 June 1842.

39 *Atlas*, 22 August 1846, probably G. H. Lewes.

40 *Morning Post*, 27 July 1850. Also see Descotes, *Corneille*, pp. 158–9. Compare Samson in *L'Art théâtrale*, part 1 (1863), pp. 146–7:

> The torrent continues to overflow, with fury: / She insults her brother and his faction. / The name of Rome, that city proud of its terrifying exploits, / She pronounces four times / Taking from the rage that bears her along, / Four different accents, each of thundering hate.

41 *Examiner*, 23 May 1841.

42 'As Rachel interpreted her, Camille seemed to be propelled beyond the Corneillian conflict between public and private virtue into an empyrean of triumphant, transcendent, romantic self-assertion.' Brownstein, p. 124.

43 See the summary of François Guizot in W. D. Howarth, *Sublime and Grotesque. A Study of French Romantic Drama* (London: Harrap, 1975), p. 81.

44 See Maurice Descotes, *Les Grands Rôles du théâtre de Jean Racine* (Paris: Presses Universitaires de France, 1957), p. 27.

45 *Examiner*, 20 July 1850.

46 *Morning Post*, 21 June 1842.

47 *Ibid.*

48 *Examiner*, 16 May 1841.

49 *Morning Post*, 6 August 1855.

50 *Atlas*, 15 May 1841.

51 *Morning Post*, 21 June 1842.

52 *Atlas*, 15 May 1841. Probably G. H. Lewes.

53 *Morning Post*, 21 June 1842.

54 *Examiner*, 16 May 1841.

55 *Morning Post*, 16 July 1850.

56 *Ibid.*

57 *Morning Post*, 16 July 1846.

58 *Atlas*, 15 May 1841.

59 *Morning Post*, 6 August 1855.

[60] *Atlas*, 15 May 1841.

[61] *Morning Post*, 21 June 1842.

[62] *Atlas*, 25 July 1846.

[63] *Morning Post*, 21 June 1842.

[64] *Leader*, 20 July 1850.

[65] *Examiner*, 16 May 1841.

[66] *Atlas*, 15 May 1841 and *Morning Post*, 11 May 1841.

[67] 22 July.

[68] *Morning Post*, 21 June 1842.

[69] See Samson, *L'Art théâtrale*, part 1, p. 85:
> A bitter irony draws on the language, / Every word she pronounces is not only a bloody insult / Always accompanied by an insolent smile / But casts doubt on her burning flame. / More irony: a cry escapes her soul, / A cry of love; suddenly her pride gives in: / She seemed to exhale a long moan, / And she is no longer, alas, a plaintive lover . . .'

[70] 25 February, 1848, *Histoire de l'art dramatique*, 5th series, p. 236. Compare Balzac: 'The Jews, though so often debased by their contact with other peoples, yet present among their numerous tribes strains in which the sublimest type of Asiatic beauty is preserved', *A Harlot High and Low* (Harmondsworth: Penguin, 1970), p. 51.

[71] Trans. Alan Hollinghurst, *Bajazet* (London: Chatto and Windus, 1991), p. xiv. I have also benefited from this version when making my own literal translations of the play text.

[72] Phillippe Jullian, *The Orientalists* (Oxford: Phaidon, 1977), has material on Chasseriau who designed Rachel's costume, and mentions *Bajazet* in the context of changing ideas of the East. Janin compares Racine with Byron in terms of their mutual fascination with the Orient, *Rachel et la tragédie*, pp. 259–61.

[73] *Morning Post*, 4 July 1850. It is said that Clairon refused to wear Turkish costume, see Maurice Descotes, *Le Drame romantique et ses grands créateurs* (Paris: Presses Universitaires de France, 1956), p. 30.

[74] *Morning Post*, 4 July 1850.

[75] My analysis of this speech is based upon *The Times*, 5 July 1842.

[76] Samson, *L'Art théâtrale*, part 1, p. 89.

[77] *Era*, 10 July 1842.

[78] *Morning Post*, 5 July 1842.

[79] *Era*, 23 May 1841.

[80] *Examiner*, 30 May 1841.

[81] *Morning Post*, 4 July 1850.

[82] *Atlas*, 8 August 1846.

[83] *The Times*, 5 July 1842.

[84] *Morning Post*, 4 July 1850.

[85] Interestingly *The Times* in 1842 thought that this would have made an excellent pose for the portrait of the actress.

[86] *Examiner*, 30 May 1841.

[87] *The Times*, 5 July 1842.

[88] See, for example, *Théâtre de Jean Racine*, Orné de cinquante-sept estampes (Paris: de l'imprimerie de P. Didot l'ainé, 1813).

[89] G. H. Lewes in *Leader*, 6 July 1850.

[90] *Era*, 23 May 1841.

[91] G. H. Lewes in *Leader*, 6 July 1850.

[92] *Morning Post*, 5 June 1851.

[93] *Morning Post*, 5 July 1842.

[94] Edouard Devrient, quoted by Chevalley, *Rachel*, p. 77.

[95] *Orientalism* (Harmondsworth: Penguin, 1985), p. 1.

[96] For Mademoiselle Maxime's precedent see Chevalley, *Rachel*, p. 127.

[97] See Gérard de Nerval, 'Théâtre-Français', *La Revue des lettres modernes*, no. 58 / 59, vol. 7 (Winter 1960–1), pp. 424–32, for comparisons with precedents such as Duchesnois and Dorval.

[98] 23 January 1843, *Histoire de l'art dramatique*, 2nd series, p. 328.

[99] *Actors and the Art of Acting* (London: Smith, Elder, and Co., 1875), p. 25.

[100] *The Times*, 16 July 1846 and *Morning Post*, 2 June 1853.

[101] *The Times*, 3 August 1855.

[102] *Atlas*, 14 July 1846.

[103] *The Times*, 2 July 1880.

[104] *Era*, 8 June 1851.

[105] 16 July 1846.

[106] *The Times*, 3 August 1855.

[107] *Morning Post*, 16 July 1846.

[108] *The Times*, 3 August 1855.

[109] *Era*, 8 June 1851.

[110] *The Times*, 2 June 1853.

[111] A vision that English critics regularly compare with Juliet imagining confronting the murdered Tybalt.

[112] *The Times*, 3 August 1855.

[113] *Morning Post*, 3 June 1851.

[114] *The Times*, 16 July 1846.

[115] Janin, *Rachel et la tragédie*, p. 226.

[116] Brownstein, p. 166.

[117] The relation between the play and the real Adrienne Lecouvreur is discussed by Sainte-Beuve in *Causeries du lundi*, vol. 1 (Paris: Garnier Frères, nd), pp. 119–20, and in the *Leader*, 13 July 1850, probably by G. H. Lewes.

[118] *Morning Post*, 9 June 1851.

[119] *Era*, 15 June 1851.

[120] *The Times*, 9 July 1850.

[121] *Morning Post*, 18 July 1850.

[122] *The Times*, 9 July 1850.

[123] Nina Auerbach, *Private Theatricals* (Harvard: Harvard University Press, 1990) relates Victorian death scenes to changefulness and to the organic idea of character.

[124] *The Times*, 9 July 1850.

[125] 'Actors and Acting', *Papers on Acting*, ed. Brander Matthews (New York: Hill and Wang, 1969), p. 186.

[126] Not all were so impressed. G. H. Lewes said, in *Leader*, 13 July 1850:
Phèdre is separated from Adrienne by a chasm as wide, deep and impassable as that which separates Phidias from Tussaud . . . If you really prefer that loud exhibition of physical agony with which the poisoned Adrienne excites your applause, to the exhibition of mental agony in 'Phèdre', 'Camille', 'Hermione', or 'Roxane', say so; we have no objection; we merely tell you that it is the pathos of the Hospital, not the pathos of Art!

For Janin *Adrienne Lecouvreur* was the exception that proved the general rule that the actress should have kept herself for the classics, although this was because 'she has applied her faith in ancient drama to a frivolous story' (*Rachel et la tragédie*, p. 433).

[127] See Samuel Irving Stone, 'Rachel and Soumet's *Jeanne d'Arc*', *PMLA*, no. 4, vol. 47 (December 1932), pp. 1130–49.

[128] Jules Michelet, *Histoire de France* (Paris: Librairie Classique et Elémentaire de Hachette, 1841), vol. v (1841), pp. 20–1.

[129] Janin, *Rachel et la tragédie*, p. 330.

[130] *Atlas*, 15 August 1846.

[131] Joanna Richardson, *Rachel* (London: Max Reinhardt, 1956), p. 81.

[132] *Atlas*, 15 August 1846.

[133] *Joan of Arc. The Image of Female Heroism* (London: Vintage, 1992), p. 246.

[134] *Histoire de l'art dramatique*, 5th series, pp. 241–3. There's a particularly good description in Madame de B-, *Memoirs of Rachel* (London: Hurst and Blackett, 1858), vol. 1, pp. 313–20.

[135] *L'Artiste*, 9 April 1848, p. 75.

[136] Falk, *Rachel the Immortal*, pp. 188–9.

[137] Mrs Arthur Kennard, *Rachel* (London: W. H. Allen, 1885), p. 143.

[138] *Ibid.*, p. 144.

[139] The Dean of Windsor and Hector Bolitho, eds., *A Victorian Dean* (London: Chatto and Windus, 1930), p. 50.

[140] See M. Agulhon, *Marianne into Battle: Republican Imagery and Symbolism in France. 1989–1880* (Cambridge: Cambridge University Press, 1981). Also see Eugene Weber, 'Who Sang the *Marseillaise?*', in *My France. Politics, Culture, Myth* (Harvard: The Bellknap Press of Harvard University Press, 1991), pp. 92–102, and Hemmings, *Culture and Society*, p. 51. Brownstein's conclusion is wisely circumspect: 'If her timely fervor of patriotism was self-serving and pragmatic, it was also appropriate to the shifting state she served' (p. 192).

[141] Daniel Stern, *Histoire de la révolution de 1848* (Paris: Gustave Sandre, 1850), Tome Deuxième, p. 349. Dutton Cook, *Hours with the Players* (London: Chatto and Windus, 1881), vol. 11, p. 223, says that she did it 'to please the Revolutionists'.

[142] Agulhon, *Marianne into Battle*, p. 91.

[143] See, for instance, Marcia Pointon, 'Liberty on the Barricades', in *Naked Authority* (Cambridge: Cambridge University Press, 1990), pp. 59–82.

[144] Janin, *Rachel et la tragédie*, p. 469.

[145] E. Legouvé, *The Art of Reading*, trans. Edward Roth (Philadelphia: Claxton, Remsen, and Haffelfinger, 1879), p. 154.

[146] E. Legouvé, *M. Samson et ses élèves* (Paris: J. Hetzel, 1875), pp. 20–1.

[147] Legouvé was the author of *Histoire morale des femmes* (Paris: Gustave Sandré, Editeur, 1849).

[148] *M. Samson et ses élèves*, pp. 25, 23.

[149] Princess Lazarovich-Hrebelianovich (Eleanor Calhoun), *Pleasures and Palaces. The Memoirs of Princess Lazarovich-Hrebelianovich* (New York: Century, 1915), pp. 213–14.

[150] See, for example, the comparisons made with Rachel in Harriet Beecher Stowe's 'Sojourner Truth, the Libyan Sibyl', first published in 1863. In France the process is embodied in the figure of 'Marianne' about whom Marina Warner makes the chastening point that, 'If

women had had a vote or a voice, Marianne would have been harder to accept as a universal figure of the ideal', *Monuments and Maidens. The Allegory of the Female Form* (London: Weidenfeld and Nicolson, 1985), p. 292. Warner's book is essential reading on this topic.

[151] See my '"Rachel's Terrible Beauty"' and Brownstein, chapter 5, *passim.*

[152] See my 'The Modernity of Aimée Desclée', *New Theatre Quarterly*, no. 24, vol. 6 (November 1990), pp. 365–78.

ADELAIDE RISTORI

All translations, unless indicated, are by the author.

The Ristori papers are held in the Museo Biblioteca dell'Attore di Genova. Some scholars have begun the task of editing and publishing some of the documentation, and details are given below.

[1] Letter to Tommaso Salvini, 29 December 1899, in 'Eleonora Duse and Adelaide Ristori: A Tale of Two Actresses', trans. Susan Bassnett, *Women and Theatre: Occasional Papers*, no. 1 (1992), pp. 1–18, quote p. 16. Italian version by Mirella Schino, in *Teatro archivio*, no. 8 (September 1984), pp. 123–82.

[2] Letter to Giuseppe Primoli, first published in *Le Gaulois*, Paris, 26 May 1897, entitled 'La Duse jugée par la Ristori', in Bassnett, *ibid.*, p. 14,

[3] *Ibid.*, p. 15.

[4] *Ibid.*, p. 15.

[5] Adelaide Ristori, *Studies and Memoirs* (London: W. H. Allen, 1888), p. 272.

[6] *Ibid.*, p. 274.

[7] *Ibid.*, pp. 298–9.

[8] *Ibid.*, p. 140.

[9] *Ibid.*, p. 164.

[10] *Ibid.*, p. 165.

[11] *Ibid.*

[12] Document 143, in Paola Bignami, ed., *Alle origini dell'impresa teatrale: dalle carte di Adelaide Ristori* (Bologna, Nuova Alfa, 1988), p. 209.

[13] *Ibid.*, document 141, p. 206.

[14] *Studies and Memoirs*, p. 91.

[15] *Ibid.*, p. 91.

[16] Alessandro D'Amico, 'La monarchia teatrale di Adelaide Ristori', in Siro Ferrone, ed., *Teatro dell'Italia unita* (Florence, Il Saggiatore, 1980), pp. 49–55.

[17] *Ibid.*, p. 53.

[18] Henry Knepler, *The Gilded Stage* (London: Constable, 1968), p. 107.

[19] *Studies and Memoirs*, p. 61.

[20] *Ibid.*, p. 66.

[21] *Ibid.*, p. 67.

[22] *Ibid.*

[23] *Ibid.*, p. 74.

[24] *Ibid.*, p. 73.

[25] *Ibid.*, p. 101.

[26] *Ibid.*

[27] Unpublished letter from Cavour, 20 April 1861, held in the Museo Biblioteca dell'Attore, Genova.

[28] *Studies and Memoirs*, p. 5.

[29] Knepler, *The Gilded Stage*, p. 64.

[30] Ristori claims she was aged fourteen, but the *Enciclopedia dello Spettacolo* entry on Ristori gives her age as twelve, which is followed by Marvin Carlson.

[31] Marvin Carlson, *The Italian Stage. From Goldoni to D'Annunzio* (London: McFarland, 1981), p. 100.

[32] *Studies and Memoirs*, p. 9.

[33] *Il vessillo della liberta*, Vercelli, 21 January 1856.

[34] *Ibid.*

[35] *Il Diavoletto*, Trieste, 7 February, 1856.

[36] Bignami, *Alle origini dell'impresa teatrale*, pp. 21–22.

[37] *Studies and Memoirs*, p. 22.

[38] D'Amico, 'La monarchia teatrale di Adelaide Ristori', p. 50.

[39] Alphonse de Lamartine, 'À Madame Ristori' (August 1855), in *Œuvres poétiques complètes* (Paris: Gallimard, 1963), p. 1786: Alfred de Vigny, 'A Madame Ristori' (September 1855), in *Œuvres complètes* (Paris: Gallimard, 1950), p. 205; Alfred de Musset, 'Stances à Madame Ristori', in *Poésies complètes d'Alfred de Musset* (Paris: Gallimard, 1957), pp. 546–7.

[40] Knepler, *The Gilded Stage*, pp. 68–72.

[41] Tracy Davis, *Actresses as Working Women: Their Social Identity in Victorian Culture* (London and New York: Routledge, 1991), p. 69.

[42] *Studies and Memoirs*, p. 38.

[43] Letter from Adelaide Ristori to Giuliano Capranica, 19 / 20 March, 1855. Document 42 in Bignami, *Alle origini dell' impresa teatrale*, pp. 70–1.

44 *Studies and Memoirs*, p. 211.

45 *Ibid.*, p. 251.

46 *Ibid.*, p. 253.

47 *The Spectator*, 7 June 1856, p. 609.

48 *Studies and Memoirs*, pp. 207–8.

49 Unpublished letter, quoted in Eugenio Buonaccorsi, 'Adelaide Ristori in America (1866–1867), Manipolazione dell'opinione pubblica e industria teatrale in una tournee dell'Ottocento', *Teatro archivio*, no. 5 (September, 1981), pp. 156–88.

50 Elaine Aston, 'Ristori's Medea and her Nineteenth Century Successors', *Women and Theatre: Occasional Papers*, no. 1 (April, 1992), pp. 38–48.

51 Handwritten note dated 9 June 1856, cited in G. Rowell, *Queen Victoria Goes to the Theatre* (London: P. Elek, 1978), p. 68.

52 *Studies and Memoirs*, p. 223.

53 *Ibid.*, pp. 32–3.

54 *Ibid.*, p. 178.

55 *Ibid.*, p. 193.

56 Unpublished letter from Ristori to Carlo Balboni, 12 January 1859, held in the Museo Biblioteca dell'Attore di Genova.

57 Teresa Viziano, 'Dall'Europa a Napoli: Adelaide Ristori', in *Il teatro Mercadente, la storia, il restauro* (Naples: Electa Napoli, n.d.), p. 165.

58 Bignami, *Alle origini dell' impresa teatrale*, p. 123.

59 Parmenio Bettoli, *Adelaide Ristori*, in *La Lettura*, November 1906.

60 Letter from Gustavo Modena to Francesco Dall'Ongaro, 31 December 1857, in *Epistolario di Gustavo Modena* (Rome, 1955), p. 289.

61 Eugenio Buonaccorsi, 'Adelaide Ristori in America (1866–1867)', pp. 156–88.

62 Knepler, *The Gilded Stage*, p. 111.

63 Letter from Maddalena Ristori to Adelaide Ristori, 12 July 1855, in Bignami, *Alle origini dell' impresa teatrale*, p. 117.

64 *Studies and Memoirs*, p. 128.

65 E. Peron Hingston, *The Siddons of Modern Italy. Adelaide Ristori, a Sketch of Her Life and Twenty words Relative to Her Genius* (London: T. H. Lacy, 1856), p. 16.

66 Giovanna Buonanno, *Adelaide Ristori's Shakespeare*, unpublished MA thesis, University of Warwick 1992, p. 31.

67 *Studies and Memoirs*, p. 255.

[68] *Ibid.*, p. 257.

[69] *Ibid.*, p. 264.

[70] I*bid.*, p. 267.

[71] I*bid.*, p. 268.

[72] Cited in G. Ward and R. Whiting, *Both Sides of the Curtain* (London: Cassell, 1918), p. 188.

[73] Fernando Taviani, 'Alcuni suggerimenti per lo studio della poesia degli attori nell' Ottocento', in *Quaderni di teatro*, nos. 21/22 (1983), pp. 69–96.

[74] Letter from Adelaide Ristori to her son Giorgio, 14 December 1901, in Bassnett, trans., and Schino, ed., 'Eleonora Duse and Adelaide Ristori: A Tale of Two Actresses', pp. 1–19.

[75] From *Colloqui con la Duse*, in Silvio D'Amico, *Tramonto del grande attore* (Milan: Mondadori, 1929), p. 56, cited in Bassnett, *ibid.*, p. 18.

Select Bibliography

SARAH SIDDONS

The two major early biographies of Sarah Siddons are James Boaden, *Memoirs of Mrs Siddons* (London: Henry Colburn, 1827), reprinted in 1893, and Thomas Campbell, *Life of Mrs Siddons* (London: Edward Moxon, 1834). Boaden places Siddons in a fuller theatrical context than Campbell and is more specific about her acting, but the latter's biography is more 'official' in the sense that Campbell had access to the actress' private papers – of which, however, he made insufficient use. Boaden's *Memoirs of the Life of John Philip Kemble* (London: Longman, Hurst, et al., 1825), contains more relevant, but overlapping, material. Mrs Siddons' account of her early career is informative but brief; it has been edited by William Van Lennep as *The Reminiscences of Sarah Kemble Siddons 1773–1785* (Cambridge, Mass.: Widener Library, 1942). There are several twentieth-century biographies, which concentrate largely on her private life. The best of these are Yvonne Ffrench, *Mrs Siddons, Tragic Actress* (London: Derek Verschoyle, 1936), expanded in 1954, and Roger Manvell, *Sarah Siddons* (London: G. P. Putnam and Sons, 1970). Manvell's is the more scholarly, but neither really comes to grips with the acting. An earlier work, Mrs Clement Parsons, *The Incomparable Siddons* (London: Methuen, 1909), possesses some valuable insights. One chapter of Sandra Richards, *The Rise of the English Actress* (London: Macmillan, 1993) contains a summary of her life and career. The most scholarly and informed single account of Siddons' life and career is the long and detailed entry in vol. XIV (1991) of *A Biographical Dictionary of Actors, Actresses, Musicians, Dancers, Managers, & Other Stage Personnel in London, 1660–1800*, eds. Philip Highfill Jr, Kalman A. Burnim, and Edward A. Langhans (Carbondale, Ill.: Southern Illinois University Press).

As for the acting itself, the most useful contemporary source, aside from the comments of Boaden and Campbell, is the notes by G. J. Bell, first edited by H. Fleeming Jenkin under the title 'Mrs Siddons as Lady Macbeth and

Queen Katharine' in *Papers Literary, Scientific, Etc.* (London: Longmans, 1887)
and most recently reprinted in *Papers on Acting*, ed. Brander Matthews (New
York: Hill and Wang, 1958). Another helpful contemporary source, James
Ballantyne, *Characters of Mrs Siddons* (Edinburgh, 1812), is mostly a collection
of *Edinburgh Courant* newspaper reviews. The long review of Siddons' 1782–3
Drury Lane season by Thomas Holcroft in the *English Review* (March 1783) and
the letters relating to her appearance in Dublin in 1785, collected under the title
The Beauties of Mrs Siddons (London, 1786), both contain valuable information
about particular aspects of characterisation and technique; Holcroft's article is
the more thoughtful and general. Several reviews by William Hazlitt and Leigh
Hunt are essential reading. These are gathered in two books edited by William
Archer and R. W. Lowe: *Dramatic Essays: William Hazlitt* (London: Walter Scott,
1895) and *Dramatic Essays: Leigh Hunt* (London: Walter Scott, 1896), and in
Hazlitt's *A View of the English Stage* (London: Stodart, 1818), edited in the next
century by W. Spencer Jackson (London: George Bell, 1906), and also in *Leigh
Hunt's Dramatic Criticism 1808–1831*, eds. L. H. and C. W. Houtchens (New York:
Columbia University Press, 1949). The best and most extended modern
treatment of the acting is an unpublished Ph.D. thesis by Patricia McMahon,
'The Tragical Art of Sarah Siddons: An Analysis of Her Acting Style' (Yale,
1972).

Two modern studies can complete this selection. Shearer West, *The Image
of the Actor* (New York: St Martin's Press, 1991) makes illuminating connections
between acting and painting in the eighteenth century; one section relates
specifically to Kemble and Siddons. Pat Rogers, '"Towering Beyond Her Sex":
Stature and Sublimity in the Achievement of Sarah Siddons', in *Curtain Calls:
British and American Women and the Theater 1660–1820*, eds. Mary Anne Schofield
and Cecilia Macheski (Athens, Ohio: University of Ohio Press, 1991), a rare
feminist commentary on Mrs Siddons, deals interestingly with the
contemporary critical vocabulary used to describe her acting and the
importance to women of her achievement in the theatre.

RACHEL FELIX

Rachel M. Brownstein's *Tragic Muse. Rachel of the Comédie-Française* (New York:
Alfred Knopf, 1993; Durham and London: Duke University Press, 1995) is
remarkable in several ways: for its exemplification of a trend in contemporary
biography that finds myth as meaningful as fact; for the political importance it
attributes to Rachel as a woman and as a Jew; for the ways in which the author
weaves her own story in with that of her subject; finally, but not least, for the
exhaustive thoroughness of its documentation. Brownstein's bibliographies are

the best and her 'post-modern' book is unmatched as an account of Rachel's life and significance. The only criticism from the point of view of a theatre historian is that it sometimes forgoes detailed analysis of what occurred on stage.

The best book on Rachel in French is also the most recent: Sylvie Chevalley, *Rachel* (Paris: Calmann-Lévy, 1989). The author's position as 'conservatoire honoraire de la bibliothèque de la Comédie-Française' ensures that the coverage of Rachel's relations with France's national theatre is exceptionally careful. The book maintains a sensible balance between the actress's private and professional lives and has a discriminating attitude to such predecessors as Georges d'Heylli, *Rachel d'après sa correspondance* (Paris: Librairie des Bibliophiles, 1882) and the various memoirs of Arsène Houssaye. Nicole Toussaint du Wast, *Rachel* (Paris: Stock, 1980) is considerably less comprehensive. Sylvie Chevalley is also the editor of a promised edition of *Correspondance de Rachel (1832–1858)*.

Some quite early French books have been translated, for example Madame de B– (A. de Barrera) *Mémoires* (London: Hurst and Blackett, 1858), and Léon Beauvallet, *Rachel et le Nouveau-Monde* (Paris: Alexandre Cadot, 1856) translated as *Rachel and the New World* (London, New York, Toronto: Abelard-Schuman, 1967).

An immense amount of ephemeral material – pamphlets, caricatures, magazine articles – was produced about Rachel during her lifetime. Much of this is to be found in specialist archives such as those held by the Comédie-Française and the Bibliothèque Nationale. Otherwise the main source of information is likely to be the collected writings of her contemporaries. Jules Janin, *Rachel et la tragédie* (Paris: Amyot, 1859) will always be central, a comprehensive study of Rachel's performing career, and one of the very first French books to be illustrated with photographs. There are important commentaries in: Théophile Gautier, *Portraits contemporains* (Paris: Charpentier, 1881); Ernest Legouvé, *Soixante ans de souvenirs* (Paris: Hetzel, 1886); Alfred de Musset, *Mélange de littérature et de critique* (Paris: Charpentier, 1867); Gérard de Nerval, *La Vie de théâtre*, ed. Jean Richer (Paris: Lettres Modernes, 1961); Joseph-Isidore Samson, *Mémoires de Samson, de la Comédie-Française* (Paris: Ollendorf, 1882); and *Rachel et Samson, souvenirs de théâtre par la veuve de Samson, avec une préface de M. Jules Clarétie* (Paris: Paul Ollendorf, 1898).

Essential for the history of the Comédie-Française are A. Joannides, *La Comédie-Française de 1680 à 1900*, 2 vols. (Paris: Plon-Nourit, 1901) and Albert Soubies, *La Comédie-française depuis l'époque romantique* (Paris: Librairie Fischbucher, 1895). The more recent catalogue, *La Comédie-Française 1680–1980*

(Paris: Bibliothèque Nationale, 1980) lists pictures and documents relevant to Rachel. Two books by Maurice Descotes: *Les grands rôles du théâtre de Corneille* (Paris: Presses Universitaires de France, 1962) and *Les grands rôles de théâtre de Racine* (Paris: Presses Universitaires de France, 1957) usefully trace major interpretations over the years.

For French theatrical background in general see Marvin Carlson, *The French Stage* (Metuchen, N.J.: The Scarecrow Press, 1972), F. W. J. Hemmings, *The Theatre Industry in Nineteenth Century France* (Cambridge: Cambridge University Press, 1993) and *Theatre and State in France 1760–1905* (Cambridge: Cambridge University Press, 1994). For the intellectual context see F. W .J. Hemmings, *Culture and Society in France 1789–1848* (Leicester: Leicester University Press, 1987) and W. D. Howarth, *Sublime and Grotesque. A Study of the French Romantic Drama* (London: Harrap, 1975).

Before Brownstein the most up-to-date life in English was Joanna Richardson's *Rachel* (London: Max Reinhardt, 1956). This is a competent account that, although it pays particular attention to Rachel's English appearances, benefits from its author's expert knowledge of French Romanticism. In the nineteenth and early twentieth centuries English writers produced a steady stream of books, some of them with an interestingly feminist emphasis. These include: James Agate, *Rachel* (London: Gerald Howe, 1928); Bernard Falk, *Rachel the Immortal* (London: Hutchinson, 1933); Francis Gribble, *Rachel. Her Stage Life and her Real Life* (London: Chapman and Hall, 1911); Mrs Arthur Kennard, *Rachel* (London: W. H. Allen, 1885). Henry Knepler's *The Gilded Stage* (London: Constable, 1968) is particularly close to the concerns of this study because it places Rachel in the context of her successors: Ristori, Bernhardt, Duse.

Best of all are the records provided by English witnesses: G. H. Lewes, *Actors and the Art of Acting* (London: Smith, Elder, and Co., 1875); Dutton Cook, *Hours with the Players* (London: Chatto and Windus, 1881); William Charles Macready, *Reminiscences* (London: Macmillan, 1875); Sir Theodore Martin, *Monographs* (London: John Murray, 1906); Henry Morley, *The Journal of a London Playgoer, 1851–1866* (1891, reprinted with an introduction by Michael R. Booth by Leicester University Press in 1974). All contain vivid testimony to Rachel's unique powers.

ADELAIDE RISTORI

The principal sources of information on Ristori are provided by her own memoirs and by the largely unpublished Ristori archive held at the Museo

Biblioteca dell'Attore di Genova. Ristori's *Ricordi e studi artistici* (Turin: Roux, 1887) was published in an abridged English version a year later as *Memoirs and Artistic Studies* (New York: Doubleday, 1888).

Research on the Ristori archive has resulted in a number of very useful extended essays that have appeared in *Teatro Archivio*. These include E. Buonaccorsi, 'Adelaide Ristori in America (1866–67). Manipolazione dell'opinione pubblica e industria teatrale in una tournee dell'ottocento', *Teatro Archivio* no.5 (1981), pp. 156–88, a study of Ristori's strategic management of American audiences, and Cristina Giorcelli, 'Adelaide Ristori sulle scene britanniche ed irlandesi', *Teatro Archivio* no.5 (1981), pp. 81-147, an account of Ristori's tours in Britain and Ireland The same journal has also begun to publish some of the Ristori letters. P. Galli Pellegrini has edited some of Ristori's correspondence with Legouvé – 'Lettere de Ernest Legouvé ad Adelaide Ristori', *Teatro Archivio* (no. 1, 1979), pp. 4–23 and Mirella Schino has edited the correspondence with Eleonora Duse: 'La Duse e la Ristori', *Teatro Archivio* no. 8 (1990) pp. 59–98. An abridged version of Schino's essay and a selection of the correspondence, translated by Susan Bassnett, appeared as 'Eleonora Duse and Adelaide Ristori: A Tale of Two Actresses', *Women and Theatre: Occasional Papers* no. 2 (1992), pp. 1–19. Claudio Meldolesi has edited letters between Ristori and Gustavo Modena: 'Adelaide Ristori e Gustavo Modena: Lettere inedite', *Bollettino del Museo Biblioteca dell'attore de Genova*, no. 1 (1970) pp. 5–15.

There is no recent biography of Ristori. E. Boutet's hagiography, *Adelaide Ristori* (Rome: 1899) is still readable, as is Kate Field's *Adelaide Ristori. A Biography* (New York: Gray and Green, 1867), though as period pieces. Even more arcane, though worthy of note, is E. Peron Hingston, *The Siddons of Modern Italy. Adelaide Ristori, a Sketch of her Life and Twenty Words Relative to Her Genius* (London: T. H. Lacey, 1856). Ristori's descendant, M. Capranica del Grillo, analyses the Ristori genealogy in 'La genealogia di Adelaide Ristori', *Teatro Archivio* no. 8 (1984), pp. 120–2.

An excellent essay on Ristori in English is to be found in Henry Knepler's *The Gilded Stage* (London: Constable, 1968). Knepler looks at four nineteenth-century performers, and locates Ristori in a comparative context. Also useful is Marvin Carlson's *The Italian Stage. From Goldoni to D'Annunzio* (New York and London: MacFarland, 1981), which discusses Ristori's contribution to the theatre of her time.

Four studies of Ristori as a performer, see Marvin Carlson, *The Italian Shakespeareans. Performances by Ristori, Salvini and Rossi in England and the United*

States (Washington: Folger Shakespeare Library, 1985). Alessandro D'Amico discusses Ristori's penchant for queenly roles in 'La monarchia teatrale di Adelaide Ristori', in S. Ferrone (ed.) *Teatro dell'Italia unita*, Atti dei convegni (Dec. 1977 and Nov. 1978) (Milan: Il Saggiatore, 1980), pp. 49–54. Elaine Aston has written a very insightful study of Ristori's playing of the role of Medea, 'Ristori's Medea and Her Nineteenth-Century Successors', *Women and Theatre: Occasional Papers*, no. 1 (1992), pp. 38–48.

Paola Bignami's *Alle origini dell'impresa teatrale. Dalle carte di Adelaide Ristori* (Bologna: Nuova Alfa, 1988) brings together a range of documents that trace Ristori's progress as actress-manager. Alessandro D'Amico has edited the catalogue of an exhibition of Ristori's costumes, *Mostra dei costumi di Adelaide Ristori: Catalogo ufficiale* (Genoa: Edizioni Teatro Stabile di Genova, 1967). The as-yet-unpublished doctoral thesis, *A Stage Under Petticoat Government. Actresses in the Age of Queen Victoria* (University of Warwick, 1996) by Giovanna Buonanno, contains a detailed analysis of the roles selected by Ristori for her British tours.

Index

Page numbers in *italic* refer to illustrations.